"Next up, Tom Bennet!"

The rodeo announcer's voice boomed over the arena. "Tom's a local cowboy, ladies and gentlemen, and he's won every prize you can think of."

Eleven-year-old Kelly Bennet sprawled on her stomach on the roof of the camper, rested her chin on her hands and stared over the fence. From there, she had an unobstructed view of the bucking chutes. Although she hated to watch her father ride, it was worse not to know what was happening.

The gate swung open, and the bull carrying her father surged into the ring, twisting and leaping madly. Music blared overhead, its frenetic beat matching the rhythm of the bull's wicked hooves.

Suddenly her father's body loosened and flopped to one side. He was holding on by sheer effort of will while he struggled to regain control. The bull lunged to the side again, and her father slipped down toward the crushing hooves.

The crowd gasped, then waited in horrified silence as a group of cowboys gathered to stand around their fallen comrade.

"Please, please, let him be okay. Please, God, I can't look after Casey all by myself. Please, God, let him get up and walk away."

But her father didn't get up.

ABOUT THE AUTHOR

Margot Dalton grew up in Alberta, Canada, on a ranch that
had been operated by her family since 1883. As she says, her
home was "where my great grandmother once traded flour
and sugar to wandering Indian tribes in exchange for buffalo
robes and beaded moccasins."

Now recently returned to Alberta after spending many years in
British Columbia, Margot has written more than thirty books
since 1980 when her first Harlequin Superromance novel was
published. *A Man I Used To Know* is set in her native
province—an area Margot writes about with authenticity and
great affection.

Books by Margot Dalton

HARLEQUIN SUPERROMANCE
664—MAN OF MY DREAMS
693—THE HIDING PLACE
714—A FAMILY LIKENESS
749—MEMORIES OF YOU
794—COTTONWOOD CREEK

MIRA BOOKS
TANGLED LIVES
FIRST IMPRESSION
SECOND THOUGHTS
THIRD CHOICE

Don't miss any of our special offers. Write to us at the
following address for information on our newest releases.

Harlequin Reader Service
U.S.: 3010 Walden Ave., P.O. Box 1325, Buffalo, NY 14269
Canadian: P.O. Box 609, Fort Erie, Ont. L2A 5X3

A MAN I USED TO KNOW
Margot Dalton

HARLEQUIN®

TORONTO • NEW YORK • LONDON
AMSTERDAM • PARIS • SYDNEY • HAMBURG
STOCKHOLM • ATHENS • TOKYO • MILAN • MADRID
PRAGUE • WARSAW • BUDAPEST • AUCKLAND

ISBN 0-373-70831-9

A MAN I USED TO KNOW

Copyright © 1999 by Margot Dalton.

This edition published by arrangement with Harlequin Books S.A.

® and TM are trademarks of the publisher. Trademarks indicated with ® are registered in the United States Patent and Trademark Office, the Canadian Trade Marks Office and in other countries.

Printed in U.S.A.

A MAN I USED
TO KNOW

CHAPTER ONE

THE MEDICINE HAT STAMPEDE was held at the end of July, when the prairie grass was bleached pale gold.

The sunshine seemed so pure and brilliant it was almost a tangible thing, spilling softly over plains and fields that drowsed in the midday heat.

Medicine Hat, in the southeastern corner of the province of Alberta, was one of the oldest cities on Canada's western plains, with a proud heritage of exploration, ranching, industry and rugged independence. That colorful history was celebrated with energy and gusto during the annual stampede, which attracted professional cowboys from as far away as Texas.

On this July afternoon, the hundred-acre expanse of fairgrounds hummed with noise and activity and glittered vibrantly with color. People waited in line for tickets at booths under the grandstand, while others swarmed the fairgrounds, rode the Ferris wheels and visited the stock displays.

From the huge loudspeakers on the rodeo announcer's covered wooden perch, the twangy voice of Willie Nelson washed over the eager faces of the spectators, over the glossy horses and the waiting tiers of seats. It drifted above the midway rides and the glittering acres of parked cars, fading at last in the sweep of silent prairie that lay beyond.

The rodeo opened its final day with a serpentine ride. More than a hundred mounted cowboys and cowgirls, all contestants in the rodeo, galloped in and circled the arena in a tight intricate pattern, weaving a web of color and magic in the sunny afternoon, a whirling kaleidoscope of rhythm and movement, of leather and horsehide and bright silken fabric.

After the contestants exited the arena, the rodeo events began, wild and spectacular, incredible feats of physical daring and horsemanship. The crowd clapped and cheered, intoxicated by the beauty of the warm summer day and the holiday atmosphere all around them. Urged on by the rodeo announcer, they applauded every ride and rewarded every cowboy's performance with their stamping feet, shouts and hand clapping.

Near the rear gate where riders entered and left the arena, a big dusty truck equipped with a camper van was situated behind a rope barricade.

Coils of rope, extra boots and spurs, little bags of powdered resin and masses of leather strapping, even some medical supplies, were arranged neatly on the tailgate of the truck. Next to the equipment sat a skinny child in jeans and ragged T-shirt, a baseball cap pulled low over wary blue eyes.

Most casual passersby would have glanced at the child's dirty callused hands, wiry little body and withdrawn, self-contained air and assumed this child was a boy.

But in fact it was Kelly Bennet, age eleven—at the moment the sole caretaker of her little brother, four-year-old Casey, who was having his afternoon nap inside the camper.

Kelly stood up on the tailgate, opened the door and peeked inside at Casey. He slept deeply, his curly brown hair spilling over the pillow and making him look like an angel, though he was dressed as a miniature cowboy in a little pearl-buttoned shirt, tooled-leather belt with trophy buckle and small leather boots. His battered straw cowboy hat lay on the floor where he'd tossed it before climbing into the bunk.

Kelly edged forward to pull off his boots, not overly concerned about waking him up. Casey slept like a log once he finally dropped off.

She set the boots aside, covered her brother with a blanket and examined his face, which was still smeared with a sticky mess from the caramel apple he'd eaten after lunch.

It was always such a chore to wash his face. He fought and yelled and tried to run away from her. Once he'd even bitten her hand.

Briefly she considered cleaning him up now, while he was asleep, but she was reluctant to take the risk. A face-washing might just be disturbing enough to wake him up. Kelly cherished the times when her brother slept and she could have a few moments to herself.

When he turned over in his sleep and kicked the blanket aside, she noticed that he had a hole in his blue jeans again, torn right through the knee.

Kelly sighed. She was gradually learning to sew well enough to fix Casey's clothes, but she could still only do big ragged blanket stitches that looked awful. Despite her best efforts, Casey never seemed as tidy as most of the other little kids around the rodeo circuit. And even when they bought him new clothes, they usually looked as bad as the old ones before a week had passed.

"Kids!" she muttered under her breath, closing the door and climbing up the side of the camper.

Kelly sprawled on her stomach on the sun-warmed roof, rested her chin on her hands and stared over the fence into the rodeo arena. This vantage point gave her an unobstructed view of the bucking chutes, and her father was entered in the next section of bull-riding.

"Next up, Tom Bennet!" the rodeo announcer called. "Tom's a local cowboy, ladies and gentlemen, and he's won every prize you can think of, and a few he'd probably rather forget."

The crowd of several thousand rippled with laughter, then roared in excited applause when they saw their local favorite climb up the side of the chute and settle gingerly on the back of a heavy Brahma bull. The big animal shuddered and bellowed as he stood captive in the narrow enclosure.

"Tom's been away from the rodeo business for the past few years. Nowadays he's back full-time and we all sure appreciate him," the announcer went on, leaning over from his stand to peer into the bucking chutes. "And he's drawn Vampire today. Now, folks, that's a mean ol' bull if ever there was one."

Kelly stuffed the heel of her left hand into her mouth and bit down on it hard enough to make a row of neat red marks.

She hated watching her father ride, but it was worse to look away and not know what was happening....

Tom Bennet was wearing a gray plaid shirt, and it strained taut across his broad shoulders. She could see him clearly through the rails of the chute. His jaw was tense, his teeth gritted as he slipped his gloved fingers into the woven handhold and settled himself on the bull's wide dusty back.

Vampire bellowed in rage and flung his head, aiming viciously upward with one of the curved horns. Kelly's father ducked his head aside, then settled his hat more firmly, sat erect and nodded to the men lined up on the chute behind him.

Simultaneously the flank strap was tightened and a last hitch was taken on the handhold. The gate swung open and the bull surged into the arena, leaping and twisting madly.

Music blared overhead, its frenetic beat matching the rhythm of the bull's wicked hooves as he pounded and gyrated. Dust rose in suffocating clouds, almost obscuring the whirling animal and the man clinging to his back.

Suddenly, to Kelly's horror, she saw her father's body loosen and flop to one side. Tom was out of balance, holding on by sheer effort of will while he struggled to regain control.

The bull lunged to the side again and her father slipped down toward the crushing hooves. But his hand was still fastened into the braided rope that encircled the animal's body.

Kelly scrambled to her feet and danced in terror on the roof of the camper.

"He's hung up! Hey, you guys!"

She cupped her hands around her mouth and screamed into the arena.

"He's hung up! Hurry and get him away!"

The rodeo clowns swarmed nearer to the bull, leaping in and skipping away, one trying to distract the crazed animal while the other tugged at Tom's hand, still trapped in the rope.

The cowboy's body flopped alongside the bull like a rag doll, receiving regular kicks from the blunt hooves. At last the rope loosened enough to let him fall away, and he lay unmoving in the dirt of the arena.

But before the clowns could distract the bull again, Vampire shifted his massive rear quarters with cruel deliberation and planted both hooves full on the midsection of the man who lay prone in the dirt. He kicked again at Tom's head and galloped the length of the arena, where he entered the holding pen and stood placidly among the other bulls.

The crowd gasped, then waited in horrified silence as a group of cowboys gathered to stand around their fallen comrade.

Kelly strained to peer over them, her heart thudding with alarm.

"He's all right," she whispered to herself. "He's okay. It's just…he got the wind knocked out of him, that's all."

She made no move to climb down from the camper and approach the group around her father. Instead she sank into a small, tight bundle, wrapped her arms around her knees, buried her face against them and prayed with all her heart to anybody who might be willing to listen.

"Please, please, let him be okay, let Dad not be hurt. Please, God, I can't look after Casey all by myself...please, God, let him get up now and walk away.''

But her father didn't get up.

She raised one arm and peeked underneath it, terrified by the way he looked, crumpled on the arena dust, blood coating his blond hair and dripping from his face.

Kelly's father was the strongest man in the world. Things like this didn't happen to him.

''I can't get hurt,'' he often told Kelly with a sunny grin. ''I have two lucky charms, you know, and I take them everywhere.''

''What are they?'' she would ask.

''You and your brother.'' He'd hug her then and give her a noisy kiss. ''You kids are my lucky charms, sweetheart. You protect me no matter what I do.''

But they hadn't protected him now, Kelly thought with a shudder that made her stomach turn upside down.

''Get up, Daddy,'' she whispered. ''Please, please get up.''

The ambulance came rolling into the arena, its lights flashing. Tom's body was examined by the paramedics, then braced, splinted and moved carefully onto a waiting stretcher.

Kelly knew how much cowboys hated to be carried from the rodeo arena on a stretcher. Even if he collapsed once he got behind the chutes, a cowboy always wanted to walk out under his own steam.

But her father was lying on the stretcher, unmoving, his long legs still, hands folded on his chest. A few cowboys walked slowly next to the stretcher to shield their companion's body from the eyes of the spectators in the grandstand. One of them carried Tom's hat.

Kelly stuffed her hand into her mouth again and bit down hard enough to cause a sharp pain. The sky whirled around overhead, and the harsh sun stabbed knives of fear into her brain.

LATE SATURDAY AFTERNOON, the Medicine Hat hospital drowsed in the summer heat. But things were as bright and noisy as ever in the children's ward where Lila Marsden was visiting several of her patients.

One of them, a little girl in a miniature yellow armchair by the bookcase, sat forcing a pair of doll-size overalls onto a teddy bear. She frowned in concentration, her lower lip jutting, small hands fumbling with the snaps. In the fluorescent lights overhead, her bald head gleamed as pale and fragile as an egg.

Lila paused and knelt by the chair, watching gravely. "Do you need some help with those overalls, Carrie?" she asked.

"Stupid things won't fit," the little girl muttered.

"Won't they? Well, maybe if we just…"

Lila made a deft adjustment to the straps on the overalls, then pulled the legs down so the fasteners lined up properly.

"There," she said. "Try it now."

Carrie tossed her an absent smile and began to work on the snaps.

"How are you feeling this morning?" Lila asked, stroking the child's head. A blue pulse throbbed just beneath Carrie's bald scalp, giving an impression of intense vulnerability.

"I threw up," Carrie said in a matter-of-fact tone. "All my breakfast."

"Oh dear." Lila sat back on her heels and studied a notation on the clipboard she carried. "I was hoping that sort of thing was all over with."

Carrie finished doing up the snaps on the overalls, then examined her bear. "Teddy and I want to go home," she said after a moment.

Lila hugged the little girl, who felt thin and frail in pajamas and dressing gown. "Soon you can go home, sweetheart," she murmured. "It's going to be just a few more days."

Carrie wriggled free to settle back in the armchair, feet stiffly extended in her furry slippers. She took a picture book from the shelves beside her, opened it on her knees and cuddled the bear, pretending to read aloud to him.

Again Lila stroked the little girl's head with a lingering caress, then moved across the room to the toy shelves, where an older boy, about eight or nine, sat in a wheelchair watching a couple of other children constructing a tower from plastic blocks. One of his legs was encased in a foam-padded brace, and he held a metal pole next to his chair, containing an IV apparatus suspended from an overhead bar.

"Hi, Tony," she said, pausing next to the wheelchair. "I'll bet you wish you could get down on the floor and help them, don't you?"

The boy turned to grin up at her. His blue eyes were darkly shadowed and his face was pale under a drift of freckles.

"I like riding in the chair," he said. "It's better than being in bed all the time like I was at first. And sometimes the other kids push me down the halls really fast.''

''Well, I'm not sure that's such a good idea.'' Lila gestured at the intravenous needle taped to a vein in the back of his hand. ''We certainly don't want anything to come loose while you're out there drag racing.''

She consulted another chart, frowning thoughtfully.

''How did you sleep last night, Tony?''

''I got really hot and felt kind of sick,'' the boy said. ''But the nurse came in and gave me something and I fell asleep again.''

''Did your leg hurt?''

''It hurts all the time,'' he said cheerfully. ''But not as much anymore.''

''That's good.'' Lila smiled at him and smoothed his cowlick.

A week earlier, after a fall from a bicycle, Tony had suffered a sudden onset of osteomyelitis lodged deep in the marrow of his upper left tibia, just below the knee. The injured area was pumping a rare form of staph infection into the boy's bloodstream, so virulent that his body temperature had spiked to dangerous levels every few hours during his first three days in hospital.

Tony's infection had resisted all of the antibiotics they'd tried. Panic was settling in among Lila and her fellow doctors before their last available antibiotic had finally begun to show signs of killing the infection.

''So, is your mother coming in again today?'' Lila asked, bending to examine the fastenings on the brace.

Tony nodded. "She's bringing a bunch of school-work for me. I'm missing all kinds of stuff," he added, looking pleased.

Lila chuckled and stood erect again. "Well, you'd better start working hard to catch up. I'm afraid we'll have to keep you here for a few more weeks while we get that sore leg looked after."

"That's okay." Tony inched his wheelchair closer to the other children, moving his IV stand deftly along with him. "I like it in here."

"You're a good boy, Tony."

She patted his shoulder, then turned when a distur-bance arose at the entrance to the playroom.

"Jamie's here!" the other children were shouting. "Hey, look at Jamie!"

A chubby baby stood in the doorway, beaming hap-pily, wearing nothing but a diaper. He was about twenty months old with a golden halo of curls, a pair of sturdy dimpled legs and bright blue eyes. In his hand he gripped a small plastic soldier.

"Oh, Jamie." Lila tucked her clipboard under her arm as she hurried toward him. "You're not supposed to be in here. Did you get out of your crib again?"

The baby chuckled hoarsely and went into a par-oxysm of coughing. When he recovered, he tossed his doll onto the floor and looked up at her with a spar-kling grin.

"Frow a man," he said solemnly.

Lila picked up the doll, then scooped the baby into her arms and cuddled him. "Yes, you threw the man." She nuzzled Jamie's plump neck. "You're al-ways throwing that poor little man around, and if you don't stop, you're going to lose him someday. Then there'll be a big fuss, won't there?''

Jamie giggled and tugged at her hair.

Lila carried him down the hall to one of the infant rooms, where a pair of nursing assistants were making up the cribs with fresh sheets. She sat in a rocking chair by the window, took a clean flannel sleeper from a stack on one of the trolleys and fitted it onto Jamie's body while he nestled contentedly in her arms.

The head nurse came into the room and paused, hands on hips, looking down at the baby, then at Lila.

''There he is,'' she said. ''I've been looking all over for this young man.''

''Hi, Marie. He came into the playroom and threw his dolly,'' Lila said, fastening the sleeper under Jamie's chin.

''Did he, now?'' Marie picked up the baby and placed him in one of the cribs, where he immediately set up a hoarse, mournful howl, then began to cough again.

Lila watched him with sympathy as he stood clutching the metal rails, tears streaming down his fat cheeks. ''Poor little fellow,'' she said. ''He hates being stuck all alone in that crib.''

Marie relented and lifted him into her arms again, cuddling him tenderly. ''But we can't let him into the playroom. He's still infectious.''

Lila checked another of the charts on her clipboard. ''I think I'll release him tomorrow. We've got his temperature mostly under control, don't we? And he's not nearly as dehydrated.''

''No, but he's in day care, you know.'' Marie handed Jamie to one of her assistants, then patted his bottom and smiled. "If we release him early, his parents will have to make some arrangements to care for him at home the next few days."

Lila sighed and got up, looking at her watch. "Do you have time for a coffee?" she asked the nurse. "I need to eat something before I go home. I'm starving."

"That sounds great."

Marie glanced at her young nursing assistant, who still cuddled Jamie. The baby's tears had stopped and he was laughing again as he peered over the girl's shoulder at his little plastic doll, which he'd just dropped onto the floor.

"Frow a man," he murmured happily.

"His mother's taking the afternoon off work, Carla," the head nurse said. "She should be getting here soon, and then Mr. Jamie will give the rest of us some peace for a while."

The nursing assistant grinned shyly. "It's okay. I like holding him."

Lila and the nurse left the room and moved off down the tiled corridor, a study in contrasts as they walked side by side.

Lila Marsden was a slender woman, taller than her friend by at least five inches. She was wearing black pleated slacks and a gray turtleneck beneath her white doctor's smock. Her dark hair was pulled smoothly back and tied at her nape with a silk scarf, and her blue eyes were calm under even eyebrows.

In repose, Lila's face often seemed withdrawn, almost cool, but when she spoke, a dimple in her left cheek gave her an engaging and unexpected sparkle.

Marie Korman, the head nurse in the pediatric

ward, was small and brisk in her pink uniform and thick-soled white shoes. She had curly gray hair, bright dark eyes and deep laugh lines around her eyes and mouth. But at the moment she looked subdued.

"Carrie's throwing up again," Lila said, holding the cafeteria door open for her friend.

"I know." Marie shook her head. "Poor little mite. She's having an even tougher time with the chemo than most of them do."

"But she's a real fighter. You should have seen her struggling this morning to get those overalls on her teddy bear."

Lila followed Marie through the lineup, selected a pot of tea, a ham sandwich and a slice of carrot cake and found a table near the window.

"Tony's better today," Marie said. "He spiked up to a hundred and four during the night, but only once. Have you seen his lab tests this morning?"

Lila nodded, munching hungrily on her sandwich. "The antibiotic's started to work, but he's going to need a long course of treatment, the poor kid. IV's at four-hour intervals around the clock for at least another week, then oral medication for another month. I'm not taking any chances of recurrence on this one."

"That was so terrifying, when nothing we tried could stop his infection. These new superbugs are my worst nightmare, Lila."

"I know. If that last antibiotic hadn't been effective…"

Both women were silent for a moment. Finally Marie shook her head and watched as Lila attacked the carrot cake with its gooey icing.

"Is that lunch or dinner?" she asked.

"I guess it's sort of both." Lila sighed and stretched her arms. "I'm so tired, I can't remember."

"You and I are getting to be such pitiful creatures," the nurse said briskly. "Look, let's cheer ourselves up. It's Saturday, you know. We should go out and have some fun tonight. It'll do us both good."

Lila smiled at her friend and started to pack dishes and utensils neatly on her tray. "That does sound like fun. A couple of wild single girls out on the town. What should we do?"

"Well, the stampede's on." Marie got up, holding her own tray. "We could drive out to the fairgrounds. It's the last day of the rodeo."

Lila stiffened, her hands tightening on the tray. "What did you say?"

"The rodeo," Marie said patiently. "The annual Medicine Hat Stampede and Fair. Haven't you noticed," she added dryly, "that this whole city is decorated like a frontier town, Lila? Haven't you seen everybody in the stores and restaurants wearing embroidered shirts and cowboy hats?"

"I just ignore it every year," Lila muttered, her heart pounding. "I look on it as an annual insanity that goes away in a few days."

"You don't like the rodeo?" Marie said curiously. "I thought everybody loved it."

"Not me." Lila moved away to deposit her tray in a metal rack. "I hate everything about it. Look, let's just go to a movie, okay?"

"Why don't you like the rodeo?" Marie asked, following her toward the door. "Don't you love all those cowboys in their tight jeans and Stetsons?"

Lila was immediately assailed by a memory so vivid and painful that she was afraid she might burst into tears. She saw a pair of wide shoulders, blue eyes shaded by a broad-brimmed hat, a teasing grin…

"I'll call you later," she said a little desperately. "Maybe we can go to dinner before the movie, if I finish up here in time. Okay?"

"First you have to tell me what you've got against rodeos," Marie said. "I can't believe a girl who's spent her life in Medicine Hat isn't a rodeo fan."

"It's just because…"

Lila faltered, glancing anxiously toward the door. The pain was intense now, and she needed to escape and be alone.

"It's because of a…a man I used to know," she whispered.

She turned abruptly and hurried out of the cafeteria, leaving Marie standing in the hallway, watching her in surprise.

CHAPTER TWO

NEAR THE RODEO ARENA, Ward Lincoln appeared at the side of the camper and looked up at Kelly, shading his eyes with his hand. He was a bull rider, too, a squat, bowlegged little cowboy with big ears and a gentle smile.

His wife stood next to him. Jenny Lincoln had a lot of freckles and was heavily pregnant, wearing a flowered smock over her blue jeans.

"Come on down from there, Kelly," she said. "Ward and I will take you and Casey over to the hospital."

Kelly hesitated, then scrambled down from the camper roof and stood silently next to them, digging into the dirt with the toe of her sneaker.

Jenny touched her shoulder, but Kelly didn't respond. She knew she'd probably start crying if she tried to talk, and that would be just awful, to have people see her crying. So she stayed silent and jerked away from the woman's hand.

"Jenny will drive your truck to the hospital," Ward said, "because your daddy's going to need it when he gets better. I'll follow in our vehicle."

"Where's Casey?" his wife asked.

Kelly jerked a thumb over her shoulder. "He's asleep in the back."

Ward and his wife exchanged a glance. "Will he fall out of bed while we're driving?"

Kelly shook her head and addressed the ground, not looking at them. "Dad built a rail on the bunk to keep him in. He's safe."

"All right, let's go."

Jenny settled her bulk behind the wheel of the Bennets' truck. Kelly climbed into the passenger seat and stared out the window, resisting all the woman's efforts to draw her into conversation while they drove across the city to the hospital.

"I'll stay here at the truck with Casey," Ward volunteered when they parked both trucks at the edge of the big lot. "Jen, you take Kelly inside and let Tom know what we're doing."

"Okay." Jenny reached for the girl's arm but Kelly resisted, jamming both hands deeper into the pockets of her jeans.

Inside the hospital she stood looking around at the soaring entry foyer, roofed in glass and filled with greenery. There were toys and books scattered around, and groupings of brightly colored furniture. It looked nice and homey, not at all like a hospital.

Jenny made inquiries at the admissions desk and then took Kelly upstairs to a ward that was pale and very quiet. Nurses and doctors bustled around, looking grim.

"Mr. Bennet's in ICU," the head nurse said. "No visitors allowed at the moment."

"This is one of his kids," Jenny said. She leaned forward and murmured something to the woman, whose eyes widened.

"All right," the nurse said, looking curiously at Kelly. "But just for a minute, all right?"

"Thank you," Jenny said. She knelt to look directly into Kelly's eyes under the brim of the baseball cap. "Listen, sweetie, you can go see your daddy for a minute. Tell him that Ward and I are going to take you and Casey out to Falkland and then Cloverdale with us. He can catch up with us on the road by calling any of the rodeo offices in British Columbia."

Kelly nodded, avoiding the woman's gentle, concerned gaze.

"Okay, I'll tell him," she muttered, edging toward the door where the nurse stood.

"Don't forget, Falkland and then Cloverdale!" Jenny called.

Kelly felt a brief flare of scorn. As if she could forget.

Everybody on the circuit knew where the next rodeos were. Half the cowboys at Medicine Hat were going on to the same string of rodeos in British Columbia, and the rest were heading back down to Montana and then east to the Dakota plains.

Entries were booked, rodeo fees paid in advance, traveling arrangements looked after. Nobody could afford to wait around in Medicine Hat for an injured bull rider to get better, and nobody expected them to.

Kelly tiptoed into the room behind the nurse, then paused in sudden terror. Her father lay on a long metal bed with side rails like a crib. He wore some kind of cotton dress and was covered by a blue sheet. All kinds of tubes and wires were attached to him, and he seemed to be asleep.

Kelly glanced up at the nurse, who nodded, looking kind and concerned.

"He might be able to hear you," she whispered. "He's just resting."

Kelly approached the bed hesitantly. Her body felt stiff and jerky, strangely brittle, as if she were going to break apart and fall in a million pieces on the floor. She reached out and touched his hand, lying lifeless and pale on the blue sheet.

"Hi, Daddy," she whispered. "It's me, Kelly."

His eyelids fluttered, but he didn't speak. It was terrifying, the way he looked so weak and helpless. Kelly wanted to fling herself on top of him, batter him with her fists, make him wake up and smile at her.

She stood for a long time just staring at him, then leaned forward to kiss his cheek near the bandage that covered most of his head. His skin was cold and smelled faintly of medicine.

The nurse touched her shoulder. "That's all for now, I think, dear. You can come back later if your friends haven't left yet. He might be awake by evening."

Kelly followed the nurse out of the room, then clattered downstairs with Jenny, ignoring the woman's questions. She ran across the parking lot to their truck, where Ward sat on the tailgate sharpening a pair of spur rowels. Casey was still asleep.

"How's your dad?" the cowboy asked.

Kelly paused, thinking rapidly. "Oh, he's…pretty good," she said at last. "Dad says his stomach hurts a bit where the bull stepped on him, but he'll be fine in a day or two, I guess."

Ward and Jenny exchanged a relieved glance. "Did you tell him we're taking you and Casey on to B.C. with us?" Jenny asked.

Kelly fixed her eyes on the spur in Ward's hand and took a deep breath. "Dad said for us not to do that."

"Why?" Ward asked.

"Dad said…" Kelly paused nervously. "He said he's heading out to North Dakota when he gets better, not B.C., so we should go with Earl and Mary instead and he'll catch up with us."

"Well now, I'm surprised to hear that." Ward looked puzzled. "I didn't think Tom was planning to go east this summer."

"He just changed his mind," Kelly said, improvising rapidly. "Because since he's…since he's hurt, he might not be able to ride bulls for a while, so he'd rather go to North Dakota and do some calf roping on Earl's horse."

"Well, that does make sense," Ward said, "though I just assumed you'd come along with us, like your dad planned. But if he told you he wants to go on to the Dakotas…" He and his wife exchanged a lengthy glance and then a nod of agreement. "So you figure you can wait here for Earl and Mary?" he asked. "I know they're on their way over. Jenny and me, we're all packed and ready to head out. We need to be in Calgary before nightfall to make Falkland in the morning."

"We're fine," Kelly told him. "Daddy says thanks for all your help," she added.

Ward and his wife both hugged her. "You take care of yourself, sweetheart," Jenny murmured. "Say thanks to Earl and Mary, and tell your daddy to get well real quick, you hear?''

Kelly hated being touched, but she endured the hugs because she didn't want to raise their suspicions. She even forced a smile and stood waving as the young couple drove off, heading into the western sunset.

HALF AN HOUR LATER, she was inside the camper, opening a can of beans for Casey's supper, when Earl Hirsch arrived with Mary, his plump, sweet-faced wife. Their big truck and four-horse trailer rolled past the camper and stopped a few lanes down, taking up a whole row of parking stalls.

Earl came striding back, big and red-faced, his boots clumping on the asphalt. ''Hey, kitten,'' he said to Kelly. ''How's your daddy?''

Kelly buttered a slice of toast on the little counter, put it on a plate and spooned some beans over it, then offered the plate to Casey, who sat at the miniature table inside the camper.

''Daddy's fine,'' she said briefly to Earl, who lounged against the tailgate. ''He'll be up and around in a few days. I guess he just mostly got the wind knocked out of him.''

''Is that so?'' Earl looked surprised. ''You know, I was afraid them injuries might be a whole lot worse than getting his wind knocked out. But Tommy Bennet, he's one tough cowboy.''

''Daddy's one tough cowboy,'' Casey echoed, bean juice dribbling down his chin.

Kelly glared at her little brother. ''Don't talk with your mouth full.''

Earl's wife came up and leaned inside the camper, as well, beaming at Casey, who was a favorite of hers. "Eating dinner, are you, sweetheart?" she asked.

Kelly cut the toast up silently, hovering nearby to make sure Casey didn't get messy.

"Earl and I thought we'd go in and talk to your daddy," Mary began, "and tell him we're taking you and Casey to Montana with us, and he can catch up later when he's healed."

Kelly tensed. "He can't talk to anybody right now. The nurse said I was the only one who could go into his room."

"Well then," Earl said, "could you run in there and tell Tom you're coming with us? Tell him we'll take good care of you all, and he can catch up with us over in the Dakotas."

Kelly stared with narrowed eyes at the western sky, now glowing in swirls of purple and orange. "Daddy still wants to go out to British Columbia," she said. "He told me we should go with Ward and Jenny and he'll pick us up later."

"But aren't Ward and Jen gone already?" Earl asked. "He was in a big hurry to get to Calgary."

Kelly shook her head. "They just went downtown to get some groceries and things. They're coming back for us right away. That's why I'm giving Casey his supper now," she added, embellishing the story nervously. "Ward, he wants to get on the road, so he said for Casey to have his supper early."

Earl and Mary exchanged a dubious glance.

"Well, I dunno," Mary said. "I sure do hate to leave you kids here all alone."

"But we need to make Billings tonight," Earl told

his wife. "I have an appointment to get the horses shod down there on Sunday."

"We'll be fine," Kelly said. "Ward's coming back in just a few minutes. My goodness," she added with forced brightness. "I better start getting our stuff packed before they get here." She began to open drawers and cabinets in the little camper, stuffing her own clothes and Casey's into duffel bags.

Earl and his wife continued to hesitate. "You're sure Ward and Jenny are coming right back?" Mary asked. "In just a few minutes?"

Kelly nodded vigorously, crawling under the bed to look for Casey's boots. "Ward wants to be in the mountains by the time they stop. Goodbye," she called over her shoulder. "I'll tell Daddy you stopped by."

"You do that, and hug him for us," Mary said. "And give our best to Ward and Jen, you hear? Tell them we'll see them next month in Oregon."

Kelly held her breath, still crouched on the floor. Above her, Casey was playing with his food, lining beans up in little rows on his plate and pretending they were corral fences.

Finally Earl and Mary left and went back across the pavement to climb into their truck. Kelly stood inside the camper, watching through the window while their big unit pulled from the parking lot and headed east.

Earl was equipped for traveling, with hay bales tied to the fenders and strapped to the roof of his trailer. The outlines of the horses were faintly visible through the side windows.

"Where's Daddy?" Casey asked, his cheeks smeared with tomato sauce.

Kelly took a damp washrag and cleaned his face over his noisy protests.

"Daddy's in there." She gestured through their small window at the bulk of the hospital against a pastel swirl of clouds. "And we're staying right here till he gets better."

"All alone?" Casey asked in alarm.

"Shut up." Kelly began to unpack the duffel bags and put their clothes neatly back in the drawers.

"I don't want to be all alone!" The little boy's voice rose dangerously. Tears swam in his eyes.

Kelly sighed and sat on the bed, lifting him onto her lap. "It's like a game," she murmured against his fat cheek. "We're playing hide-and-seek in here, and we don't want any grown-ups to find us. Okay?"

Casey looked dubious but remained silent.

"And then," Kelly went on, holding him tighter, "when Daddy gets better and comes outside, it'll be a great big surprise. He'll say, 'Where are Kelly and Casey? Where could they be?'"

She imitated her father's voice, sounding gruff and worried.

Casey brightened. "And then we'll jump out from behind the truck and say, 'Here we are!' And Daddy will be happy. Won't he?"

Kelly hugged the little boy. "It'll be so much fun. But we have to be very quiet in the camper so nobody knows we're here, or it would spoil the surprise."

"Okay," Casey said, looking hushed and solemn. "Can we ever go outside?" he asked after a moment.

"Of course we can. Don't be so dumb."

Kelly was beginning to be a little frightened about this course of action she'd decided on, and her brother's questions irritated her. But she had to keep him calm, at least for the next couple of days, or they'd be discovered and sent away with the rodeo people.

And the last thing she wanted was to be taken away from her father while he lay bruised and helpless in that hospital bed.

"Tomorrow we can go to the park down the street and play games," Kelly promised. "Maybe there'll even be a wading pool," she added, drawing on a distant memory of what playgrounds were like. "And a sandbox where you can play trucks and cars with other kids."

"And we won't have to travel anywhere for a while?" the little boy asked hopefully.

"No," Kelly said. "As long as Daddy's sick, we'll just stay right here."

"I'd like to play in the park and the wading pool." Casey climbed onto the bench and knelt to peer out the camper window. "I hate riding in the truck and going to different places all the time."

"So do I," Kelly said. "Why don't we go have a look at the park right now."

She put Casey's jacket on and lifted him from the camper, making sure to pocket the key. They walked down a tree-lined street to the little park, where she spent a couple of hours playing with him on the monkey bars and pushing him on the swings until he was pink-cheeked and drowsy.

When they came back to the parking lot, the place was all but deserted. The sky was darkening and a couple of stars sparkled near the horizon. A west wind freshened and began to howl around the corners of their makeshift home.

"I'm scared," Casey muttered when she buttoned his pajamas and tucked him into bed. "I wish Daddy was here."

"Daddy will be coming back soon," Kelly told him. "And you don't have to be scared of anything, you dummy, because I'm here to look after you."

He fell asleep almost at once, clutching his teddy bear. But Kelly lay rigid in the upper bunk and stared for a long time at the black sky beyond the window.

CHAPTER THREE

AS A PEDIATRICIAN, Lila kept different working hours from most of her colleagues. She saw patients in her downtown clinic Tuesday through Saturday, and took Sunday and Monday off except for emergencies.

But she did her hospital rounds every morning, especially when she was dealing with a patient like Tony, who still battled his dangerous staph infection with mixed results.

On the way to the hospital on Sunday morning she thought about the boy in his wheelchair, and Carrie with her adverse reaction to the chemotherapy for her leukemia. And baby Jamie, who was being released to his parents the following morning and would have to be looked after by his grandmother for at least a week before he returned to day care.

As she approached the hospital, Lila noticed a pair of children walking hand in hand along the deserted sidewalk toward the park. They were all alone, a girl about ten or eleven years old and a chubby preschool boy.

Lila glanced at her watch. It was just after eight o'clock on a glorious summer morning. Nothing unusual about a pair of children heading for the park.

But there was nobody else around, and the two

children had a solitary, vaguely unkempt look that troubled her.

The girl wore a pair of faded blue jeans and a striped T-shirt, and her blond hair was cut short and combed straight behind her ears. She seemed tense and worried as she squinted at the empty park, gripping the little boy's hand as if she had all the cares of the world on her thin shoulders.

The younger child, by contrast, skipped along at her side looking happy and excited. He wore green shorts and a T-shirt with a dinosaur on the front, and carried a teddy bear in his arms. He had a mop of curly brown hair and a round, engaging face.

Lila smiled, watching the two of them run into the park and head for the monkey bars.

But as soon as she entered the hospital, all thoughts of the two children left her mind. A major emergency was just arriving. A minivan on the way to a weekend church camp had been struck broadside by another vehicle.

Four of the seven children in the van had been seriously hurt, and the staff on both the emergency and children's wards were snowed under. Lila tugged a smock over her jeans and pitched in to help.

By noon the situation was stabilized, with only one of the children remaining in ICU. She went to the cafeteria for a bowl of soup, sprawling wearily across the table from her friend Marie Korman, who was also working the weekend.

"So much for my day off," Lila said.

"I'm glad you were here." The nurse rubbed her shoulders and adjusted her cap. "It was a madhouse in there for a while."

"Oh well," Lila said with a tired smile. "It's not like I would have been doing anything all that exciting at home. Just sitting out on the porch and watching Dad whittle."

"That's a whole lot more exciting than weekends around my house," Marie said. "There's nobody whittling on my porch."

Lila poured more tea from the little metal pot in front of her. "I'm so hungry."

"You're always hungry. Did you have breakfast?"

Lila grinned. "I can't remember."

"Oh, for goodness' sake." Marie sighed. "What a trial you are."

"Dad and I always used to sit around in the kitchen and have a great big breakfast together," Lila said wistfully. "It was one of his firmest convictions, the idea that a big breakfast was essential to good health. But nowadays…"

"Isn't he any better?" Marie asked.

Lila shook her head, rendered momentarily speechless by a mouthful of soup.

"I suppose he's not any worse," she said when she was able to talk again. "But he's just…not himself. He gets quieter and quieter every day, and harder to reach."

"Does he have mood swings?" Marie asked.

"Not really, unless you count going from sad to grumpy as a mood swing."

"Archie Marsden, grumpy? That's hard to picture."

"You haven't seen him lately," Lila said.

"I had an awful crush on your father when I was a teenager," Marie said, her cheeks turning pink. For a moment the strain left her face and she looked surprisingly pretty. "But he was already a young married man at the time, you know. In fact, I think you were probably born around then. You're about fifteen years younger than I am, right?"

Lila looked at her friend, fascinated. "I never knew about this, Marie."

The nurse laughed awkwardly, her color deepening. "It was a silly schoolgirl thing. I got over it and married Howard. And," she added bitterly, "we all know how that turned out, don't we?"

"You and I," Lila said, trying to lighten the mood, "are just not good at choosing men."

"But I can still remember the way Archie Marsden used to look, walking down the street, laughing and whistling. How that man could whistle, Lila! He could charm the birds down out of the trees."

"I haven't heard him whistle since Mom died," Lila said. "In fact, I hardly hear him talk anymore. He just sits out there on the porch, whittling and staring off into space. It drives me crazy."

"He's clinically depressed." Marie drained the last of her black coffee. "You know he is, Lila. He needs to see a doctor and get some medication and counseling."

"I think you're right." Lila frowned, tracing the handle of the little teapot. "But it's just impossible. I can't knock him on the head and haul him down to the clinic. And that would probably be the only way to get him there."

"Poor girl," Marie said with a brief smile. "Always looking after everybody."

"Me?" Lila asked, startled. "But, Marie...I don't

look after a soul. I'm thirty-six years old, and all alone. I don't even have a boyfriend. In fact, I'm as solitary as a woman can be.''

''Hogwash,'' Marie said comfortably. ''You looked after your mother for years before she died. You worry and fret over every one of these little kids in here. And you're still taking care of that baby you married.''

Lila laughed, a warm peal of merriment that made others in the cafeteria turn to them with curious smiles.

''Trevor would be so offended to know you called him a baby. He thinks of himself as a very suave and cultivated man-about-town.''

''Yeah, right,'' Marie scoffed.

''Trevor has a certain boyish charm,'' Lila said idly, sipping her tea.

''You're a softheaded, gullible woman, Lila Marsden.'' But the affection in Marie's voice belied her words.

''Oh yes, I'm gullible, all right. There's no disputing that point. Here, Marie, eat the rest of this toast for me.''

''And you're good to your friends,'' Marie went on, reaching for the toast. ''If it hadn't been for you, I don't know how I'd have survived these past six months. I really don't.''

Lila waved her hand in dismissal. ''That's what friends are for. Have you heard anything more from your lawyer lately?''

''Things are just about settled.'' Marie took a bite of chocolate cake. ''Howard thought he could go off and leave me after thirty-one years of marriage and not give me a red cent. But that man has learned a thing or two, let me tell you.''

''It's not fair of him to take more than half. You've worked all these years, Marie, ever since the kids were old enough to go to school. I don't know what happens to men when they turn fifty,'' Lila said. ''I really don't.''

''They go crazy,'' Marie said flatly. ''They start questioning their manhood and searching for reassurance. Some young girl comes along who's looking for a father figure, and she makes a man feel big and strong and full of beans, just like he did when he was young. Before anybody knows what's happened, the poor old wife is gone and he's stuck in a little bilevel somewhere, raising a brand-new family.''

Despite Marie's sadness, there was a certain amount of dark satisfaction in her voice when she described the fate of her ex-husband.

''Poor Howard,'' Lila said, chuckling. ''I wouldn't want to trade places with him, and I'll bet you wouldn't, either. Admit it, Marie, you're actually enjoying the thought of him suffering through diapers and midnight feedings all over again. A tiny part of you is really tickled about it.''

Marie shook her head, then gave Lila a grudging smile. ''Well, I can't say it's not what he deserves. The silly fool,'' she added, her voice roughening with emotion. ''We could have had such a nice retirement. We could have traveled, visited the kids and grown old together in comfort. Now everybody's lives have been turned upside down.''

Lila reached out to touch the other woman's hand

in sympathy. Surreptitiously she glanced at her watch, realizing she still had to finish her rounds.

"I just wish I didn't feel so...cast aside." Marie blinked rapidly as she stared out the window. "I'm like a pair of old shoes that look too shabby to wear anymore, so you toss them into the trash and go shopping for something nicer."

"Marie, that's ridiculous and you know it," Lila said with some heat. "You're still a very attractive woman. Just because Howard's decided to start behaving like an idiot, that doesn't make you any less valuable as a person."

"Or any less lonely," Marie said.

There was a brief silence while both women looked down at the table.

Lila grinned and broke some crackers into her soup. "Marie, we really should both find a way to get ourselves a life."

"Hey, you know what I'd like to do?" Marie said wistfully.

"What's that?"

"I'd just love to go ballroom dancing. They're starting a new class in the basement at the library. Ballroom dancing for all skill levels. Meets every Thursday night. Want to come with me?"

"Oh, Lord." Lila paused with the spoon halfway to her mouth and stared at her friend in alarm. "Marie, I've got two left feet, and I'm a total klutz. I can't dance. I never could. Besides, I'm usually taller than my partner, and afraid of trampling him underfoot."

Marie sighed. "I wish I could find a partner for that class. It would be so wonderful to put on a nice swirly dress and do the rhumba and the fox-trot. I'd feel like a girl again. I used to be pretty good at that kind of dancing, you know.''

"So was my dad. He was a marvelous dancer back in his prime. But he hasn't gone dancing for years and years. Not since Mom got sick.''

"Poor Archie. You know, I really feel sorry for the man.''

"So do I. But sometimes I'd also like to hit him with a brick.''

Marie chuckled, and the two women settled in to eat their meals in the comfortable silence of old friends. Lila set her clipboard on the table and began to page through it, making notes and reminders to herself.

"I guess it's a lucky thing we didn't go to the rodeo yesterday afternoon,'' Marie said at last. "We would have got more excitement than we bargained for.''

"Hmm?'' Lila said idly, turning a page.

"Didn't you hear? There was a cowboy badly injured at the rodeo yesterday.'' Marie grimaced in sympathy. "He was riding one of those awful Brahma bulls and got trampled. Donna says they still have him up in ICU.''

Lila nodded again, barely listening to her friend's chatter as she checked on Tony's newest antibiotic treatment.

"Apparently he used to live here in the city, a long time ago,'' Marie said, taking a sip of coffee. "His name's Tom Bennet.''

"What?'' Lila flung her head up, staring. "What did you just say?''

Marie looked at her curiously. "This cowboy who was hurt. For goodness' sake, Lila Marsden,'' she said with an indulgent grin. "You haven't been listening to a single word I was saying, have you?"

Lila reached over to grip her friend's arm. "I'm listening now. Tell me about this cowboy."

"Not much to tell. His name's Tom Bennet, and he was badly hurt during the bull riding yesterday afternoon. They have him upstairs."

Lila sank back in the chair. Her throat was tight and her heart pounded noisily in alarm. "Is he...do you know how he's doing?"

Marie shrugged. "It doesn't sound good. They've had him in ICU all night, still trying to stabilize the vital signs. Blunt-force head trauma and unspecified internal injuries was what Donna told me this morning."

Lila got to her feet, clinging to the edge of the table. She gazed around at the other patrons in the cafeteria without seeing any of them.

Marie watched her in alarm. "Lila?" she asked. "What's the matter? Are you all right, sweetie?"

"I'm fine. It's just..." Lila shook her head, trying to clear it. "Look, I have to go," she said. "I'll be upstairs for a while. Page me if you need any more help on the ward, okay?"

Outside the cafeteria, she hesitated in the corridor, then ran upstairs to the ICU unit and approached the desk.

"Hello, Dr. Marsden," the duty nurse said. "How are you?"

"I'm fine, Sharon. I just wanted to know the condition of the...of your rodeo cowboy."

"Mr. Bennet?" Sharon consulted a chart. "He's

doing a little better today. Beginning to stabilize after a very painful night.''

''What are his injuries?'' Lila asked.

''Well, to start with, he has a badly bruised spleen. Dr. Weider thought it was ruptured at first. They were all ready to operate last night, but now it appears there was just surface tearing and some bleeding.''

''Well, that would certainly be painful enough,'' Lila said.

''Yes, he's in a lot of pain. But we can't sedate too heavily because we're also watching for closed-skull brain injury. We need to monitor his reactions all the time so we can be aware right away if there's any swelling in the cranial cavity.''

''So I assume you're checking his reactions every fifteen minutes?''

''For another twelve hours.'' The young nurse shook her head. ''He also has a broken right arm, a badly dislocated shoulder, several cracked ribs and a lot of cuts and abrasions. He was a real mess when they brought him in.''

Lila glanced at the closed door and darkened glass walls of the adjoining ICU room. ''Could I...see him for a minute, do you think?''

The nurse nodded. ''No problem, Dr. Marsden.'' She glanced up curiously. ''Do you know him?''

Lila clenched her hands tightly into fists to control their trembling.

''I used to,'' she said.

Inside the room she closed the door and tiptoed to the bed, standing with her hands on the metal bars while she stared down at him.

She'd tried to prepare herself, but the sight of the

man still hit her like a blow to the stomach, taking her breath away.

"Tom," she whispered. "Oh, God, Tom..."

She hadn't seen him for fifteen years.

And that last time, he'd been walking away from her with his head high, not looking back, though she could tell from the set of his shoulders how much he was hurting....

Most of his blond head and part of his face were now obscured by gauze wrappings. His shoulders were bare, and she could see the thick golden mat of hair on his chest above the white bandage around his midriff. Both arms lay on the cover sheet, brawny and tanned, one of them wrapped in a padded brace almost to the shoulder.

She knew that body so well, so intimately. Memories washed through her and left her breathless.

Lila felt weak, almost sick with yearning.

She reached toward the undamaged arm, then shivered and drew her hand back.

He hadn't changed much in fifteen years. But then, Tom had always had a boyish, engaging look.

His face was a little more weathered now, his lips harder and more sculpted than she remembered. Even in this painful sleep, one corner of his mouth turned up in a familiar ghost of a smile, and his eyelashes lay in a dense fan against the tanned skin of his cheek.

Lila pulled the sheet back to examine his midriff. There wasn't much to see, just the broad white bandage and the livid bruises above it on his rib cage where the bull had kicked him. She shuddered to think of the mess that must be concealed beneath those dressings, and the pain he was enduring.

"Oh, but you're a fool, Tom Bennet," she whispered to his handsome sleeping face. "You were always such a damn fool...."

Tears burned in her eyes and began to trickle down her cheeks. She wiped at them with the sleeve of her smock and checked the bank of instruments near his bed.

His blood pressure was low and his pulse was still light and thready, consistent with serious internal injuries and possible brain damage.

While she watched, he frowned in his sleep, moaned and shifted his long legs under the cotton cover, lifting them toward his abdomen.

Instinctively Lila pressed his uninjured shoulder, feeling her hand turn to fire when she touched his naked skin.

It's still there, she thought in despair. *Dear Lord, after all these years...*

His eyes fluttered open. He stared at her, eyebrows knit in confusion.

Lila returned his troubled gaze, willing herself to stay calm, to smile in a distant professional manner, to hold back the tears.

His eyes were so blue, with a hint of aqua like a mountain lake.

I could drown in your eyes, Tom, she'd once told him.

Well, if you do, he'd replied with a lazy grin, kissing her, *I sure hope you're skinny-dipping at the time, darling....*

He rolled his head on the pillow and looked around, then turned back to her.

"Lilabel?" he whispered, trying to reach for her

with his injured arm. He winced in pain and gingerly lowered the padded brace to the sheet again. "Is that really you, or am I dreaming?"

Lilabel.

Nobody but Tom had ever called her that silly pet name. She hadn't heard it for fifteen years.

"Yes, it's me. You seem to have landed in my hospital, Tom."

He stared at her, struggling to focus. "Lila Marsden," he murmured. "The woman of my dreams, standing close enough to touch. I guess...I guess I must have died and gone to heaven."

"Tom," she protested. "Don't try to talk."

"And here I am, too weak to lift my goddamn hand." He gave her a bleak, twisted grin. "Kind of funny, isn't it, Lilabel?"

She was spared the need to reply when a young doctor swept into the room, accompanied by a bevy of nurses.

"Hello, Lila," the doctor said, giving her a curious glance as she stood by the bed.

"Hello, Matthew. I was just visiting."

"We need to check the catheter and do a couple of other procedures," Matthew Weider told her, approaching the cowboy's bedside.

"Okay, I'll leave now."

"Lilabel?" Tom said hoarsely, causing the young doctor to give her another startled glance.

"I'll come back, Tom," she said from the doorway, trying to keep her voice casual. "I work right here in the hospital. I'll stop by to see you tomorrow when you're feeling better."

"Lila, don't go," he called weakly as the others

closed in around his bed. ''Make sure my kids are all right, Lila!''

His tone was so pain-racked and despairing that she could hardly bring herself to leave and close the door behind her.

In the corridor she paused, her heart pounding noisily, and tried to collect her thoughts. His final words rang in her ears.

Tom Bennet had children?

She went back to the desk, where the duty nurse was filling out charts.

''Sharon,'' she said.

''Hmm?'' the nurse asked without looking up.

''This cowboy, Tom Bennet…what personal info do you have on him?''

Sharon took out a file and paged through it. ''Not much,'' she said. ''They brought him over by ambulance from the rodeo grounds. A couple of the other cowboys admitted him, but they could only guess at his age and personal details.''

''Where are they now? These cowboys, I mean.''

The nurse shrugged. ''They're all gone. Apparently they've already moved on to other rodeos.'' She glanced up at Lila. ''They cover a lot of miles in a year, and have their rodeos booked for weeks and months ahead. They can't just stop when one of them gets injured.''

''It still seems pretty callous,'' Lila muttered, ''to drop him and go like that.''

''But they were all really concerned,'' Sharon said. ''A lot of them stopped by before they left the city last night. And there's been a steady stream of calls today from places all over the country, other cowboys calling in to check on how he's doing.''

''He said something about...'' Lila hesitated, looking down at the file. ''He said something to me about his children.''

Sharon nodded. ''He has two little kids who were traveling the rodeo circuit with him. A couple of little boys, I think.''

''So where are they now?''

''They went out to British Columbia with one of the other cowboys and his wife. When he's released and able to travel, he'll catch up with them.''

''What about—'' Lila swallowed hard. ''What about his wife?''

Sharon consulted the file. ''His next of kin is listed as Kelly Bennet.''

''So has she been contacted?''

The nurse shook her head. ''We don't have phone numbers to call anybody. The cowboys said they'd look after contacting anybody who needed to know about him.''

''I see. Thanks, Sharon.''

Lila quickly checked in on the last of her patients then went downstairs and out to the parking lot, her mind still whirling. She settled behind the wheel of her car, staring blindly out the window.

It had been so terribly upsetting to see Tom after all these years. To hear his voice, and even touch him...

She shook her head.

Tom Bennet was married. He actually had children. Lila could hardly encompass the reality of it, or the bitter irony.

They'd parted mostly because she craved a home and family and a settled life, but Tom had wanted only to keep rolling with the wind like a tumbleweed. Now, all these years later, he was the one who had children and she was alone.

Still dazed, she backed out of the parking lot and started toward home.

She drove by the little park near the hospital where she'd seen the girl and the small boy earlier that morning. It seemed like years ago. Lila barely noticed in passing that the park was empty now, the swings stirring eerily in the prairie breeze as if they were occupied by the ghosts of vanished children.

CHAPTER FOUR

MEDICINE HAT WAS a small city, surprisingly hilly, green and lush despite its austere prairie setting. It curved along the banks of the South Saskatchewan River, nestled in a valley formed by rugged coulees.

Lila lived with her father on an acreage west of town, sprawling along the riverbank. Their home was a two-story log house with dormers, a cedar-shake roof and a wide veranda overlooking the water. Long-eared mule deer often came right up to the fence, and a bizarre assortment of animals grazed in the pastures next to the house, including some shaggy miniature horses and a couple of llamas.

Four dogs were sleeping on the veranda when Lila pulled into the garage. Her father was there, as well, sitting in his rocking chair with a pipe clamped between his teeth. He was whittling, as usual. She could see the long curls of pine shavings as they fell to the wooden floor and dusted the coat of the black Labrador who dozed near his feet.

Archie Marsden loved animals. For years he'd been a country veterinarian with a large-animal practice that took him to most of the farms and ranches within a hundred-mile radius. He could never resist a mistreated or abandoned animal, and many of them had made their way to his home over the years.

Lila climbed the veranda steps and smiled at her father, who nodded absently and went on whittling.

Archie had a head of thick gray hair, a lined, weathered face and a rangy body that seemed to be getting thinner as he aged. He wore blue jeans and a red flannel shirt, but the rough clothes were, as usual, meticulously clean. His hands, holding the wood and the knife, were gnarled but graceful.

Lila had always loved her father's hands. Throughout her life she'd been supported by their strength and soothed by their tenderness.

She settled into the opposite chair and looked down at the river, where a couple of pelicans swooped above the water with their effortless, graceful flight.

One of the dogs, a liver-spotted spaniel, woke and padded across the veranda to settle heavily at her feet. Lila reached down to stroke his long silken ears.

"Nice afternoon," she said to her father, watching the sunlight sparkle on the water.

He grunted and went on whittling.

Lila sighed. These days, grunts were just about all the communication she got from him. It was sad to remember what a happy person Archie Marsden had once been, a man who'd loved to joke and dance, with a booming laugh that could fill a room.

But since his wife's illness and death a few years earlier, her father had sunk so deep into himself that Lila didn't know how to reach him anymore. Increasingly she missed the man he'd once been, with an ache that never went away.

"Guess what, Dad?" She leaned back in the chair and squinted at the cliffs beyond the river, towering against the sky.

He said nothing, just went on whittling. Lila glanced at the wood in his hands and decided he was making an owl. He worked constantly on these replicas of the prairie wildlife all around them, finely carved and exquisitely detailed.

Archie labored over the carvings with thoughtful care, but seemed to lose interest in them as soon as they were finished. Every few months Lila filled a box with the little wooden animals gathered from around the house and took them to a gallery in the city, where they sold for an astonishing price.

She put the money into a bank account and used it to care for the dogs and other animals. Archie never commented on her disposal of the finished carvings, or her handling of the money.

"I said, guess what?" she persisted, turning to look at him.

He kept his eyes on his work and ignored her as if she hadn't spoken.

Lila looked back at the river where a herd of cattle was making its way down through brush and willows to the water's edge.

"Tom Bennet is in the hospital in town," she said, feeling a deep shiver of emotion when she spoke the name aloud. "He was hurt at the rodeo yesterday."

Archie looked up, his blue eyes widening in surprise. Though he turned away again immediately and went on with his work, Lila was encouraged by the brief flare of interest.

"He was entered in the bull riding," she went on. "Apparently he got bucked off and hung up in the rope, and he was badly trampled."

"What's wrong with him?" Archie asked.

Lila glanced at her father, startled. Often he went a whole day without saying this much, or showing interest in anything that was happening.

"He has a bruised spleen," she said. "Also a dislocated shoulder, a broken arm, several cracked ribs and possible brain injuries."

Archie carved a long curl of yellow wood from around the owl's tufted ears.

"The damn fool," Lila went on, feeling tears stinging behind her eyelids. "He's thirty-seven years old, Dad. Why is he still riding bulls as if he were a teenager?"

"Did you see him?" Archie asked.

"Yes, I went up to his room this morning. Apart from being so beat-up, he still looks pretty much the same as he did when we…"

She looked down at her hands while Archie went on whittling.

"He has kids," Lila said at last, needing to share the fierce pain she was feeling. "I couldn't believe it. The ICU nurse said Tom has two little boys who were traveling the rodeo circuit with him. I never even knew he was married."

Across the river the cattle splashed into the water, hides gleaming in the afternoon sunlight as they swished their tails lazily at flies. Upriver about a hundred yards, a coyote approached the water daintily and stood with ears pricked, watching one of the calves. When its mother saw the coyote she lowered her horns and moved forward a few steps, bellowing. Her challenge carried on the still air with a faintly musical note.

"Can you imagine Tom Bennet as a father?" Lila

asked. "Home and family were always the furthest things from his mind. In fact, that's why we broke up. He just refused to think about settling down."

She looked at Archie but he didn't seem to be listening any longer. He concentrated on the wood in his hands, making quick little flicks with his knife to outline the owl's tail feathers.

Lila was suddenly overwhelmed by a flood of loneliness and misery, a sense of wasted years and lost opportunities.

AN HOUR OR TWO LATER, Lila put on a pair of ragged denim shorts and a T-shirt, found a book and wandered down to the river, seeking out a flat rock in the shade of a cottonwood tree that had been one of her favorite places since childhood.

She looked around for a while, trying to enjoy this rare moment of leisure, watching the sun-dappled water and listening to the drowsy murmur of insects in the afternoon heat. But thoughts of the man in the hospital room kept intruding, along with sweet wistful memories that she'd kept repressed for so many years.

She opened her book and forced herself to concentrate, but soon a rustle on the path startled her. She looked up to see a handsome, dark-haired man standing just a few feet away.

"Trevor!" she said. "God, you scared me. I didn't hear you coming."

Her ex-husband grinned and settled next to her on the rock. "The only way I can ever get close to you these days is to sneak up on you."

Lila smiled, recognizing a core of truth in his

words. Years of painful experience had made her a little wary of Trevor Applegarth.

"You're looking well." She glanced at his open-necked polo shirt and khaki shorts, his bare feet in handmade leather deck shoes. "Is that a new hairstyle?"

Trevor swept his hand through his hair. "I'm wearing it longer these days," he said. "Do you like it?"

"It's very fashionable." Lila stretched her legs in the sun, wondering what on earth had ever possessed her to marry this vain, immature man.

Less than a month after the ceremony, she'd realized what a dreadful mistake she'd made. But she stuck with the marriage for two more years, mostly out of a reluctance to fail. Only when she began to realize that Trevor was becoming damaged by his dependence on her did she finally leave him, with as much gentleness as she could muster.

Probably the marriage had been the result of a combination of things. She'd been almost thirty at the time, had finished medical school and was starting her practice, able at last to look around and realize how empty her personal life was. After Tom left, she'd never had a really serious relationship with anybody, just immersed herself in her studies and tried to forget.

Trevor had actually suited her quite well, because he wasn't a man who could make any real claim on her mind or heart. He was more like an expensive, attractive toy. Subconsciously, she'd always known that after loving Tom Bennet, she couldn't give herself as completely to any other man.

"What do you want, Trev?" she asked, squinting at the cliffs across the river.

He looked injured. "Why do you always assume I want something?"

"Because," Lila said, smiling at him to soften her words, "you never stop by these days unless there's something you need."

Trevor shifted on the rock and rubbed a smear of dust from his shoe. "Actually," he said, "I was hoping to borrow five hundred dollars. Otherwise I'll miss another payment on my car."

Lila sighed. "I thought you had a good job these days, selling commodities."

"It is a good job," he said defensively. "But I invested a bit of my own money in some grain futures and it didn't work out. I'll know better next time."

"I'm sure you will." Lila set the book aside and leaned back. "Why do you need such an expensive car, anyhow? Five hundred dollars is awfully steep for a lease payment."

"I need to impress clients," he said. "You can't make money unless you look like you've got it. Everybody knows that, Lila."

"Do they?" she asked pointedly.

They sat together in silence, looking out at the water.

"Archie just told me about Tom Bennet being in the hospital," he said after a moment.

Lila stared at him in disbelief. "I'm always amazed the way Dad talks to you. He never tells me anything. Or anybody else, for that matter."

Trevor grinned. "I guess Archie thinks I'm harmless."

Lila smiled in reply, then sobered when she remembered the man in the hospital room.

"Is he pretty badly hurt, Lila?"

"Well, it doesn't look good. He might even have brain injuries. He was always so strong," she added, "but he's not exactly a kid anymore. Too bad he can't seem to remember that."

Trevor glanced at her curiously. "You never really got over him, did you?"

"Of course I did," Lila said with a brief flare of annoyance. "That was just a girlhood crush, nothing more. I'd known Tom since we were little kids. Besides," she added, "I was the one who broke it off."

"Why?"

"For a lot of reasons. None of which I care to discuss at the moment."

"That's my Lila," he said cheerfully. "Never talks about her feelings. Buttoned up and buttoned down. In some ways you're just as bad as your father."

The words stung, but Lila didn't want him to see how much. Instead, she turned to give him a cool, appraising glance.

"I'll make a deal with you, Trev," she said.

"What kind of deal?" he asked.

"I'll loan you five hundred dollars if you'll do something for me in return."

He looked suspicious. "What could I ever do for you that's worth five hundred dollars?"

"You could take Marie out ballroom dancing."

"Who's Marie?"

"Marie Korman. You remember her, Trevor. She's the head nurse in the pediatric ward."

"Small, pretty woman, gray hair, smiles all the time?" he asked.

"Not anymore," Lila said. "Her husband got his secretary pregnant. He and Marie divorced in the spring after a thirty-one-year marriage, and she's terribly lonely."

"So I'm supposed to take her dancing?"

"Oh, come on," Lila pleaded. "You're such a great dancer. And Marie's really a fun person when she's not so unhappy."

"But just a bit old for me, don't you think, sweetheart?"

Lila punched his arm. "Look, I'm not trying to fix you up. Marie doesn't want a man, just a dance partner."

He pondered for a moment, then sighed. "Where can you go ballroom dancing in Medicine Hat?"

"There's a group starting up in the basement at the library," Lila said promptly. "They meet every Thursday night."

"My God," he muttered.

Lila got up and gathered her book. "Well," she said, "if you don't want the money…"

"Okay, okay. I'll do it."

"So you'll call her?"

"I'll call her," he said gloomily.

"And you'll make up some kind of tactful story?" Lila asked. "Like, for instance, that you've been wanting to do some dancing to keep from getting rusty, and I told you she might be looking for a partner?"

"I'm nothing if not tactful, Lila."

"Yes," she agreed. "You're always very smooth.

Come on,'' she added, starting up the path toward the house. ''I'll write you a check.''

NIGHTTIME WAS the worst of all.

During their first full day on their own, Kelly had pretended they were just at another rodeo, and the camper in the hospital parking lot was the same home they'd known for such a long time. She was even able to keep Casey amused, though they were very much alone, and a couple of times he got scared and cried, frightening her, as well. But she never showed her fear, just bullied or teased her small brother until he cheered up again.

At night, though, when the parking lot emptied and darkness closed over the city, she realized how solitary they were and how much responsibility rested on her shoulders. It was all she could do not to start crying herself when she saw the moon shining through the window and heard the wind begin to howl again.

Kelly knew how to work the little stove in the camper. She'd even cooked a supper for them, eggs from the minifridge and beans and potatoes, which Casey liked to eat with lots of butter.

But that was another worry. Soon they would run out of food, and she didn't know where to get any more.

Money wasn't a problem, because her father kept quite a lot of cash under the floor of the compartment where he stored saddles and other equipment. But she didn't know where to find a store and wasn't sure if she could carry the groceries home after she bought them.

And Casey couldn't walk very far without getting tired and starting to whine.

As night closed in, she ran warm water into the sink and gave her little brother a sponge bath. Casey shivered and complained, jumping from one foot to another and ducking away from the washcloth. Kelly wrapped his small naked body in a towel and dried him, then bundled him into his pajamas, put him in his bunk and read aloud from his favorite book, the one about the toy soldiers who came to life and made friends with each other.

He begged for another story but Kelly shook her head and turned off the light, fearful that somebody would notice it and come to investigate.

Casey lay in the darkness, clutching his teddy bear and staring up at her. "Where's Daddy?" he asked.

"Don't keep asking the same thing, you dummy." Kelly got up impatiently and jerked open the door of their little fridge. "I've told you a million times, Daddy's in the hospital."

"Is he hurt?" Casey's voice began to quiver. "Will he die?"

Kelly turned from her examination of their sparse food supplies. "Of course he won't die," she said, feeling a sharp clutch of fear. "He just has a sore arm, that's all. He'll probably get out tomorrow."

"I'm scared." Casey gripped his bear. In the dim glow of the street lamps outside, she could see tears glistening in his eyes. "I want Daddy."

"Shut up!" Kelly said roughly. "Don't be such a baby." But that was a mistake, because he started to cry so loud she was concerned about being heard.

She closed the fridge and went to sit next to the little boy, stroking his soft curls.

"Don't cry, Casey," she murmured. "Daddy's going to be just fine, and I'm looking after you. Nobody can hurt you. Do you want me to sing?"

Casey hiccuped and jammed his thumb into his mouth, something he hardly ever did anymore. Kelly began to sing in a low, halting voice, the same song her father sang to Casey.

It was "Danny Boy," but he'd changed it to "Casey Boy," which always made her brother happy.

While she watched, his eyelids began to droop, and before long he was asleep, still sucking his thumb.

Kelly was amazed at how fast Casey could fall asleep. She lay awake for hours sometimes, staring into the darkness while she tossed and turned and worried about things.

But then, she was eleven and Casey was only a baby.

Being older made a big difference.

When she was certain he was deeply asleep, Kelly tucked the blankets up around his shoulders, pocketed the key and slipped out of the camper, locking the door behind her.

She approached the hospital, which loomed hugely against the star-dazzled sky, like a massive ship with its banks of lighted windows.

People lay behind every one of those windows. Lots of them were awake at this very moment. They were having babies, or in pain, or dying…

She shivered and pushed the morbid thoughts aside, concentrating instead on how to get in without being seen.

After his injury, Tom's camper had been left far to one side of the parking lot, half-obscured under shady cottonwood trees. The nearest hospital door was the emergency entrance, which Kelly figured was probably open all the time, since people could have emergencies in the night as well as the daytime.

She hesitated briefly, then started forward. Hurrying before she could lose her nerve, she opened the door and ducked inside the lighted vestibule. Two nurses sat behind a tall counter, half-concealed by several huge bouquets of flowers. They were talking and laughing and didn't notice Kelly at all as she darted along the corridor.

A series of lines was painted on the floor, all of them different colors. On the wall, a chart showed where each color led. Kelly began to trot along the yellow line that went to the lobby, reasoning that once she got there she could find her way to the third-floor room where she'd seen her father the day before.

Nobody seemed to be around except a few janitors, who were mopping the floors, and nurses carrying trays and charts. Whenever anybody approached, she ducked into a doorway or alcove and flattened herself against the wall until they passed.

Finally she reached the lobby, which was completely deserted. Stars glittered coldly through the soaring glass roof. Kelly ran over to the elevator, slipped inside and pushed the third-floor button.

She came out of the elevator almost beside her father's room, and felt a slight easing of the tension that was making her stomach feel queasy. A nurse sat in a pool of light behind the tall desk, working at a counter. Only her hair and cap were visible.

So far, so good, Kelly thought.

She slipped out of the alcove and into a washroom, leaning against the cold tiled wall.

Once inside the washroom she realized that her nervousness was making her feel the need to go. She locked herself into one of the stalls, then came out to wash her hands and examine herself in the mirror. She was so scared, her face was white as paper and all the freckles stood out like marks made by a felt pen.

Kelly dried her hands, thinking about Casey alone out there in the camper, trying not to worry about what might happen if there was a fire or something while she was gone. Or if he woke up and got scared and wandered into the night searching for her....

Kelly had always been used to her father looking after both of them. She'd had no idea Casey would be such a huge responsibility.

Finally she left the washroom and huddled in the recessed entry, taking stock of the situation. To her immense relief, the nurse got up in response to a buzzer on a panel near her desk and hurried off down the hall in the opposite direction.

As soon as she was gone, Kelly raced across the corridor and into her father's room, soundless in her running shoes. Holding her breath, she closed the door carefully behind her and approached his bed.

The room was dimly illuminated by a shadowed light panel above him, and by the flickering glow of the machines at the head of the bed.

A metal rack fitted with a plastic bag of clear liquid stood on the other side of the bed, attached to his arm.

His eyes were closed, and he looked very pale in

the ghostly light, somehow smaller than Kelly remembered.

For a dreadful, heart-stopping moment, she wondered if he was still breathing. The bottom dropped out of her world in dizzying fashion. She felt her throat tighten, as if somebody were choking her.

In panic, she gripped his arm and squeezed it tightly.

"Dad!" she whispered, leaning over the bed. "Dad, wake up!"

His eyelids fluttered open. He rolled his head toward her, frowning in confusion.

"Kelly?" he muttered.

She was so relieved to hear him speak that she felt weak and shaky, afraid she might fall down. Instead, she bent forward and rested her head on his chest, burrowing into him for comfort.

But he didn't even smell like her father, who usually had a pleasant scent that was a mixture of clean cotton, sunshine, dust and horses. Now there was only a faint tang of medicine and disinfectant.

And his skin felt so cold...

He lifted his free hand, the one that wasn't encased in plaster, and touched her hair clumsily.

"What's going on, Kelly? Am...am I dreaming?" His voice was thick and slurred, so unlike him that she was terrified all over again.

She pulled away to stare at him. Her father looked and sounded like some of the other cowboys when they had too much beer. But her father didn't drink, so Kelly had never seen him this way.

They must be giving him something in the hospital

that made him talk really weird, she decided. It had to be some kind of medicine.

"Do you feel better today?" she asked. "I hope you start getting better pretty soon, Dad, because it's kind of hard for me to look after Casey all by myself. He's a real pain sometimes, you know."

"Kelly, why are you here?" he whispered, then struggled to focus on her, as if he were peering through a pane of dirty glass. "I thought you and Casey were... Ward was supposed to take both of you out to..." His voice trailed off.

"We didn't go away with Ward and Jenny." Kelly stroked his arm again, since it looked to be the only part of him that wasn't injured. "I couldn't leave you here all alone, Dad."

"But what are you..." He shifted in the bed, looking agitated.

"It's okay," Kelly said gently, pressing his shoulder. "Everything's okay, Daddy."

"But...where's Casey?"

"He's asleep right now," Kelly said. "Casey's just fine. Today I taught him to print his name, Dad. You should see how good he can do it. He printed the whole thing—Casey Bennet—and it's really good except he still can't make the *B* very good. It looks kind of squashed but he..."

She realized that she was chattering out of nervousness and forced herself to stop talking. She glanced anxiously at her father.

Tom gripped her arm and held on tightly, but his eyelids were drooping shut again. He looked like Casey when he was fighting sleep, trying to stay awake even though it was an hour or two past his bedtime.

Kelly smiled briefly, then gulped and realized she was crying at the same time. Tears ran down her cheeks and dripped off her chin. She wiped at them with the sleeve of her jacket.

Tom's eyes fluttered open and struggled to focus.

"Sweetheart," he whispered.

"Yes, Dad?"

But he couldn't seem to say any more. Instead he closed his eyes and lay very still, holding her arm.

After a while, still sobbing and gulping, Kelly eased herself out of his grasp and placed his hand carefully at his side.

She rested her ear on his broad chest again to make sure he was breathing, then huddled near him for a while, comforted by the steady thudding of his heart under the cotton blanket.

At last, startled by the sound of footsteps and voices out in the corridor, she pulled away and tiptoed to the door. A couple of nurses were out there a few doors away, talking together quietly. When their backs were turned, Kelly slipped down the hall to the elevator, rode downstairs and made her way out through the deserted lobby and back across the parking lot.

Casey was sound asleep but had kicked off his blankets. She covered him again, then changed into her own pajamas, climbed to the upper bunk and lay staring for a long time at the shadows that played across the walls and ceiling of the camper.

CHAPTER FIVE

TOM WAS DREAMING.

In his dream he was young again, a boy enjoying the pleasure of a warm summer day. He made his way along the river, strolling on the damp gravel at the water's edge. The cottonwoods rustled above him and fish splashed nearby, rising lazily to feed on insects at the sun-dazzled surface of the water.

He rounded a bend in the river and saw a girl sitting on a flat rock at the water's edge. It was Lila Marsden. She had on a pink T-shirt and baggy shorts rolled up on her slim, tanned legs, with one of her father's old straw hats jammed on her head.

She was fishing for goldeye with worms and a bobber, singing quietly to herself because she thought nobody was around.

Tom flattened himself against a stand of chokecherry bushes and watched her, dry-mouthed and tense with excitement, wondering how to find the courage to approach her.

This girl was his fantasy, his dream, the most desirable creature in all the world, and she was alone by the water. Tom was suddenly confronted by the big chance he'd been waiting for since they were in grade school together.

But his feet were rooted to the gravel and he couldn't lift them. His heart began to pound in alarm.

In a minute Lila would see him. She'd get up, put her fishing rod aside and come over to him, and her level blue eyes would express her concern and puzzlement. Maybe she'd even laugh at him because he was stuck here and unable to move, though Lila didn't tend to laugh at people. She was too gentle.

Tom made a last frantic effort to pull himself away in time but it was no use. Just as he'd feared, she turned and saw him, then climbed down from the rock and picked her way across the gravel toward him.

Even trapped in this humiliating situation, Tom was dazzled by her beauty, the way her young breasts thrust upward under the faded pink cotton and her legs were slender and silken-smooth.

He hesitated, torn between a longing to reach out and touch her face and an even more urgent desire to escape. But his feet remained stuck fast, making it impossible to move. He felt his face warming with embarrassment.

"Tom?" she said. "Tom, can you hear me?"

He blinked at her, confused. The sunlit river and the cottonwoods faded to a pale shimmer, replaced by painted walls and a faint gleam of metal.

And Lila's old straw hat and pink T-shirt had mysteriously vanished, as well. Instead she wore a white coat over a blue silk blouse. She looked older somehow, but still gentle, even more beautiful.

"What happened to your hat?" he whispered.

"My hat?"

"It was Archie's hat, but you were wearing it to keep the sun out of your eyes."

Her forehead puckered with concern. Tom thought he saw tears sparkling in her eyes.

"It's okay, Lila," he whispered. "Don't be scared, I won't bother you. I'd go away right now but I can't move," he added, feeling abashed. "I'm sort of...stuck here. My feet are stuck."

"You'll be better soon, Tom," she murmured. "Your vital signs are beginning to stabilize, but you've had a pretty nasty blow on the head."

"On the head?"

Gradually the mists cleared and he began to realize he wasn't dreaming anymore.

This place was real. In fact, it looked a lot like a hospital room. And Lila Marsden, of all people, was standing next to his bed. He had a confused feeling maybe she'd been here yesterday, as well, but he couldn't remember.

"Lila," he said, reaching toward her with his un-injured hand. "It's really you."

"Yes, it is." She tensed a little but didn't pull away from him. Instead she placed a hand on his forehead.

Her touch was infinitely soothing. Tom sighed and realized how desperately he'd yearned for her all these years, like a man wandering through an endless desert and longing for a drink of cool, fresh water.

She'd always seemed like that to him, ever since he was a little boy. And in their late teens when they started dating, then became lovers, Lila had been a miracle, a blessing, the light of his life.

But somehow he'd lost her...

Pain began to throb behind his temples along with a new and disturbing scrap of memory.

"Lila," he muttered, lifting and flexing his legs

restlessly under the blanket, conscious now of all the
other pain in his body.

"Try to lie still," she said. "What is it, Tom?
What's bothering you?"

"I think...Kelly was here. It was dark, and she
came to see me."

"Your wife was here?" Lila asked.

He stared at her blankly. "No," he said at last.
"Not my wife. It was Kelly."

"Who is Kelly?"

The pain was beginning to suck at him, washing
over him in dark waves that pulled him under. His
eyelids drifted shut. He yearned to go back to sleep,
to escape the pain and return to that peaceful sunlit
river where Lila was fishing.

But this was important, so he forced his eyes open
again and looked up at the woman beside him.

"Kelly's my...she's my little girl."

Again Lila seemed confused. "Tom, they told me
you had two boys."

He shook his head and the quick stab of pain made
him wince. "My boy is named Casey," he muttered,
grinning briefly as he pictured Casey's fat cheeks and
winsome smile. "He's four years old."

"And Kelly's your daughter? You have a boy and
a girl, then?"

"Yes. She was here in my room."

"Tom, the kids have gone to British Columbia with
some of the other rodeo people. They left right after
you were hurt."

"Kelly was here. She put her head on my chest."
Tom forced himself to look up and focus on Lila's
face, which blurred and wavered in front of him. "I'm

worried, Lilabel. I'm worried about my kids. Where are they? Who's looking after them?''

''They're in another province, Tom,'' she said patiently. ''Your kids are both fine. You'll be with them soon.''

He couldn't keep himself awake any longer. The darkness pulled him down, but even as he drifted away he felt a growing fear, and an urgent need to make her understand.

''Kelly was *here*,'' he whispered, closing his eyes. ''Lila, you have to do something. I'm so worried about my...''

HE WAS ASLEEP AGAIN, his handsome face pale and still against the pillows. Lila hovered over him, touching his shoulder anxiously, checking the bank of instruments at the head of the bed.

''The man's as strong as an ox,'' Matthew Weider had told her earlier when she arrived at the hospital. ''After all the abuse to that poor body of his, he's already stabilizing and beginning to recover. He'll probably be riding bulls again in a couple of weeks.''

Not if it was possible to talk some sense into the man, Lila thought grimly, watching him sleep.

Dr. Weider hadn't been as confident about Tom's possible brain injuries, now being monitored by two of the staff neurologists, although Matthew said the other doctors, too, were encouraged by their patient's vigorous responses.

But Lila felt increasingly worried when she recalled Tom's agitation, his disjointed, confused speech, and especially the fantasy about one of his children visiting him in the night.

Hallucinatory episodes in a concussive patient were a particularly dangerous sign....

At last she left the hospital room, let herself quietly out into the corridor and rode the elevator upstairs to the chief neurologist's office. Wilson Clark was a plump, bearded man, sprawled in a chair with his feet on a file cabinet and a folder open in his lap.

"Hi, Will." Lila lowered herself into one of the leather-covered chairs. "I'm a little worried about Tom Bennet."

"Amazing powers of recovery." Wilson tossed the file aside and whirled his chair around to smile at Lila, his eyes sparkling above the bush of beard. "In fact, that cowboy is an impressive physical specimen."

"It's his mental powers of recovery I'm mostly concerned about."

The neurologist looked quizzical, obviously wondering what involvement a pediatrician had in this case.

"It's a personal thing," Lila told him. "Tom's an old friend of mine. We...went to school together."

"Ah, I see." His face cleared. "Well, the X rays look pretty good. Only a bit of nominal swelling, and well controlled at this point."

"But his speech seems very disjointed, and I think he's hallucinating." Lila told the doctor about Tom's conviction that one of his children had visited him during the night.

"That's not good," Wilson said, getting to his feet and rummaging through the file cabinet. "Not good at all. Unless he's having some vivid dreams and isn't able at this point to separate them from reality."

"I suppose that could be," Lila said thoughtfully.

"The medication would possibly have that effect, right? But he seemed so certain the little girl had been in the room. He got very agitated, worrying who was looking after his kids."

"They're traveling with friends, I believe?" The neurologist cast her an alert glance.

"Yes, I understand they left the city the same day he was injured."

"And nobody has been able to contact their mother?"

"Apparently not. There's no personal information about the man, including his marital status or current home address. Tom and I grew up together, but I haven't seen him for fifteen years, Will. I have no idea what he's been doing, or where."

"If you grew up together, he must have lived here in the city at one time."

"Yes, he did."

"So does he still have family here?"

Lila thought about the shack on the edge of town where Tom was raised, and the drunken, violent man who'd been his father.

"I could check," she said at last. "But I doubt if it's going to do much good."

"It's important to set his mind at rest. Fretting about things is very bad for him."

"Okay," she said reluctantly. "I'll go out there as soon as I can and see if I can learn anything." She got up to leave, then paused and glanced at the neurologist.

"Take good care of him, Wilson," she said. "Tom's a...a special kind of man."

"Is he now?"

She hurried to change the subject, conscious of the doctor's bright-eyed, speculative glance. "Wilson...what can one do for a family member with clinical depression?"

"There are so many levels of the illness, and so many treatments," he said. "Some cases take a year of counseling and drug therapy to restore chemical balances in the brain. Others can respond to a single climactic encounter that helps the patient engage with reality again."

"But what if the patient refuses to seek medical help?"

"Then there's nothing you can do," the doctor told her. "Nothing at all."

She nodded and left the office.

EARLY EVENING the following day, when the last of her patients had been seen and the bulk of the follow-up paperwork done for the day, Lila changed into khaki shorts, sandals and a loose cotton shirt, then went outside to the staff parking lot at the clinic.

The summer twilight was warm and rich. Traffic had thinned and the birds sang in the trees nearby. The western sky arched overhead like a golden canopy, swirling with clouds of pink and turquoise. The air seemed hushed, somehow expectant.

Lila stood for a moment by her car, remembering how much she'd always loved these enchanted moments when she was a child. In that magical time between sunset and the appearance of the first stars, she used to feel as if anything could happen.

A handsome prince might ride over the hill on a black stallion glittering with jeweled trappings and sweep you into the saddle to take you off to his castle. Or a wizard could fly down on a magic carpet and gaze at you with his smoldering eyes under a turban decorated with plumes and gold....

Lila sighed, wondering when she'd stopped believing in magic.

Probably it was after she'd sent Tom away and begun learning to live without him for all these lonely years.

She tossed her handbag onto the seat, then got in, started her car and drove west into the golden sunset, gripping the wheel tensely.

Lila hadn't spoken to Howie Bennet after Tom left the city, until one night when he'd appeared in the ER with a knife slash on his chest after a bar fight. But he hadn't mellowed any. The old man had been even more foulmouthed and abusive in the hospital than she'd remembered him from the past.

He was treated and released, and she never saw him again, hadn't even thought of him until now.

The road narrowed as she reached the edge of the city, and rows of houses gave way to a straggle of mobile-home parks, then scattered "acreages" with shabby houses and yards full of trash. She parked by a small building, not much more than a tar-paper shack with a few broken windows. A rusting old car sat up on concrete blocks in the front yard.

Lila got out, her heart pounding, and looked at the place. Painful memories and sympathy for Tom made her catch her breath.

The shack where Tom Bennet grew up had been directly across the river from Archie Marsden's beautiful house on the river. Even now, if Lila looked to the north, she could faintly make out her own home, see the redbrick chimneys and the outline of the veranda behind the rows of cottonwoods on the opposite shore.

"Whenever things got too hard at home," Tom once told her shyly, "I used to go over to that ridge with a pair of binoculars I bought at a secondhand store. I'd sit there and watch your house for hours, just hoping to catch a glimpse of you."

"How old were you?" Lila had asked, cuddling into his arms.

"About twelve or thirteen, I guess."

"And you could afford binoculars, Tom?"

He'd shrugged and grinned. "I was a hardworking kid, Lilabel. By the time I was ten, I had two paper routes and worked evenings cleaning the grease rack at Jacob Dinsdale's garage. But," he added cheerfully, "I always had to hide my binoculars from my old man. He'd have sold them to buy whiskey."

Oh, Tom....

The warm colors in the sky began to fade. A star twinkled above the western horizon and the breeze freshened, chilling her arms. Lila shivered and pulled a sweater from the car, then stood erect to look across the river again.

In later years, the swift-flowing South Saskatchewan had been no obstacle to Tom Bennet. As a teenager he swam across it, made rafts and poled his way to the other side, even hiked over the ice in the wintertime. And when he got to the northern shore, he became a different person from the sullen, angry child who lived in that shack with a loutish father.

On Lila's side of the river, Tom was a normal,

carefree boy, high-spirited and full of imagination. He loved to help Archie with the chores or lie in a hammock on the veranda and talk with Lila about everything under the sun. He also chopped firewood tirelessly and did other chores for her mother.

Lila's parents had always liked him. But gradually a subtle warning tone crept into Bella Marsden's voice when she watched her daughter's childhood friendship begin to take on a grown-up edge.

"You have to be very careful, Lila," her mother had often said. "Even though Tom is a charming boy, and probably a fine enough person..."

"What is it, Mom? What exactly are you trying to say?"

"Well, your backgrounds are very different, you know. And that's certainly not the best basis for a serious relationship."

But Bella's warnings went unheeded. Lila Marsden and Tom Bennet were lovers by the time she was eighteen. In the few precious years that followed, she was drunk with his sweetness, lost in the wondrous discovery of his muscular young body and her own, and the shattering excitement of their lovemaking.

Back then, Lila had paid scant attention to her mother's concerns.

At least, she thought she hadn't....

The wind whipped at her hair, tearing it loose from the scarf at her nape. Strands blew over her face and she pulled them back and fastened them, still gazing across the river.

Nearby, a couple of skinny pigs nosed around the veranda of Howie Bennet's shack, then squealed and fought with each other when they discovered the carcass of a long-dead gopher near the cracked water barrel.

"Here, you two, get outta there!" A woman appeared from the direction of a neighboring shack. She was fat and walked with a limp, leaning heavily on a cane.

The newcomer wore denim overalls, a checked shirt and a man's slouch hat. Only the braid of hair hanging over her shoulder, and an incongruous smear of lipstick, gave any indication that she was a woman.

She lifted the cane and waved it threateningly at the pigs. They squealed in alarm and trotted away, casting resentful looks over their shoulders.

"Damn pigs," the woman told Lila cheerfully. "Can't never keep them two animals penned up. I swear, them pigs could figure a way to crawl through the eye of a needle if there was a corncob on the other side."

"They're very clever animals," Lila agreed with a smile, having also met a pig or two in her time.

"Lookin' for somebody?" the woman asked.

"I wondered if..." Lila glanced at the weathered shack with its broken windows. "I used to know the people who lived here about fifteen years ago, but it's obviously empty now."

"Howie Bennet, he died five or six years ago."

The woman settled herself with a gusty sigh on an overturned keg and braced her stick in the ground, then looked up at Lila.

"He drunk himself to death, and good riddance. What a mean old sucker that man was. I'm sorry to say that if he was a friend of yours," she added, "but it's still the truth."

"I only met him a few times. But I certainly don't remember him as...as a very nice person."

Lila recalled a few occasions when they'd been out for a drive and stopped by Tom's home to pick up spare clothes or something he needed for work.

Poor Tom, he'd been so edgy during those times, tense and ashamed about having Lila see how he lived.

And once when Howie stumbled out of the shack and shouted some drunken abuse at them, Lila had sat frozen in horror, afraid the boy and his father were going to come to blows.

"What business did somebody like you ever have with Howie Bennet?" the woman asked curiously. "Are you a social worker?"

"No, I used to... I was a friend of his son," Lila said. "We went to school together."

"Now, Tom, he was a different matter altogether." The woman smiled broadly. "That boy was a real sweetheart. He grew up and turned into a rodeo star, you know. And no wonder," she added, her smile fading. "Living with old Howie made him tough enough to handle any Brahma bull, I'd guess."

"He was riding in the rodeo here in the city just a few days ago," Lila said. "In fact, he was quite badly hurt."

"He was?" The old woman gripped her stick.

"Yes, he's in the hospital where I work. I'm trying to find out if there's anyone who knows where his family is, so we can contact them."

"What family?" The woman spat noisily in the dust at her feet, then wiped her mouth on her sleeve. "There never was no family but old Howie and poor little Tom. His mother died when he was just a baby. Howie broke the poor girl's spirit, I'd reckon.''

"Did Howie ever tell you anything about what happened to Tom after he grew up and left the city?''

"You mean besides being a rodeo star?''

"I'm thinking about his personal life. Did Tom have a wife or girlfriend that you know of?''

The woman squinted, then raised the hat and scratched her head. "I remember once Howie told me Tom was doing real well for himself, dating a local girl from a rich family. Howie said she was a real looker, too. But then something happened and Tom just up and went away, and we never saw him again after that.''

Lila nodded, her heart aching. "Yes, that's true," she said. "He just left and didn't come back. But did Howie ever tell you what happened to him after that?''

The old woman frowned and hitched up the strap of her overalls. "You said you work at the hospital?''

"I'm a doctor.''

"No kidding?'' The woman gaped at her, clearly impressed. "Well, Tommy went on the rodeo circuit for quite a while. Howie used to tell me where he was. All over the place, Texas and Oklahoma and Nebraska. Tom even went to Australia once.''

Lila waited while the garrulous neighbor collected her thoughts.

"Then Howie started bragging about how rich Tom was getting. He said Tom was going to be looking after him real good in his old age.''

Lila looked at her, startled. Dusk was settling in

around them and the old woman's face looked darkly shadowed under the hat brim, almost sly.

"He was getting rich from the money he won at rodeos?" she asked.

"No, it was something else. Tom had a real big business and he was going to be a millionaire. That's what Howie bragged."

"But he's riding the rodeos now," Lila said. "And he doesn't seem like a millionaire. He also has a couple of small children."

"Tom has kids?" The woman looked up, her mouth hanging open in surprise. "Well, who'd have thought it? He sure never seemed like the type to be a daddy. That boy always was a rolling stone."

A rolling stone, Lila thought. That was Tom Bennet, all right....

"Didn't Howie ever mention his grandchildren?"

Lila's informant barked with laughter. "Howie never cared two cents about any kid, including his own. Poor young Tommy, he lived through some hell with that old man when he was just a little fellow. It was enough to break a person's heart, but what can you do?"

Apparently losing interest in the conversation, she heaved herself from the keg and set off in pursuit of her pigs.

Lila got behind the wheel of her car and sat in the gathering darkness, looking at the decrepit shack while her eyes blurred with tears.

What a desolate childhood Tom must have had, indeed.

Worst of all, Lila wasn't even sure at this point

why she'd really broken off their relationship all those years ago.

Was it only because of Tom's restless, wandering life-style and his reluctance to think about settling down and having a family? That was what Lila had told him, and what she'd truly believed.

But had there been a deeper reason, something she hadn't even wanted to think about back in those days? Something, perhaps, relating to her mother's subtle snobbery and Lila's own fears about Tom's family background?

Finally, grim-faced and silent, she put her car in gear, backed down the rutted gravel road and headed back.

CHAPTER SIX

WHEN LILA GOT HOME her father was at the kitchen table eating a solitary dinner, with several of the dogs lying on the floor nearby.

He looked up and grunted as she came in, then gestured with his spoon in the direction of the stove, where a pot of stew simmered.

"Hi, Dad." Lila filled a plate with coleslaw from the fridge and sat opposite him, eating hungrily. "How was your day?"

He shrugged and mopped his plate with a crust of bread. Outside, darkness rolled across the river and washed into the quiet valley. An owl hooted mournfully in a cottonwood near the water, and a coyote howled from the ridge.

Lila got up to cut herself a slice of bread, then filled a plate with stew and turned the heat off under the pot.

"I was out at the old Bennet place just now," she said, returning to the table. "But I guess you're not interested, are you, Dad. Nothing much seems to interest you anymore."

Archie glanced up at her. His eyes under their craggy eyebrows looked so bleak that Lila regretted her impatient words.

She reached out to touch her father's hand, but he

withdrew it hastily and turned away, tossing a piece of bread toward the spaniel.

"Howie Bennet's dead," he said.

As always these days, Lila was a little startled to hear his voice.

"I know." She took a mouthful of stew and savored the rich flavor. "One of the neighbors told me. Poor Tom," she added after a moment. "He led such an awful life with that old man, didn't he?"

"How is he?" Archie asked, surprising her again. "Tom, I mean."

"He's getting stronger, but they're still worried about the concussion. He seems to be having hallucinations, and that's not a good sign at all."

Since he appeared at least mildly interested, Lila told her father about her early-morning visit to the ICU the previous morning, and Tom's insistence that one of his children had been in his room during the night. When she'd looked in on him today, he had been asleep.

Archie listened but made no comment. As soon as she stopped talking he got up and wandered from the room. The spaniel padded quietly behind him.

Lila sighed, watching them leave. For the next several hours Archie would sit alone in the study, whittling and staring blankly at the television set. Then he'd make his way upstairs to bed, looking so withdrawn and morose that her heart ached for him.

Every night was the same.

Feeling lonely and increasingly hopeless, she got up and cleared the big pine table, then washed the dishes and set out plates and silverware for breakfast. Just as she was finishing, the phone rang.

"Oh, damn," Lila muttered, expecting an emergency that would require her to hurry back to the hospital. These nighttime calls were a part of life when you had a pediatric practice.

In fact, nowadays the phone seldom rang in the evening unless it was something related to Lila's job.

Archie had once had dozens of friends who clamored for his attention. But he'd been so withdrawn and crusty since Bella's death that even the most faithful of them had gradually stopped calling.

"Hello," Lila said into the telephone receiver, wiping her hands on a gingham dish towel.

"Hi, it's me."

"Hello, Marie." Pleased, Lila settled onto a stool and reached for her coffee mug. "How are you?"

"You'll never guess what just happened!"

Lila smiled at the bubbly tone in her friend's voice. Marie, at least, sounded happier than she'd been in recent months.

"Okay, so tell me," Lila said.

"First I want to know if you had anything to do with this."

"Marie, if I don't know what it is, how can I tell you?"

"Have you talked to your ex-husband lately?" Marie asked.

"Sure, I talk to him frequently. As a matter of fact, Trev was out here on the weekend."

"I see," Marie said darkly. "And did you by any chance mention anything to him about ballroom dancing, you bad girl?"

Lila grinned at the dark square of window and the

trees rustling in the summer wind. "I think the subject may have come up."

"How exactly did it come up?"

"Well…" Lila hesitated.

She hated telling outright lies, but she also didn't want to spoil Marie's happiness by telling her a man, even a notorious lightweight like Trevor Applegarth, was being bribed to dance with her.

"I think the way it happened," she said cautiously, "was that I was telling Trev you'd mentioned these ballroom-dance classes were starting up at the library, and he said something about how much he loved dancing. Trev's a great dancer, Marie. You should see him do the tango. It's sheer poetry."

"So you were telling him about the dance classes at the library," Marie prompted.

"And I said you didn't have a partner. I told him you wanted me to go with you, and he laughed like crazy. Trevor knows," she added in a wry tone, "all about my dancing skills. Once when we were in Acapulco, he…"

"Don't try to change the subject, kiddo. Just tell me what happened."

"That's pretty much all of it," Lila said, crossing her fingers. "I told him you were looking for a partner, and he said he hadn't done any serious dancing for a long time, and maybe he should call you. I didn't know," she added truthfully, "that he planned on doing it quite this soon."

In fact, Trevor must really have been in desperate need of that five hundred dollars.

Or maybe he intended to be back soon for more, and wanted to stay in Lila's good graces.

"I'm so excited," Marie was saying. "This is the first time I've done anything for ages except go to the movies with you."

"I see," Lila said teasingly. "And what am I? Chopped liver?"

"You know what I mean."

"Marie, I don't think this is… I mean, I think Trevor's just interested in…in the dancing," she concluded lamely.

"Well, of course he is," Marie said, sounding exasperated. "What do you take me for, some kind of idiot? But since the nice boy is actually willing to be my partner, I can still buy a new dress and go out and have some fun. It's going to be wonderful. I haven't felt this good for months."

"I'm glad," Lila said. "I'm really glad to hear it, Marie. And I hope you and Trevor have all kinds of fun."

After they said their goodbyes, she hung up and sipped her coffee, staring out the window with a bemused expression.

If only it were as easy to find some way of making Archie happy again. But that problem, unfortunately, was going to be a lot harder to solve.

Lila sighed again, then smiled when the black Labrador got up and came across the room, his toenails clicking softly on the hardwood floor, to lay his big head on her knee.

She patted him gratefully, listening while the coyotes howled across the river.

KELLY WAS in a parking lot in the middle of the city, so she didn't know coyotes were singing on the moonlit ridge. All she could hear was the drowsy chirp of crickets on the lawn, and the noise of traffic passing on the street nearby.

She sat cross-legged on the bench in the truck camper, looking at Casey while he slept. His eyelashes cast dense shadows on his cheeks, and his face was painted silver by the moonlight shining through the little window. Maybe it was just the light, but Kelly was scared to see the way her plump little brother suddenly looked so delicate and fragile.

By now, Kelly had grave doubts about the wisdom of what she'd done. Casey was getting more tired and fretful all the time. To make matters worse, they'd run out of food so he was also hungry, which made him even harder to look after.

The days seemed to last forever, and the nights were lonely and terrifying.

At first it had seemed like an adventure, being on their own and staying close to Dad to make sure he was all right.

But Kelly was growing more afraid that her father wasn't all right. She remembered the way he'd looked so strange and confused, all hooked up to machines in that cold hospital room. The thought made her shiver and she bit down on her hand again, then buried her face against her knees so she wouldn't cry.

They should have gone to British Columbia with Ward and Jenny. At least they'd be safe. Now everybody they knew was hundreds of miles away. If she went to the people in the hospital and asked for help, who knew what they'd do to her and Casey?

They might even split them up and put Casey in a foster home.

And how would Dad feel when he got better and found out that Kelly had lost her little brother?

She sobbed a couple of times, then clenched her hands into fists and rubbed them against her eyes. Slipping from the bench, she edged her way across the camper, trying not to think about her rumbling stomach.

There'd been just one small can of beans left in the cupboard, along with two dried-out slices of bread. She had to let Casey eat almost everything before he could fall asleep. Now she was so hungry that she could hardly stand up.

Kelly knelt on the other bench to stare idly out the window, wondering how much longer she had to wait before it was safe to go up and see her father. She hadn't been able to leave Casey the night before, he'd been so fretful, so she was determined to see Tom tonight. But people were still coming and going, and all the...

She tensed and stared, wide-eyed. A couple of young men in white smocks came out a back door of the hospital carrying boxes and trays of food, which they began to load into a square metal trash bin.

Kelly strained, trying to see.

It looked like all kinds of stuff. Buns and bread, fruit, even pieces of cooked meat...

Her stomach lurched and growled, so noisily that she clasped her hands over her middle, afraid Casey might wake up.

But it was still too risky to check out the trash bin. People were using the emergency doors and a lot of cars were parked around them in the parking lot.

The garbage trucks didn't come to empty the trash

cans until morning, around dawn. In fact, the rumble and clanging usually woke Kelly, who was a light sleeper.

I'll get the food later tonight, she thought in rising excitement. *After I've gone up to see Dad, I'll stop by there and pick up a whole lot of stuff and bring it to the camper.*

Feeling optimistic for the first time in days, she sat tensely near the window, counting cars as they went by on the street. When a hundred cars had gone by, it would be late enough to slip unseen into the hospital.

Seventeen, eighteen, nineteen...

With grim determination, Kelly ignored the pain in her stomach and went on counting.

LILA WAS DOWNSTAIRS in her father's study, wearing a plaid nightshirt and tennis socks, looking for a book to read.

Archie had already wandered up to bed, though it was still quite early. He spent a lot of time sleeping these days, both at night and during frequent daytime naps. Lila recognized this as yet another symptom of clinical depression.

She turned away from the bookshelves and bent to pick up the owl he was carving. Archie had left it on one of the coffee tables, almost completed. The little wooden bird was an exquisite replica with huge eyes that stared back at her, eerily lifelike.

Lila stroked its detailed feathers, feeling a wave of sadness. As she stood erect, the phone rang.

This time it was Vivian Ashcroft, the mother of

little Jeremy, age three and a half, who was having a violent asthma attack.

"They were...they were paving the street in front of our house today," the woman sobbed, almost hysterical. "We tried to keep him inside all day, Dr. Marsden, but he got away from the baby-sitter for a few minutes and opened the front door to watch, and the fumes were..."

"Vivian," Lila said, gently but with enough firmness to staunch the anxious flow of words. "Vivian, listen to me. Take Jeremy to the ER right now. They'll know what to do. I'll call and tell them you're coming, and get there myself as fast as I can. All right?"

"All...all right."

"Good. Now hurry!"

Lila replaced the phone and made a call to the doctor on duty in Emergency, then raced upstairs to pull on a pair of jeans and a T-shirt. In the hallway of the loft, she called to her father from outside his closed door.

There was no answer, but she hadn't really expected one.

Finally she ran downstairs and out into the summer night, driving along a moonlit road toward the city and the lighted bulk of the hospital.

TWO HOURS LATER, Jeremy was settled peacefully in one of the metal cots in the children's ward. He cuddled his stuffed lamb and slept, taking shallow, rasping breaths while his parents slumped in chairs nearby.

"Well, that was a bad one." Lila checked the boy's

pulse one last time, then smoothed his hair back from his damp forehead. "Those asphalt fumes can be so dangerous for kids with asthma. Will you both be staying all night?"

"As long as we can," Steven Ashcroft said. "And during the day we'll have to coordinate our jobs so we can take turns."

Lila smiled at the young couple. Vivian was a stockbroker and Steven was a computer systems analyst. They had plenty of money to care for their beloved little boy, but they struggled constantly to find enough time, which was a far more precious commodity.

"Well," she said, moving toward the door, "I'm testing this new inhaler on him, and I have a lot of hope for the formula. I think it might be just the thing for our little Jeremy."

"Thank you, Dr. Marsden," the young father said with quiet sincerity. His chair was close to his wife's. Lila noticed that their hands were linked.

She smiled and waved, then left the children's ward, pausing for a few minutes to chat with the duty nurse. Afterward, she wandered up to the doctors' lounge, took off her smock and settled back to drink a cup of coffee, reluctant to go home to her lonely bed after so much excitement.

But there was nobody around to talk with and her eyes were beginning to feel heavy. Finally she gathered her jacket and handbag and went downstairs, letting herself out through a side entrance.

The rear parking lot was almost empty of cars now, and moonlight washed over the smooth pavement, turning it ghostly white. The leaves of the trees along the street were brushed with platinum, but under each one was a dark pool of mystery.

Lila paused by the trash bin at the side door, rummaging for her keys.

Suddenly she heard a noise, loud enough to startle her. It seemed to come from inside the bin, which stood next to her at about chin height. She stared at the dark rusted metal, her eyes widening in alarm.

Could it be a couple of mice in there? Or even…

Lila shuddered, remembering the noise.

Even something larger, like a rat?

This part of western Canada still prided itself on being rat-free. Businesses and institutions were careful with their waste, trying to maintain the status. Lila wasn't sure she'd ever seen a rat near her home.

The trash bin was silent now, but she still had the impression of something in there, trapped and silent. She pictured bared teeth in the moonlight, and whiskers quivering.

"What nonsense," she muttered aloud. "More likely it's somebody's cat. Poor kitty climbed in and now it can't get out."

She put her handbag down on the pavement, gripped one of the projections on the edge of the bin and hoisted herself up to peer in, then gasped.

What she saw was half a face.

In fact it was part of a small pointed face, a child's face, but only the mouth and chin were visible because, she realized, the rest was shadowed by the brim of a ragged baseball cap.

The child huddled tensely in a dark corner of the trash bin, staring up at her.

Lila gazed back in horror, trying to fathom the situation.

This small person might be boy or girl, she had no way of telling. The intruder had been filling a box with buns, cake and pieces of fried chicken. This last treasure was still gripped firmly in a pair of small greasy hands.

"Are you hungry?" Lila asked, beginning to recover her senses. She peered over the edge of the bin. "Please, come out of there and I'll see that you..."

But as Lila spoke, the child erupted from its hiding place with the swiftness and agility of a cat, grasped the side of the bin and vaulted to the ground, trailing scraps of food, then disappeared around the corner of the ambulance garage.

Lila shouted and gave chase.

She didn't know why she was running, except that she felt appalled at the thought of any child eating food from a garbage bin in the midst of this prosperous city.

Beyond the hospital's auxiliary unit, she could still make out the dim running shape as it fled across the lawns and in and out of shrubbery.

It was really a very small child, Lila realized, struggling and panting. This shadowy wisp she pursued was probably the same age as poor little Tony, back there in the hospital with his staph infection.

When I find out who's responsible for this kid, there's going to be hell to pay, she thought grimly.

The running shape barged through a lilac hedge and back into the parking lot. Lila followed, muttering in distress as the gnarled branches tore at her hair and clothes.

But when she fought free of the hedge, there was no sign of her quarry. Lila's heart lurched with disappointment. She bent to grasp her knees for a moment, still heaving and winded from the chase, then stood erect and looked around at the silent parking lot.

Suddenly she tensed.

A big dusty truck and camper stood off to one side of the lot. As she watched, the camper rocked and swayed briefly, then settled again, as if somebody had just climbed inside.

Lila ran over to the vehicle and pounded on its aluminum side. "Open up!" she yelled. "Who's in there? What are you doing?"

Too late she realized the rashness of her action. This big vehicle might be dusty and well traveled, but it was also a newer model and looked expensive.

What if the occupants were just moving around, preparing for sleep?

Or worse yet, she thought, her cheeks turning hot, what if somebody was making love in there?

But there was no response from the camper, and the deliberate silence emboldened her to try again.

"Please," she called. "I don't want to bother anybody, but I'm looking for a child I just saw running away from the hospital. Could you open the door for a minute?"

Again there was a hushed stillness. After a moment Lila thought she could hear a muffled sound, like the whining of a sleepy child. Then, leaning close to the camper wall, she detected an urgent whisper. It sounded as if somebody were trying to soothe the child, who nevertheless began to whimper more loudly.

Lila hesitated, wondering how far one's personal responsibility extended in a situation like this. There was clearly more than one person in the camper, so presumably somebody was in charge.

Maybe it was none of her business.

Frowning, she squared her shoulders and glared at the mud-smeared sides of the vehicle. When a child was reduced to rummaging through trash cans late at night, somebody had to make it their business.

"Look," she called. "I don't want to make trouble for anybody. I just want you to open the door and talk to me. If you don't, I'm going to call the police on my cell phone and wait right here until they come."

There was another long, tense silence. Finally the door opened and a small person stepped out on the tailgate, then jumped down to the pavement, glaring at Lila from under the brim of a baseball cap.

Lila looked at the child in confusion. "You're the one who was in the…"

"My brother's really hungry," the child interrupted sullenly. "I didn't think there was anything wrong with taking that stuff for him. People already threw it away, right? Tomorrow it's going to the landfill, so why can't we eat it?"

"How old is your brother?"

"He's four."

"And you?"

"I'm eleven." The child looked up again, and Lila realized, despite the grubby clothes and cap, that she was a girl.

''I see. And who is looking after you and your brother?''

''I am.'' The girl cast her a scornful glance. ''We don't need anybody to look after us. We're fine.''

''May I see your brother?'' Lila glanced upward as the sleepy complaint from within the camper began to get louder.

''No!'' The ragamuffin jumped up to block the entry door, but Lila set her aside with gentle firmness and climbed into the camper.

On the bed, an enchanting little boy with round flushed cheeks and a mop of curls sat clutching a teddy bear. He sniffled and gazed at Lila through a sparkle of tears.

''I'm hungry,'' he said. ''My tummy hurts.''

''Shut up, Casey!'' the older child hissed. She too had climbed into the camper and stood close behind Lila, her hands clenched tensely into fists.

The boy's name struck a dim chord in Lila's memory but she couldn't stop to think about it now. Instead she sat on the bed and lifted the little fellow onto her lap, touched by the way he burrowed gratefully against her.

He smelled pleasantly of soap, and his curls were shiny. The camper, too, looked surprisingly clean and neat considering where Lila had recently discovered one of its occupants.

''What's your name?'' she asked the older child.

The girl shrugged and looked down stubbornly at the toe of her sneaker.

But her brother took his thumb from his mouth and gave Lila a hopeful, winsome smile. ''She's Kelly,'' he said. ''And I'm Casey. We were...''

"If you don't shut up," Kelly told her brother fiercely, "I'm going to smack you, Casey. No kidding, I really am."

He cowered against Lila, who held him close, stroking his rumpled curls. At that moment something dawned on her.

"Kelly? And Casey?" Lila stared at the two children, thunderstruck. "You're...but you must be Tom's kids, then. Isn't that right? Your father is Tom Bennet."

CHAPTER SEVEN

WHEN LILA SAID Tom's name, the little boy began to cry again. "I want Daddy." He burrowed against Lila, sobbing. "I want my daddy."

Lila looked at the girl, who stood tensely in the doorway. Her face remained mostly hidden by the brim of the cap so it was impossible to see her expression.

"Kelly, where's your mother?" Lila asked. "Does she know where you are?"

But the child stared down at her feet and refused to answer.

"Could you just give me her phone number so I can call and let her know you and Casey are all right?"

The silence lengthened, grew strained and tense.

"Are the two of you all alone here?" Lila said. "You have no adults looking after you?"

Still no answer. The only sound in the small enclosed space was Casey's muffled howling.

Lila held him and patted his back, feeling increasingly helpless.

"Look," she said at last, "you can't stay overnight here, eating food from a trash bin. I'll take you home with me and talk to your father tomorrow about..." She paused awkwardly.

Kelly looked up, and Lila caught a flash of fear and panic in the shadowed eyes.

"We're not going anywhere with you," the little girl said. "You must be crazy. I'd never let a stranger take me and Casey away."

"Of course you wouldn't. But I'm not a stranger," Lila said patiently. "I'm a doctor in this hospital. Looking after children is what I do for a living. Besides," she added, "I've known your father all my life. We played together when I was younger than you are."

"Well, Dad never said anything about you," the child muttered. "So why should I believe you? You might just be one of those crazy people who likes to steal kids and hurt them."

Lila realized the rudeness came out of fear, so she kept herself from giving a sharp reply.

"I'm not a crazy person, Kelly," she said quietly. "I'm a doctor, and I live with my father in a nice house in the country with lots of animals. The kitchen is full of nourishing food," she went on, "and there are warm beds for you and Casey to sleep in. And that's where I'm taking the two of you, so I'm afraid you'll just have to get used to the idea."

Suiting actions to words, she got up, still holding Casey, wrapped a blanket around his small body and began to carry him toward the door.

But Kelly barred the way, glaring up at her fiercely from beneath the cap. "We're not going with you," she said. "Put him down."

Lila saw how the girl's thin body quivered with fear and tension. She felt a wrench of sympathy.

"Kelly," she said gently, bending to get a clearer

look at the face under the cap, "if I don't take you and Casey home, I'm required as a doctor to notify the child welfare authorities about you. Then somebody from their agency would come and take charge of you. Don't you think it's better to come with me?"

Kelly hesitated, then turned away with a shrug of defeat. Her chin trembled and jerked as if she was fighting back tears.

Lila remembered Tom as a child. Sometimes he would come to school with welts and bruises on his arms, but the last thing he ever wanted from anybody was pity. This little girl was a lot like her father.

"Maybe you could bring a few clothes," she said casually, "so you and Casey will have something to wear in the morning."

Silently, Kelly took a small duffel bag from under the bed and began to jam it full of jeans, T-shirts and shoes. She seemed expert at packing for herself and her brother, selecting items with practiced ease and stacking them neatly in the bag.

They stepped down from the camper. Still holding the boy, Lila watched while Kelly took a key from the pocket of her jeans and locked the door, then stood rigidly in the moonlight.

"My car is over here," Lila said, leading the way across the parking lot. "But you know what?" she added, hefting Casey into a more comfortable position in her arms. "I left my handbag by that trash bin. Could you run and get it for me, please?"

The girl cast her an inscrutable glance, then trotted off across the pavement to pick up the handbag, hoisted it onto her shoulder and came running back to Lila, who waited beside her car.

"Thank you," Lila said. "Now, if you'll look in that small compartment on the outside, you'll find a set of car keys."

Kelly rummaged in the zippered case and found the keys. Without being told, she moved around the car to unlock both the driver's and passenger's doors.

Lila watched her over Casey's tousled curls, thinking what a competent and unusual child she was. Again she was reminded of Tom at the same age.

"You'd better put Casey in the front," Kelly muttered, holding the passenger door open. "It's easier to buckle the seat belt on him that way. Dad and I never let him ride without a seat belt."

"That's a very good idea." Lila bundled the sleepy boy into the car, assailed by a sudden feeling of unreality.

What was she doing, driving around in the middle of the night with a couple of little kids? And how would she care for them?

She also had a sharp moment of anxiety when she pictured Archie's reaction to all this. It wasn't too hard to imagine what her father was going to say when he woke up and found a couple of lively children occupying his house.

These days Archie Marsden seemed unable to tolerate any kind of disruption to his daily routine, no matter how minor.

But at the moment, there was simply no other choice. Lila stood erect, watching while Kelly climbed into the back seat and buckled her own seat belt. The girl leaned back and stared straight ahead, her jaw grim and set.

Lila started the car and drove out of the parking lot, then headed west along the river.

The motion of the car made Casey nod off again almost immediately. He slumped within the straps of the seat belt, his curly head bobbing to one side, a thumb jammed into his mouth.

"Have you been out there in the camper ever since your father was hurt?" Lila asked, trying to see Kelly's face in the rearview mirror.

No answer from the back seat.

"I thought you and Casey were going to British Columbia with some of the rodeo people. That's what the nurses told me."

Lila kept her voice deliberately casual, hoping to disarm the wary child, who stared out the window at the darkened countryside.

"But your father told me you came to visit him in the night," Lila went on. "We all thought he was imagining things, but I guess he was right."

As she spoke, this fact dawned on her with sudden relief. Tom hadn't been hallucinating, after all. His daughter really had come creeping into his room while the hospital was dark and still.

Lila thought about the prickly, independent child looking after her little brother all alone, then slipping into the hospital to check on her injured father. She felt a lump in her throat, and tears stinging her eyelids.

Finally, since it was clear that Kelly wasn't going to answer any of her questions, Lila fell silent and concentrated on driving.

As they drove down the valley road and parked in front of the house by the river, she could sense

Kelly's interest sharpening. The child leaned forward and stared at the water gleaming dull silver in the moonlight, then at the big house with its veranda and gables.

But she still said nothing, just climbed out of the car, opened the front passenger door and leaned inside to unbuckle Casey's seat belt.

Lila joined her and lifted the sleeping boy into her arms, then carried him up the veranda steps, handing the keys to Kelly.

"It's the one with the blue tab," she murmured.

Kelly unlocked the front door and Lila freed her hand briefly to switch on the hall light, then took Casey to the study, put him down on the couch and pulled the blankets up cozily around his pajama-clad body.

"I think he'll be all right here, don't you?" she asked Kelly. "There's a guest room upstairs that you can use."

The girl shook her head and indicated the Navajo carpet. "I'll just sleep on the floor," she said. "Right here beside him."

Lila was on the point of arguing, but changed her mind and nodded. It would be frightening for Casey to wake up and find himself alone in a strange place. Kelly was right, it would probably be better if she slept near him.

"I'll go downstairs and get you an air mattress and sleeping bag," she said.

"I don't need any of that stuff," Kelly muttered, sounding sullen again. "I'm not a baby."

By now Lila was getting more accustomed to this difficult little person. In fact, it was so much like dealing with Archie when he was in one of his moods that she had to struggle to keep from smiling.

"I'll get them, anyway," she said calmly. "But first we'll go to the kitchen and find you something to eat. I'll bet you've been giving all the food to Casey, haven't you? And now you must be starving."

The girl cast her a startled glance. Casually, Lila pulled off Kelly's baseball cap, then caught her breath.

Except for a delicacy of the bone structure and a girlish cast to the eyes and lips, this could be Tom Bennet at ten years old. Kelly had the same strawblond hair, clipped boyishly short, the cocky lift to her chin, the wide blue eyes and freckled nose, the air of toughness and vulnerability that Lila remembered so well.

"My goodness," she murmured, reaching out involuntarily to touch the smooth golden hair. "Kelly, you look so much like your father."

But Kelly ducked away and stared up at her suspiciously, looking uncomfortable without the protection of her cap.

"Let's find you something to eat," Lila said, getting up and heading for the kitchen. "And after that, it's time for everybody to get some sleep."

Kelly hesitated to look again at her sleeping brother. She tucked the blankets closer under his chin, then followed Lila to the kitchen. Without being told, she crossed the room to wash her hands at the sink.

Two of the dogs woke up and thumped their tails sleepily on the floor. Kelly smiled at them, startling Lila. But as soon as the child realized she was being watched, she masked her expression and stared blankly out the window.

While Lila sliced bread and filled a plate with stew to heat in the microwave, Kelly squatted on the floor and patted the big spaniel. He lifted a sleepy eyelid and rolled over, waving his paws in the air, pleading for his belly to be scratched.

Kelly complied gravely, then got up and washed her hands again while Lila was putting the dishes of food on the table.

They've been well brought up, Lila thought, watching the child's thin little back as she stood at the sink.

Kelly's shoulder blades jutted like fragile wings through the soft cotton T-shirt, and her nape looked narrow and vulnerable.

"I wish you could help me a little," Lila began, sitting opposite the girl with a cup of coffee. "I really need to find out where your mother is so she can be notified."

Kelly was eating with quick motions, clearly torn between good manners and voracious hunger. But the training won out, apparently, because she buttered her bread with tidy strokes and cut the meat carefully into bite-size pieces.

She chewed and swallowed, wiped her mouth on a napkin and gave Lila a level glance. "Don't talk about my mother anymore," she said. "'Specially not around Casey, because it upsets him."

"But I don't understand..."

Kelly's small face went blank and cold, as if a shutter had dropped over it. Lila realized there was going to be no information coming from this source.

She could see the child's tension as Kelly gripped her fork and stared at the table.

The mother of these two children seemed to be a painful topic. Obviously, all was not well in the Bennet household.

"How did you happen to be out in that camper, anyhow?" Lila said, trying another tack. "Didn't the rodeo people get upset about leaving you behind?"

"I lied to everybody," Kelly said calmly. "I told Ward and Jenny that Earl was taking us to the Dakotas. Then I told Earl we were going to Falkland with Ward. But we stayed right at the hospital."

"Why?" Lila asked.

The child flashed her a look of scorn and disbelief. "Because my dad was hurt. Why would I go anywhere else and leave him behind?"

"I see," Lila said.

She sipped her coffee and tried to make small talk about the dogs, the wildlife along the river and the games she and Tom had played as children. She sensed that Kelly was beginning to relax and listen to her, though the girl made no visible response.

When Kelly finished eating, she took her plate to the sink, rinsed it and put it neatly on the rack, then wiped her hands on a dish towel.

Lila took her back to the den, made up a bed for her on the floor next to Casey and showed her where the bathroom was.

At last she turned to the door.

"Well, it's past bedtime for all of us," she said. "My room is right at the top of the stairs if you need me. Oh, and I might be gone to work by the time you get up, but my father will be here to look after you."

"Whatever," Kelly said with a shrug. "We don't need anybody to look after us."

But as Lila climbed the stairs to her room, she was already brooding over this new problem. Taking a deep breath, she paused outside Archie's room, then knocked reluctantly and went in.

He lay in bed reading, the bedside lamp casting a soft glow over the covers and the rough-hewn log walls.

Lila felt a fresh surge of impatience. He'd probably heard everything, right from the moment they arrived at the house. There'd been all kinds of activity, footsteps and, of all things, a child's voice, but he hadn't even bothered to get up and see what was going on.

She sighed and came over to sit by the bed, looking at his rugged face, shadowed by the lamp.

In the old days, Archie Marsden would have charmed both these little kids. By now he would probably have had Kelly sitting beside him, laughing as he did magic tricks.

Instead, Lila was all on her own. Even worse than alone, because nowadays she had to worry about her father, as well.

"Dad," she said, "something's come up. I'm going to need your help."

He watched in silence, his face unreadable, while she told him about Tom Bennet's children, including their reluctance to talk about their mother and Kelly's rash plan to stay behind with Tom while the rodeo people moved on to other locations.

When she finished, Lila couldn't tell if he'd heard. There was no expression on his face, not the slightest flicker of interest.

"Dad?" she asked, leaning forward. "Do you understand me? These kids are here in our house right now, and they're probably going to stay at least a week or two, until Tom gets stronger or we can manage to locate their mother."

Archie turned his gray head on the pillow to look at her, his face so empty that she felt like crying for him. "What's all this got to do with me?" he asked.

"You'll have to watch over them while I'm at work, Dad. Kelly's pretty good at looking after her little brother, but I still won't feel really secure unless you're keeping an eye on these kids."

For the first time he showed some emotion.

"Lila," he said, "what do I know about looking after kids?"

She tried to smile, reaching out to squeeze his shoulder. "Well, as I recall, you were the most wonderful father in the whole world. So you must have taken pretty good care of me at one time."

But there was no answering smile from Archie. Even the look of fear had faded to blankness again. "I don't want any little kids running around here," he said. "They'll make a lot of noise and upset the dogs. Take them away, Lila."

She struggled to keep from making an impatient reply. "They're very nice kids, Dad," she said at last. "The girl's name is Kelly, and the little boy is Casey. And you won't believe how much Kelly looks like Tom at that age. It's just uncanny."

"I don't want them here," he repeated stubbornly.

"Well, I'm afraid you have no choice for the moment." Lila got up and started out of the room. "They'll be here when you wake up, and if I'm gone,

I expect you to look after them. I'll call from the hospital as soon as I can after my rounds. Okay?''

She looked at him but her father made no answer, just rolled over and turned his face to the wall.

Lila sighed and left, trudging down the hall to her own room.

CHAPTER EIGHT

NEXT MORNING before her early hospital rounds, Lila ran upstairs to Tom's room and found it empty. The bed was neatly made and all the monitoring equipment had been disconnected.

Numb with shock, she swayed on her feet and stared at the smooth bedcovers.

A nurse passed by, carrying a tray of instruments. She paused and smiled. "Good morning, Dr. Marsden. Looking for somebody?"

"The patient who was in this room…Mr. Bennet. Where is he?"

"Oh, the cowboy, you mean? We've moved him onto the ward. He's much stronger this morning. And looking gorgeous," the nurse added, dropping her voice. "My God, that man has the most beautiful eyes."

"I know," Lila said, then smiled awkwardly when the nurse gave her a curious glance.

"Well, you'll find him down on the second floor. Room 207."

"Thank you." Lila hurried to the elevator.

When she arrived at Tom's semiprivate room, the curtains were drawn around his bed and Dr. Weider was inside with a nursing assistant. Lila sat on a chair with her clipboard on her knees and waited a few minutes for them to emerge.

"Good morning, Lila," the young doctor said. "We've just removed the catheter. Your friend is feeling a whole lot better today."

"That's good news," Lila said. "May I see him for a few minutes, Matthew?"

"Help yourself." The male nurse emerged, as well, carrying tubes and catheter bottles, and the two men left the room.

Lila ventured behind the curtain and found Tom lying in a pool of sunlight near the window, looking pleased with himself. Already the fragile, precarious air he'd had in the ICU was gone. The bandage had been removed from his head, revealing a livid bruise on his temple and a scrape that ran upward into his thick hair.

He seemed like the man she remembered, brawny and confident, and even more dangerous to her studied composure.

"Good morning, Tom. You're looking a lot... stronger," she ventured, coming near the bed and looking down at his face.

The summer tan had faded a bit, but there were still warm crinkles around his eyes and a dimple that flashed near the edge of his jaw when he smiled. A lock of thick blond hair flopped over the scrape on his forehead, and Lila had to fight the urge to smooth it back.

Long ago, she'd loved to stroke that thick silky hair....

"I feel a whole lot better." Tom smiled at her. "Especially to find out you weren't a dream. It's really you.'' His smile faded but his eyes remained intent, fixed hungrily on her face. ''You look wonderful, Lila. Time has made you even more beautiful.''

''Oh, come on,'' she said, trying to laugh. ''Pretty soon I'll be forty years old. I'm not the little girl you used to play with.''

''Yes, you are.'' He touched her hand, then ran his fingers up under the sleeve of her smock to caress her wrist. ''The very same little girl. I've missed you so much all these years, Lilabel.''

She shivered at his touch and drew her hand away. ''Tom, there's something we have to talk about.''

''We have lots to talk about.'' He grinned again. ''Fifteen years of news to catch up on.''

''This is about your children, Tom.''

''My kids?'' The teasing smile vanished. ''What about them?''

Sitting next to his bed, Lila told him how Kelly had deceived everybody and managed to remain alone and undetected in their camper out in the hospital parking lot for three days.

He was so agitated and upset that she had to tell the story all over again as soon as she'd finished, and reassure him several times that the children were physically safe.

At last he began to relax, then grinned ruefully and shook his head. ''What a kid. She's one in a million, that Kelly.''

Abruptly he frowned and looked up at Lila.

''But it was such a crazy thing to do when she had Casey to look after. Are they both okay now, Lila? You're sure?''

"I told you, they're at my house," Lila said patiently. "I took them there last night."

"Thank God. If anything happened to those kids…"

"Look, you're going to have doctors coming around soon," she told him, "but later in the morning I'll have one of the nurses bring a phone in so you can call and talk with the kids, all right?"

"Thanks, Lila." He forced a smile. "I have to admit, I'll feel a whole lot better after I've heard their voices."

Lila couldn't resist giving his shoulder a reassuring pat.

He took her left hand and stroked it with his thumb again, smoothing the bare ring finger. "And where's your house, Lilabel? Where are you living these days?"

His touch was almost more than she could bear. She'd always had this same reaction to him, as if all the nerves in her body came alive and began to tingle when he was near.

With forced casualness she freed her hand and moved to consult the chart at the foot of the bed. "Actually, I'm still living with Dad in the old house by the river," she said. "I moved back there a couple of years ago, after Mom died."

"Your mother died?" His face softened. "I'm sorry, Lila. I hadn't heard."

"She had cancer. It was a long hard battle, and I'm afraid it took quite a lot out of the family. Especially Dad."

"I'm sorry," he said again. "You know, Bella never liked me much, but I always thought she was a fine woman. And a great cook," he added wistfully. "She fed me the best meals I ever ate when I was a kid."

Lila smiled. "We had fun in those days, didn't we, Tom? Do you remember the fort we built down in the cottonwoods, and our secret-club charter?"

"I sure do." Laughter made his face light up. "Remember how we used to fight over whose turn it was to build the fire?"

"We were both firebugs in those days. But we loved that clubhouse of ours," Lila said fondly, remembering. "Every scrap of carpet or bit of lumber we could lay our hands on, it all went into that clubhouse. We made it really nice and cozy over the years, didn't we?"

"Yeah." He studied her face, suddenly intent, his eyes sparkling. "Our clubhouse was a nice cozy place, Lilabel."

Her cheeks flamed with embarrassment when she realized what he meant.

The old clubhouse wasn't just their childhood hideaway. It had also been the place where they first made love, one summer night by the river when she was eighteen and he was a year older....

"That's not what I mean," she said hastily, leafing through the chart she held to hide her confusion. "I was thinking about when we were little kids, just Kelly's age. I'd forgotten about...all those other things," she concluded awkwardly.

"Forgotten, Lilabel?" he asked softly, grasping her arm. "You've really forgotten?"

It was ridiculous the way she still responded to his words and his touch. Almost as if she hadn't grown up at all, and was still subject to those same adolescent passions.

"Yes, Tom." She freed her arm and moved over to stand by the window. "Actually, I have. It was all a long time ago."

She glanced down at the file to avoid his probing gaze.

"But you're still not married, Lila," he said. "You live at home with your father?"

"I've been married and divorced. It's fifteen years since I last saw you, Tom. I've lived half a lifetime since then, and so have you."

"Yes," he said quietly, glancing out the window beyond her with a sudden look of fatigue and sadness. "We've both lived half a lifetime, haven't we?"

There was a brief, awkward silence.

"I couldn't get Kelly to tell me anything about her mother," Lila said, "so we still don't know who to notify about your accident and the children's situation."

His face hardened, and a muscle twitched in the tanned line of his jaw. "Their mother is dead. I have sole custody of them. There's nobody else to notify."

"I see."

Lila consulted the chart again, wishing she could ask for more information, but something in his face made her reluctant to pursue the topic. Instead, she glanced up and gave him a level glance.

"So you have sole custody and this is how you're looking after them, Tom? Hauling them around to rodeos with you, all over the country?"

"They have a good life," he said. "The best I'm able to give them."

"Last night it didn't look so good when I found them all alone in that camper. Poor little Casey was terrified and crying."

She saw the brief spasm of pain that touched the man's face, then vanished. He looked at the window and said nothing.

"Does Kelly go to school?" Lila asked. "Do you ever settle down in the winter long enough for them to have some stability in their lives?"

"She takes correspondence courses," he said coldly. "We work on them together in the evening after Casey's in bed. She's a whole grade level ahead of other kids her age."

"Oh, Tom." Lila shook her head. "You haven't changed at all, have you?"

"What do you mean by that?"

"You're still a drifter. Nothing but a tumbleweed, rolling around with the wind." She waved a hand at the hospital bed and his injured body. "But you have responsibilities now. Did you ever give a thought to what happens to these children if you aren't able to care for them?"

"I had all the arrangements made in case something happened to me." He met her eyes with a look of angry challenge. "How could I have known Kelly was going to take matters into her own hands?"

"They should have a home and neighbors," Lila said. "And a whole network of support in case something happens to you. I really don't think you're being very responsible, Tom."

"And I don't think you have the right to tell me how to live my life. You waived that right a long time ago, didn't you, Lila?"

"I guess I did."

For a moment the old tension hung between them, as charged as a summer afternoon before a thunderstorm.

Finally she forced herself to relax and smile.

"Well, I'm certainly not exhibiting the best in bedside manners," she said lightly. "Fighting with patients is not good medical practice. And you're right," she added, replacing the chart. "How you live and what you do with your children is none of my business."

"Are they really okay?" he said, looking anxious again. "Has Casey settled down? He can be really touchy when he's upset."

"They were asleep when I left." Lila moved toward the door, checking her watch. "But I imagine everybody's awake by now and having breakfast. I'll call soon to make sure they're doing all right."

"Thanks for looking after them, Lila. I'm…sorry I yelled at you."

"I'm sorry, too. But there are some things we'll just never agree on, Tom. It's probably best not to talk about them."

He watched her with that disconcerting blue gaze. "I guess you're right. You always disapproved of me, didn't you, Lila?"

No, she thought sadly. I loved you, Tom. Practically all my life, since I was a little girl. But I could never, ever live the way you do.

He settled back and adjusted his broad shoulders against the pillows. "They'll probably be getting along just fine," he said with a fond smile. "Archie was always great with kids."

Lila paused in the doorway, wondering what to say. How could she explain all that had happened in recent years, and the way Archie was nowadays? Tom would hardly recognize the man.

"Yes," she said at last, her heart aching. "He was always good with kids. Look, I'll drop by later and let you know how they're doing. Now that you're out of the ICU, they can probably come for a visit tomorrow."

"Thanks, Lila." He gave her one of his old sunny smiles, as if the moment of angry tension had never happened. "This is great, what you and Archie are doing for my kids. I really appreciate it."

"No need to thank me, Tom. Anybody would have done the same."

"Well, I'll settle up with you when I'm on my feet again. And the way I'm feeling this morning, that won't be long."

"Don't rush anything," she said. "You've had some pretty serious injuries, you know. We'll want a reasonable amount of recovery time before you can travel again. In the meantime, there's lots of room at our house for Casey and Kelly."

"Lucky kids," he said with a reminiscent smile. "I wish I could be ten years old again and going fishing with Archie Marsden."

Lila opened her mouth to speak, then thought better of it, closed the door quietly and hurried off down the hallway to begin her rounds.

KELLY WOKE UP and blinked in confusion, wondering what was wrong. Somebody had come along while she was asleep and moved the window of the camper. Or else she'd fallen onto the floor.

In sudden panic she leaped to her feet, looking for Casey.

But the little boy was nowhere to be seen. She was in a strange place, standing on an air mattress and sleeping bag in the middle of the floor. The walls were lined with books and framed oil paintings of horses and dogs. On a couch nearby was a rumpled nest of blankets.

She knew Casey had been sleeping there, but no trace of him remained.

Kelly grabbed the duffel bag and rummaged through it, pulling on her jeans and T-shirt. As she dressed, she recalled the dreamlike events of the previous evening, the pretty lady who'd chased her away from the trash bin, then said she was a doctor and served up bread and stew in a kitchen where dogs slept on the floor.

But where was Casey?

She left the den and made her way down the hallway, trying to find the kitchen from memory. As she walked, Kelly gazed around in awe.

After living so long in the little camper, she found this house as big as a palace. The floors were shiny wood, and most of the furniture was made of leather, soft and inviting. Big windows looked out onto a peaceful morning, with views of trees, rugged cliffs and a river that sparkled in the sunlight.

Finally she came to the kitchen and stood barefoot in the entryway on the cool wood floor. A couple of dogs sprawled in a square of sunlight near the outer door. The big spaniel sniffed the air, then got up and padded over to lick Kelly's hand.

Casey sat at the table with an awed and frightened expression. He wore the Star Trek pajamas she'd dressed him in last night, and his curly hair stood on end. His eyes were wide and dazed, the way they always looked when he wasn't quite awake yet. Silently, he watched an old man who stood by the counter buttering toast.

Kelly looked around, taking stock of the situation. When Casey caught sight of her, his face crumpled and he seemed on the verge of tears.

If he started crying, she didn't know what she'd do. It was hard to concentrate on anything else when Casey was making a fuss.

Kelly crossed the room hastily and slipped into a chair beside him, leaning forward. "Be quiet," she whispered tensely. "Don't start bawling. There's nothing to be scared of."

He gulped and swallowed hard, his brown eyes shiny with tears.

Kelly gave him another stern warning glance. Her little brother stuck his thumb in his mouth and remained quiet for the moment.

The old man turned and looked at her. Kelly was badly frightened by his unsmiling features and jutting gray eyebrows. But she quelled her fear and stared back at him with a look of cold wariness.

"What do you want to eat?" he said curtly. "Toast or cereal?"

"Toast is fine," Kelly said. "Please," she added automatically.

He carried a stack of buttered toast over to the table, along with a couple of plates. He was very thin and was dressed in clean blue jeans, moccasins and a green plaid shirt. His hands were gnarled and knotted with veins and covered with brown spots like freckles, only bigger.

When the old man set the toast down, Casey looked at it, then up at Kelly with an expression of startled distaste. The tears gathered and spilled over, running down his plump cheeks.

"What's wrong now?" the man asked gruffly.

"He doesn't like toast with seeds and hard stuff in it. He thinks they're bugs," Kelly explained for her brother, who was still crying silently.

"Well, that's just ridiculous. This is healthy whole-grain toast. Now, eat your breakfast!" the old man said, turning suddenly to Casey, his eyebrows looking very fierce.

It was too much for the terrified little boy. He began to howl in earnest, then slid down from the chair and ran back to the den, flinging himself onto the couch. Kelly followed closely behind. He curled up in a ball under the quilt so that all that was visible was his thatch of curls, and cried louder when Kelly tried to talk to him.

The man passed by, holding a knife and a piece of wood, and stood helplessly in the doorway. Kelly, who was kneeling by her brother, felt a shiver of alarm when she saw the knife.

But this old man didn't look like somebody who wanted to kill them. He just seemed upset that people were around interfering with his life.

He wants us to go away, she thought. *And I wish we could, but I don't even know where we are.*

Still, her concern for Casey made her act ruder than she'd intended.

"Now look what you've gone and done," she said angrily. "Why'd you have to yell at him like that, anyhow? He'll probably cry all day."

The man looked distressed. He opened his mouth as if to speak, then closed it again and trudged off down the hall and through the front door. After a couple of minutes she peeked outside and saw him slumped in a chair on the veranda, whittling at the block of wood.

Kelly edged nearer and flattened her face on the glass to get a better look, but it was hard to tell what he was making. The shavings fell away from his hands in long golden curls and dusted the floor of the porch. Three dogs lay around him, one with its chin resting on his moccasined foot.

He couldn't be that bad, Kelly thought, if the dogs liked him.

Despite her nervousness in the old man's presence, part of her felt a sneaking sympathy for him. She sensed that he was like her in some ways, a person who didn't fit in or do the things people expected of him, so everybody got upset.

Besides, he seemed lonely and that always tore at Kelly's heart. She knew a whole lot about loneliness.

But then she looked at Casey, still howling under the quilt, and her face hardened.

Serves him right if he's lonely, she thought. *Mean old thing.*

At that moment the phone began to ring. Kelly went back to the window, expecting the man to get up and answer it, but he didn't. He just went on whittling while the phone rang and rang in the quiet house.

Finally, she went out into the hall and lifted down the receiver.

"Hello?" she said.

There was a brief silence on the other end. "Kelly?" a woman's voice said. "Is that you?"

"Yeah."

"This is Lila. I'm the…the lady who brought you there last night."

"I know who you are," Kelly said.

"I just wondered if everything's all right out there."

"That old man made Casey cry," Kelly said. She peeked through the door of the den and held the receiver out for a moment. "Did you hear that?" she said, bringing the phone to her ear again. "He's still bawling like crazy."

"Oh dear," the woman said. "What happened?"

"That man tried to give Casey toast with bumps in it, then yelled when he wouldn't eat. Casey always cries if you yell at him."

"Well, no wonder," the woman said, sounding so annoyed that Kelly grinned in spite of herself. "I'd cry too if a stranger yelled at me when I wasn't even sure where I was. Poor little Casey."

"The old man is sitting on the veranda now," Kelly said. "He's carving something with a knife."

"And how's Casey, besides being scared?"

"Still crying. I guess he's hungry, too, because he didn't have any breakfast, but I don't know if I can get him to settle down and eat anything now."

"Oh dear," the woman said again. "Kelly, could

you wait just a minute, please? There's somebody here I have to talk with.''

''Sure.'' Kelly leaned against the wall, twisting the phone cord around her fingers and listening to a muffled conversation at the other end. She wondered how her father was feeling today, and wished she could summon the courage to ask the doctor lady.

''Kelly?'' the woman said. ''Are you there?''

''Yeah, I'm here.''

''Well, my friend Marie is a nurse who works here at the hospital in the children's ward, and she's got the rest of the day off. She's going to drive out there and take care of you and Casey. All right?''

''We don't need anybody to take care of us,'' Kelly said automatically, though Casey's howls were getting loud enough that they scared her a bit.

''I'm sending her out for my own peace of mind,'' the woman said. ''You'll both like her. She's a very nice lady who just loves kids. Oh, and Kelly...''

''Yeah?'' Kelly said again.

''Your father is feeling a lot better this morning. He's going to be fine. I can probably take you and Casey in to visit him tomorrow, if I can get away from work for a while. And he should be calling to talk with you later this morning.''

Kelly felt a flood of relief so intense that her knees turned to rubber and she was glad to have the wall for support.

''He's okay?'' she whispered. ''Really?''

''He's really okay,'' the woman said. ''Now, you go and look after Casey, and Marie will be there in a few minutes, all right? I have to run now.''

Kelly was close to tears, struggling hard to get herself under control.

Finally she said, "Okay." Then after a pause she whispered, "Thank you."

But the woman was already gone. Kelly hung the phone up and wandered back into the den to kneel by Casey's small writhing body.

CHAPTER NINE

THE DAY SEEMED interminable, filled with small emergencies, unscheduled appointments and even a staff meeting that stretched on for almost an hour.

It was well after six o'clock before Lila could drag herself away from the clinic. She stopped briefly at the hospital and ran up to check on Tom.

"He's much better," the red-haired duty nurse reported. "Out of bed and walking up and down the hall most of the afternoon."

"You're kidding." Lila stared at the pretty young woman. "With that list of injuries?"

"He's a very tough cowboy," the nurse said. "Also a very charming one. He looks great in his hospital gowns," she added with a grin. "Especially the one that opens in the back."

"We'd better get him a pair of pajamas," Lila said with a touch of irony. "Can't have the nursing staff getting distracted. Where is he now, Jane?"

"Ken took him down to X ray. He should be back in fifteen minutes or so."

Lila hesitated, then shook her head. "I can't wait that long. Could you tell him I'm taking some time off tomorrow, and I'll bring his kids for a visit in the afternoon?"

"Sure thing. That'll make him happy. He's crazy about those kids."

Lila wondered how much Tom had been chatting with the pretty young nurse, and was both amused and dismayed by her quick flash of jealousy.

Crazy, she told herself as she hurried out to the car. Just crazy...

She headed west into the setting sun, a little worried about Marie, who'd spent the whole day at the house with Archie and the two children.

Not that Marie hadn't seemed happy to volunteer. She was just beginning a long-anticipated two weeks off. She assured Lila that she didn't want to sit around in her lonely house and had no idea what to do with all the free time.

Still, Lila felt guilty about saddling her friend with two displaced children and a moody old man.

But the scene at the house when she finally arrived was pleasant, almost idyllic.

Archie sat out on the porch as usual, whittling on the ever-present block of wood. Lila glanced at the shape in his hands but it was too early to see what he was making this time.

"Where are Marie and the kids, Dad?" she asked, pausing at the top of the steps.

He jerked the handle of his jackknife toward the river.

Marie sat by the water's edge in jeans, sandy bare feet and a sweatshirt. Her gray curls glistened in the slanting rays of light. Casey squatted contentedly nearby, gripping a handful of shells, and both watched while Kelly tried to skip flat stones across the water.

Marie seemed to be giving instructions. Lila saw

her friend pick up a stone from the riverbank and hold it out, demonstrating. Kelly watched intently as the stone skipped and danced on the surface of the river. She tried again and shouted in frustration when her pebble sank after its first bounce.

Lila smiled and turned back to her father. "They seem pretty contented."

"Noisy kids," he muttered, keeping his head averted. "Turning the whole house upside down. I wish you'd get them out of here."

"Oh, Dad," she said gently, moving to touch his shoulder. "Since when did you ever mind a little noise or clutter? These are Tom Bennet's kids," she added with determined cheerfulness, "and they have nobody to look after them until he's well enough to leave the hospital. So they're staying here whether you like it or not."

Lila walked into the house, conscious of the stubborn set to his jaw as she passed. Inside, she ran up to her room and changed into khaki slacks and a cotton shirt.

She stopped in the kitchen long enough to grab a banana and drop a couple of bagels into a plastic sack, then went outside to join the little group on the riverbank.

Kelly and her brother were both at the water's edge, where the little girl was still trying to skip stones. Casey watched and did his best to imitate, but his efforts were so ineffectual that the pebbles he threw barely made it into the water.

Lila sat down on the sand next to Marie, munching one of her bagels. "They look a lot happier now," she said. "Thanks, Marie. This was so nice of you."

"It was fun." Marie lowered her voice. "But that Kelly is a pretty strange kid. Practically impossible to get close to."

Lila watched the wiry girl as she roved the beach looking for flat stones. "She seems to be getting along with you just fine."

"I think she's pretending, sort of humoring me." Marie leaned back and hugged her knees. "My guess is she's keeping up appearances for Casey's sake, because she doesn't want him to get upset or frightened. But underneath she's still being very cautious, just watching and waiting."

"For what?" Lila peeled the banana.

"I guess for the chance to escape from all of us and take charge of things again. She doesn't like having everything slip beyond her control. I sense a lot of anxiety in that child."

"Poor little girl." Lila ate her banana thoughtfully, brooding over the two children at the water's edge. "What a load of responsibility for an eleven-year-old."

Casey looked around, caught her eye and gave her a radiant smile, then turned away as if suddenly overcome by shyness.

"He seems happy, at least," she said. "Not a lot of emotional complications in Casey."

"That little boy," Marie said fondly, "is an absolute darling. I could just gobble him up, Lila. What a sweetheart."

Lila glanced over her shoulder at the silent figure on the veranda. "How's Dad been?"

"Oh dear." Marie's smile faded. "It's really sad, isn't it? I thought you were exaggerating about him, but you weren't. I can hardly believe that poor man is the Archie Marsden I once knew.''

''Has he talked to you at all?''

''Hardly a word. It's like you said, mostly grunts and mutters. But he's not rude, just so completely drawn into himself.''

''This is really hard on him.'' Lila waved a hand toward the two children. ''Having a major disruption like this in his life is so upsetting, but I just didn't know what else to do.''

Marie squinted into the fading sunlight. ''Can you believe that little girl playing such a trick on everybody, and staying all alone with a four-year-old for days on end in the parking lot?''

''I can believe it,'' Lila said, ''now that I'm getting to know Kelly.''

''You know, there's something there…'' Marie paused.

''What do you mean?''

Marie shook her head. ''Something about these kids. I can't quite put my finger on it, but they seem…I don't know.''

''What?'' Lila urged. ''What are you trying to say, Marie?''

''I don't know,'' the older woman repeated, picking up a handful of sand and letting it sift idly through her fingers. ''There's something…tragic about them. But I can't figure it out, and they won't open up and talk like other kids do.''

''Tragic?'' Lila asked. ''I don't understand.''

Marie shook her head again. ''Never mind. It's just a feeling I keep getting, that's all. Anyway,'' she added, ''how would we expect them to feel when their father's in the hospital and they're at the mercy of a bunch of strangers?''

''I talked with Tom about that very same thing just this morning,'' Lila said. ''I told him it was irresponsible to drag these kids around the country with him and not have some kind of safety network in case something happened to him.''

Marie gave her a thoughtful glance. ''And how did he react to that?''

''About the way I expected. He told me it was none of my business.''

Both women sat for a moment and watched the children running along the riverbank. They were keeping pace with a muskrat that swam parallel to the shore, its sleek body breaking the water in tiny ripples.

''Tell me again about your connection to this man,'' Marie said at last. ''He's an old friend?''

''A very old friend. We grew up together.'' Lila pointed across the river at the horizon to the south. ''Tom lived over there, but he'd already learned all kinds of ways to get across the river by the time he was Kelly's age. We played together for years.''

''Played together?'' Marie's glance was searching this time, and Lila felt her cheeks warming uncomfortably.

''Later on we...sort of dated,'' she said. ''I guess you could say Tom was my first love. But it was always hopeless, Marie. As soon as we stopped being kids, we had no chance of holding a relationship together.''

''Why not?''

''Because we were so different.'' Lila tucked her

banana peel into the empty sack. She folded the plastic edges, pleating them aimlessly in her fingers. "I wanted to go to medical school, then build a career and a stable home. Tom wanted to drift around and have adventures. And he expected me to wander along with him."

"Well, it looks like he's living just the kind of life he wanted."

"Yes, it does." Lila's face clouded with concern. "But now he's dragging two little kids along with him, and I don't think it's right."

"Where's their mother?" Marie asked. "I thought maybe he just had custody for the summer and this was a vacation for them, but Kelly says no, they live in the camper all the time."

"That's what Tom said, too. Did Kelly tell you anything else?"

"Not a word." Marie smiled without humor. "Pumping that child is about as easy as trying to get information out of Archie. I think Casey might be more willing to talk about things, but Kelly won't let him. She glares daggers at him if he even volunteers a scrap of information about their life."

"Very strange," Lila murmured, feeling increasingly troubled as she watched the two children silhouetted against the water.

"What are you going to do about all this?" Marie asked quietly.

"What do you mean?"

"Well, considering the kind of injuries Tom Bennet has, he's not going to be able to travel as soon as he's discharged. And I seriously doubt that he can live in a camper and look after his family, either. At least not right away. Are you going to bring him out here along with these kids?''

Lila looked at her friend, startled. ''I hadn't even thought about that.''

''Well,'' Marie said bluntly, ''I'd suggest you start thinking about it, kiddo. You may find you've taken on a pretty major project.''

Marie got to her feet and brushed sand from the seat of her jeans.

''And speaking of major projects,'' she added cheerfully, ''I'd better go home and practice for a while if I expect to go ballroom dancing next week.''

''That's when you and Trevor have your first class?'' Lila asked, getting up, as well.

''Next Thursday night. Lila, I can hardly wait. I plan to spend some happy days shopping for a new dress, and quite a few nights dancing with a floor mop to see if I can knock some of the rust off before then.''

Lila smiled, then hesitated, feeling awkward. ''About tomorrow…''

Marie smiled and touched her arm. ''Don't worry, I've already planned to come out in the morning. I don't think Archie is ready to look after these kids on his own just yet.''

''Oh, Marie,'' Lila said gratefully, ''that's so sweet of you. I've canceled my appointments so I can have the afternoon off,'' she added. ''I'm planning to come home and take the kids back into town to visit Tom after lunch, so you'll only have to stay until noon.''

''It's a pleasure coming out here,'' Marie said. ''Archie and Kelly might be a pretty hard pair to get along with, but that little Casey is a darling.''

She smiled fondly at the small boy who squatted by the shore, chubby hands on his knees, staring intently at the muskrat as it drifted along the riverbank.

"This is so good of you," Lila said again. "I don't know how to thank you."

Marie waved a hand airily and headed for her car. "What are friends for?" She paused and looked at the two children. "Goodbye, Kelly!" she called. "Bye, Casey. See you tomorrow, sweetheart."

Casey glanced up from his study of the muskrat and waved happily, but Kelly went on skipping pebbles in silence.

Lila watched Marie drive away, then mounted the steps and sat by her father.

"I'm really sorry about all this upset and confusion, Dad," she began. "And I'm sorry I was short with you earlier. I just don't know what else to do with these kids right now."

He carved a long curl of yellow pine, his pipe clamped between his teeth. "I don't want them sleeping in my den," he said.

Lila felt a rising helplessness. "But, Dad, we can't—"

"I took the cot up to the guest room this afternoon," he said, "and made it up with sheets and blankets. They can sleep together up there so the little fellow won't be scared."

Lila gazed at him in astonishment. "Thank you," she said at last. "Dad, that's really nice of you. I didn't expect…"

Before she could finish, he gathered up his carving and his knife, got to his feet abruptly and left the veranda, trudging into the house without a backward glance.

CASEY WOKE UP and lay rigid with terror, staring at the wall where awful things crawled and slithered toward him.

They were shapes, like wolves and bears and monsters. They moved closer, reaching for him. Outside he could hear a mournful howling that sent shivers up his spine. He whimpered and sucked hard on his thumb, but he could feel the tears welling up inside him.

Cautiously he sat up and looked around, clutching the blankets to his chin. Kelly slept in a bed near his cot. She was curled into a tight little ball, her face buried against the pillow, bright hair gleaming in the moonlight.

Casey would have felt less frightened if he could see her face, but he knew better than to wake her up.

This room was big and unfamiliar, not at all like their camper, where Daddy and Kelly both slept close enough to him that he could hear them breathing at night. The shapes on the wall danced and swayed, reaching for him, and the howling got louder.

He whimpered again and climbed down from the cot, then edged hastily through the door that stood open into a dimly lighted hallway. At least out here the shadows were gone from his sight, and he couldn't hear the terrifying noise from outside.

Casey hesitated, then sank onto the floor and wrapped his arms around his legs. He buried his face against his knees for a while, struggling not to cry.

Finally he rolled his head and peeped sideways, trying to accustom his eyes to the darkness.

The hallway opened onto a big loft overlooking a room below. Casey already knew the lower room had a stone fireplace and soft couches and pictures on the walls. The ceiling soared high above him, covered in some kind of wood.

He couldn't believe how big this house was. The vast spaces all around him felt strange and scary. He gulped and sobbed, sucking hard on his thumb, knowing that if he started to cry out loud, Kelly would be very angry with him.

Or the terrifying old man with the shaggy eyebrows might wake up and kill him.

Down the hall in the other direction was a series of doorways. The scary old man lay behind one of them, but Casey couldn't remember which.

While he watched, one of the doors opened and a figure appeared in the darkness.

The shape was tall and white, wearing a flowing robe. Casey thought it was probably an angel. He remembered one of the cowboys' wives saying that his mother was an angel now, living in heaven.

What if this ghostly figure that approached down the hallway was his mother?

The thought was too frightening to endure. Suddenly Casey's mind filled up with the Bad Thing, the memory that he never allowed himself to think about because it was too horrible.

He began to cry in earnest, rocking back and forth on the floor, his face hidden against his knees.

Arms picked him up and cradled him, and a voice murmured softly in his ear. He was conscious of softness and warmth and a sweet fragrance, and realized he was being carried somewhere. The angel took Casey through a door into a strange place and settled in a chair, cuddling him in her lap.

"Now, what's all this?" she whispered. "Why are you crying, darling?"

Casey gulped and swallowed, burrowing against her warmth. He realized it wasn't an angel at all, but the lady who'd brought him and Kelly here to this big house, the pretty lady with the dark hair and nice smile. She was wearing a nightgown and some kind of long white robe that felt soft against his face.

The lady held him tight and began to rock in the chair, humming softly. Casey felt himself soothed by the sound and motion. Gradually, mercifully, the Bad Thing began to fade from his mind, and went back into the box where he kept it locked tightly away so it couldn't hurt him.

"Casey," she said against his ear. "Are you all right? Were you having a bad dream?"

"There were monsters on the walls," he whispered. "And outside, too. I could hear them."

She kissed him. "Those aren't monsters," she said, her voice low and husky. "They're just shadows, darling. The moon is outside in the sky, smiling at you, and when it shines through the tree branches outside your window, it makes shadows on the wall."

"The moon is smiling at me?" he asked.

"It certainly is." She reached out beside her to pull back the curtains at her window. "See?"

She showed him the round moon and the face in it, and how it smiled down at him like a happy face.

Casey was so interested that he forgot to cry and snuggled happily on her lap.

"And the sounds you hear outside are the owls and the nighthawks and the crickets making music. Like a symphony concert."

He shivered again and nestled close to her. "Doesn't all sound like music. Something is screaming."

"Those are coyotes."

"Coyotes?" he asked fearfully.

She laughed. "Coyotes are nice animals. I love them. They're really gentle and playful, just like dogs. And this time of year they have fuzzy little baby coyotes, so the mommies and daddies are out looking for food. When you hear them call like that, they're just talking to each other, making sure everybody's safe."

Casey considered this, his thumb in his mouth. "Are the babies outside in the dark, too?" he asked.

"No, they aren't. They're all snug and cozy in their little dens, waiting for their mommies and daddies to bring food for them."

"Isn't anybody looking after them?" Vividly, Casey remembered the scary nights when he and Kelly were all alone in the camper and Daddy was far away in the hospital. He began to tremble again.

"They're very safe in their little dens," the lady said firmly, hugging him. "Their parents check in all the time to make sure they're all right, and the baby coyotes know there's nothing to be scared of so they just roll up into tight little balls, very close together, and sleep until morning."

He considered this, comforted by the image of the furry babies sleeping all warm and safe. Through the open window he could still hear the howling sounds, but they weren't scary at all anymore. Instead, they sounded busy and friendly, like people calling to each other at the rodeo grounds.

"Are you all right now, dear?" she asked.

He nodded against her breast, beginning to feel drowsy and content.

"Is anything else bothering you?"

She was so comforting that for a moment he considered telling her about the Bad Thing, and seeing what she would say.

But he never talked to anybody about that, not even Daddy or Kelly or the man Daddy had taken him to see afterward, who gave Casey dolls and toys to play with and tried to make him tell what he was afraid of.

If he talked about it, everything would be real again and he couldn't bear that.... .

He shook his head against her soft dressing gown.

"Well then, shall we take you back to bed now?"

"All right," he whispered.

She carried him down the hall and into the room where Kelly slept, put him down on the cot, then sat beside him, tucking the covers up around his face and smoothing his hair.

Her touch was warm and soothing. She began to sing, so softly that Kelly didn't even stir.

"Daddy sings a different song for me," Casey murmured sleepily.

"What song is that?"

"'Casey Boy.' It's about pipes. I like it."

To his amazement, the lady knew the song. She

began to sing again, in a voice so sweet that he could have listened forever. He smiled and reached out to grasp part of her robe, holding it contentedly in his hand, and felt himself drifting off to sleep.

CHAPTER TEN

AFTER LUNCH the next day, Tom closed the door of his hospital room and managed to dress himself in a pair of jogging pants and a T-shirt. Even bending and lifting his legs was agony. He felt a clammy sweat break out on his forehead and had to lower himself carefully into one of the vinyl armchairs until the wave of nausea passed.

He heard a knock on the door and the pert red-haired nurse popped her head inside. Her eyes widened when she saw him sitting in the chair, fully dressed.

"My goodness," she said. "Where did you get the clothes?"

"I asked one of the orderlies to go outside and fetch them from my camper," Tom said. "My kids are coming to see me in a few minutes. They're probably scared enough about all this without seeing their father sitting around in a dress and slippers."

"That's a pretty scary thing to see, all right," the nurse said with a grin.

Tom rested in the chair, watching as she fussed with his chart and the supplies on his nightstand.

He knew the woman was attracted to him and would have liked to draw him into conversation. But

Tom wasn't in the mood for flirting, not when Lila would be here in a few minutes, and his kids, as well.

Finally he closed his eyes and rested his head against the back of the chair, waiting for the pain to subside. The nurse looked down at him for a moment, then slipped away.

A few minutes later he heard voices in the hallway and sat erect, grasping the arms of the chair. The door opened and Lila looked inside.

"For heaven's sake, look at you," she said. "Tom, you're up and dressed!"

He grinned weakly. "I'm making progress, but you'll have to forgive me if I don't get up to greet you, Lilabel. Putting these pants on almost did me in."

"I wouldn't doubt it," she said severely, frowning at him. "Considering your injuries, you should still be in bed."

"Always scolding me," he teased. "Lila, you haven't changed much in fifteen years."

Her cheeks turned pink and she hesitated awkwardly in the doorway.

Tom watched her, his heart aching with love. "You still blush like a schoolgirl," he said.

"I know. There's nothing I can do about my blushing. It's the bane of my existence."

"Don't ever change," he told her softly. "You're so beautiful, Lila."

He was overwhelmed by love for her. All the old feelings came flooding back, stronger than ever, and he cursed the injuries that kept him from striding across the room, sweeping her into his arms and carrying her to that bed to show her exactly how he felt.

Suddenly he remembered their argument the day before, and noticed her stiff, nervous stance as she paused with her hand on the doorknob.

Oh hell, he thought wearily. *Nothing's changed at all. After all these years, she still feels the same way about me. Except that now she's had fifteen years to harden her position.*

"Did the kids come?" he asked.

"They're waiting down by the nursing station. I thought I'd better check first and make sure you were up to a visit."

"I'm anxious to see them."

She came into the room and stood looking down at him. "Tom..."

"Yes?"

"I'm really sorry about our argument yesterday. I was out of line."

"You've already apologized," he told her calmly. "There's no need to talk about it anymore."

"But I have no right to express an opinion on how you've been raising your kids. It's none of my business at all."

He'd forgotten how beautiful her eyes were, smoky blue under the dark even eyebrows.

When she was a girl, Lila's eyes had often seemed to change color. They'd be light blue when she was feeling dreamy, and darken almost to violet in the midst of anger or sexual passion.

Tom shivered, remembering the way she'd felt in his arms, all silky and fragrant...

Their lovemaking had been such a delicious mystery to him in those days. As a young man he was enchanted by the way his tomboyish playmate had become a passionate, sensual woman, and how perfect she was in every way, as if designed to satisfy the urges of his own body.

"God, I loved you when we were kids," he murmured, looking up at her. "Nothing in the world has ever felt like that, Lila."

Again her face colored. "Tom, that was all so long ago. Can't we just forget about it?"

"Can you?" He met her eyes steadily. "Can you really forget the way it felt when we held each other? I can't, Lila. Not if I live to be a hundred."

"It was a different world," she said. "And we were completely different people."

He couldn't resist a teasing grin, though he knew it would annoy her. "Damn, sweetheart, now I'm all confused. I thought your major complaint about me was that I'm still the same man I used to be. Now you're telling me I'm completely different?"

She stared at him, and he could tell that she was struggling with herself to keep from giving him a curt answer. Finally she composed her face and turned away, heading for the door.

"I'll get the kids," she said over her shoulder. "They're both excited about seeing you."

Tom's smile faded and he sat tensely in the chair, watching the doorway where Lila had disappeared. After a few minutes the door began to open a crack, then a little more.

Casey appeared, looking wide-eyed and frightened. He wore a pair of clean blue jeans, neatly patched, with a cowboy shirt, his little boots and a tooled leather belt. His hair had been brushed until it shone, and his round face was clean and bright.

"Well, hi there, cowboy," Tom said huskily. "How's my boy?"

"Daddy!" Casey ran across the room and flung himself onto Tom's lap, burrowing against him.

When the firm little body hit his midsection, Tom's rush of agony was almost more than he could bear. But he clamped his jaw and made no reaction, just shifted the small boy to a less painful position and cuddled him tenderly.

"How've you been, son?" he asked, kissing the cloud of bright curls. "I can't believe you're here. All that time I thought you were far away in British Columbia, and instead you were just outside in the parking lot."

Casey burrowed in his arms again. "It was scary, Daddy. It got dark and you weren't there, and we didn't have any food and Kelly wouldn't..."

"Shut up, Casey," his sister snapped, appearing suddenly in the room. "Quit whining about everything for a minute, can't you? Dad doesn't want to hear all that stuff."

Tom looked over the boy's head at his daughter, who'd entered silently and now stood near his chair. She, too, looked tidier than he remembered. Somebody had obviously taken a lot of care with these kids, mending and pressing their clothes, giving them haircuts and sprucing them up.

"You're wrong, Kelly," he said quietly. "In fact, I want to hear every word about what you did, including the way you lied to everybody about where you were going after I got hurt."

Kelly's face drained of color and she sat nervously on the edge of the bed. "Don't be mad at me," she pleaded. "I couldn't go away and leave you alone in the hospital. I just couldn't stand it, Dad."

Casey was beginning to relax. He sat easily in his father's lap and looked up at Tom's face. "Are you mad at Kelly?" he asked.

Tom hesitated, then shook his head and leaned back, reaching out to his daughter, who scrambled onto his other knee.

"Careful, honey," Tom murmured. "Those ribs still hurt quite a bit."

Kelly's face shone with relief. She perched carefully on his knee and reached up to give him a kiss. "I was so scared, Dad," she told him. "When I first saw you in here, right after the accident, you looked awful. It was like you were dead."

Tom hugged her with his good arm. "Well, I'm fine now. Feeling better all the time." He looked around. "Where's Lila?"

"She had to go check on one of her patients in the children's ward. She said she'd be back soon because Casey and I can only stay about fifteen minutes or you'll get tired."

Tom laughed, though it hurt his ribs. "Still ordering me around, is she? Lila's been doing that for years."

"I love Lila," Casey said with a blissful smile. "She's the nicest lady in the whole world. Last night she sang to me and told me about the face in the moon and the baby coyotes sleeping in their little houses."

"Oh, quit lying," Kelly told him rudely. "She did not."

Casey's face screwed up and turned bright red. "Yes!" he howled. "Yes, she did!"

"Okay, okay," Tom said. "Sit still, both of you, and no fighting or bouncing because your poor old dad can't take it right now." He turned to Kelly. "What about you, sweetheart? Do you mind staying at Lila's place for a while?"

Kelly shrugged, her face an inscrutable mask again. "It's okay," she said. "I like the river, and the animals are neat. Especially the dogs."

"But that old man is really, really scary," Casey told his father solemnly. "I think he kills people with his knife."

"Casey!" Tom said, genuinely shocked. "Lila's father, you mean?"

Casey nodded, his eyes round and earnest. "The old man who lives in Lila's house. His eyebrows are like this..." Casey cupped his hands fiercely over his own eyebrows. "And he growls all the time."

"Growls?"

"Grr, grr," Casey said, obviously enjoying the sound he was making.

Tom looked from one child's face to the other in disbelief. "I can't believe you're talking about Archie Marsden. He was the happiest man I ever knew. Archie loved to laugh and dance, and get down on the floor and play with kids."

Kelly and Casey exchanged a skeptical glance.

"It has to be somebody different," Kelly said at last. "This old man is the grumpiest person I ever met. He really is, Dad."

The door opened again and Lila came in to stand looking at the three of them snuggled close together in a single chair. Tom gave her a rueful despairing glance, raising one eyebrow, and she nodded with immediate understanding.

The woman had always had this uncanny ability to read his mind, ever since they were children.

"Well, I think this might be a little too much for your daddy's poor sore tummy," she said cheerfully as she sat down nearby, "having both of you on his knee at once. Each of you can give him one more kiss now, and then sit in the other chairs to visit. Okay?"

To Tom's relief and surprise, they obeyed without argument. Even Kelly kissed his cheek and then slipped dutifully to the floor and moved away to stand by the window, gazing out at the clipped green lawns surrounding the hospital.

Casey, though, went at once to Lila's chair and climbed into her lap, where he nestled as contentedly as if he'd known her all his life.

Tom watched in astonishment while she bent to whisper in the little boy's ear, then cuddled and kissed him.

Her tender beauty while she held his son was almost more than he could bear. He felt such a flood of yearning that he couldn't speak over the lump in his throat.

Lila had always loved and wanted children. Now, in her mid-thirties, she had none of her own but spent her life caring for the children of others.

And part of her loneliness was his fault. Because after he won her heart, she'd been unable to trust him enough to take his hand and follow him on his restless journey through life....

"Kelly," Lila was saying, "could you do something for me, please?"

"Okay," Kelly said without expression. She turned away from the window and waited impassively while Lila reached into the pocket of her smock to take out a small change purse.

"Could you take Casey down to the gift shop and buy a treat for each of you? I promised him a chocolate bar this morning if he'd let me wash his hair."

Casey brightened and slid off her knee, already heading for the door.

"Wait up, dummy," Kelly said to him. "You don't even know where the gift shop is."

"Do too!" Casey shouted.

They scrambled into the hallway, still arguing. The room was suddenly filled with a silence so profound that Tom could hear the gentle hiss and splash of the lawn sprinklers beyond the window.

He grinned at Lila. "Bribery?" he asked. "Is that how you're trained to deal with kids at all those child psychology seminars?"

"Not really," she said with a rueful answering smile. "But in the heat of battle we all tend to do what works, don't we?"

"Parenting is no easy job," he agreed, his smile fading. "In fact, it's just about the hardest thing I've ever done."

There was a brief silence. She seemed on the verge of asking him something, then changed her mind.

"I spoke with Dr. Weider this morning," she said at last. "He's prepared to discharge you on Sunday if I'll take custody of you for a while."

"Custody?" Tom raised an eyebrow. "What am I, some kind of homeless waif?"

"No, you're a seriously injured patient. Matthew

doesn't want to release you unless it's into the care of a professional who can monitor your condition.''

''My condition is fine,'' Tom said. ''I'm getting stronger every day. Another week like this and I'll be on the road again.''

''Oh, for goodness' sake,'' she said with a flash of real anger. ''Tom, can't you just grow up?''

''Grow up?'' He stared at her. *''Grow up?''*

''Look, I don't want to argue with you anymore. But if you're not prepared to consider your own welfare, at least please think of your children for a minute.''

''That's what I do all the time, Lila. I think about my kids.''

She met his eyes with a cool, steady gaze, and he found himself wondering what she was really thinking. The speculation made him feel wary and uncomfortable.

''These children need a lot of care,'' she said. ''They're growing fast, and they should have nourishing meals and regular sleep. I won't get into their emotional needs because that's your responsibility as their parent. But as a pediatrician...''

She took a deep breath and paused, toying with the stethoscope that hung around her neck.

''Go on,'' he said impassively. ''As a doctor, what do you think?''

''I don't think you're ready to assume full responsibility for their physical care until your injuries have healed for at least another couple of weeks, maybe even a month. Living in that camper and looking after two children would be an impossibility for you in this state.''

"Nothing's impossible, Lila."

She looked up at him with her disconcerting blue gaze. "Maybe not. But it could be very hard on the children. You do care about that, don't you, Tom?"

"Of course I do. Quit patronizing me, okay?" he said with rising annoyance. "I'm not a complete idiot, you know."

There was a brief silence. He wondered with wry humor if Lila was tempted to tell him just how much of an idiot she thought he was. But if that was in her mind, she didn't say it.

"So what do you propose, Lila?" he said at last. "I would assume you've got a plan all worked out for me and my kids?"

"I propose," she said calmly, "that you come home and stay with us for a while until you've healed. The children are already settled and fairly comfortable, and if you're there, as well, Marie won't have to come out and baby-sit in the daytime."

"Who's Marie?"

"A friend of mine," Lila said. "She's the head nurse in Pediatrics, but she has some time off now so she's been helping me look after the kids."

"I've caused an awful lot of trouble for all of you, haven't I?" he murmured. "I'm sorry, Lila."

"Under normal circumstances it would be no trouble at all." She looked down at her stethoscope, still moving it aimlessly between her fingers. "But with Dad the way he is…"

"Yes, what's that all about?" Tom asked curiously. "The kids sound like they're actually scared of the man, and I can't believe it's Archie Marsden they're talking about."

"Oh, Tom…wait till you see him."

Lila's eyes sparkled with tears. It was all he could do not to get up and take her in his arms.

"Anyhow," she said, clearly making an effort to compose herself, "I was thinking we could make up a bigger bed in the extra guest room and Casey could share it with you. Then we'd have enough space for everybody and Kelly would have a room to herself. Besides," she added, her face softening, "Casey tends to get frightened at night, so it would be best if you were there."

But Tom shook his head. "I'm not sleeping in your house, Lila. You've done enough for me and for the kids. I have no desire to be a houseguest on top of everything else. I'll pay you for whatever they've cost you so far, and then we'll hit the road."

"Oh, Tom," she said wearily, "can't you ever make something easy for a change?"

He hesitated, thinking it over, and realized she was probably right. Just getting dressed and sitting in a chair was hard for him at the moment.

"Okay," he said finally. "Since the kids are already settled in the house, they can stay there. But I'll sleep outside in my own vehicle for a few days until I'm able to travel."

Her cheeks turned pink again, but with anger this time. "That's ridiculous," she said. "Climbing in and out of that camper would be terribly painful for you in your condition."

"So what are you saying, honey?" Again he couldn't resist giving her a warm, significant grin. "Do you really want me sleeping under the same roof with you? I may be in some pain, but not enough to keep me from going wandering in the middle of the night.''

She got to her feet, glaring at him. ''That,'' she said angrily, ''is not only absurd, it's the least of my worries. As far as I'm concerned, Tom Bennet, you can sleep wherever you damn well please, as long as those two kids are safe.''

He watched her, awed by her beauty and the emotion he was still able to arouse in her, even though most of it seemed to be negative.

''Lila,'' he whispered huskily, his groin stiff with a sudden hot rush of sexual need. ''God, Lila, how can we ever—''

But they were interrupted by the arrival of the children, who burst into the room, both carrying chocolate bars and arguing bitterly about something. Lila turned away to tend to them. Speaking softly, she settled the fight, whatever it was, with a few well-chosen words.

Then she looked at Tom. ''We'll go now,'' she said. ''Sunday's my day off, so I'll come in and pick you up around noon. Dad will come along to drive your camper back to the house. All right?''

''Whatever you say, Lila. You're the boss.''

He tried to sound casual and sardonic, but he was still so gripped by sexual passion that it was hard to sit in the chair, and impossible to stand up.

At least, he thought with bleak humor, there were parts of his body that still worked.

His discomfort was so intense that he was actually grateful when she herded the children out and left him alone in the bleak, silent hospital room.

CHAPTER ELEVEN

A FEW DAYS LATER, a peaceful Sunday morning in the country, Lila ate her breakfast at the kitchen table in the midst of unusual activity.

Marie was with them already, having volunteered to come out and watch the children while Lila did her morning hospital rounds, then went down to the ward to collect Tom and get him discharged.

"It'll be my only chance to see them," she'd told Lila on the phone the night before, sounding a little wistful. "Now that their father's coming home, I guess you won't need me anymore."

"You can come out and visit anytime," Lila had told her. "They love you."

Remembering, Lila glanced at the little girl, who sat at the table eating cereal with a book propped in front of her. Kelly had been fascinated by the walls of books in the den and was now reading her way voraciously through the *My Friend Flicka* series.

"I loved those books," Lila said to the child. "You know, Kelly, when your father and I were kids, we used to sit down on the riverbank with our fishing rods, and I'd read aloud to him. We went through all three of those books one summer, and spent hours arguing about whether anybody could really ride a wild stallion."

Kelly glanced up at her with the familiar shuttered expression, then lowered her eyes to the book again, eating mechanically.

By now Lila was getting to know this child well enough to understand that Kelly was excited about Tom getting out of the hospital today, but was holding her emotions in check even more tightly than usual to keep those feelings from showing.

Casey, however, obviously had no such concerns. The boy was pink-cheeked and bouncing with excitement. He laughed aloud as Marie held him in her arms, gripping one of his fat hands, and swooped around the kitchen with him.

"And this is the fox-trot," she was saying, taking long, elegant steps. "We keep our backs very straight and hold our chins like this..."

She flung her head back haughtily, still dipping and twirling with the little boy in her arms. Casey shouted with laughter.

"Do the tango!" he urged. "Marie, do that tango thing!"

Lila chuckled, wondering how much Marie had taught the children during their few days together.

The nurse complied, making a sultry face and dropping her head to one side. She extended her arms stiffly and danced Casey toward the door, then back, while he squirmed happily in her arms.

"This is the way I'm going to look," Marie told her chubby partner, "when I go dancing with Trevor on Thursday night. Except that I'm not going to be wearing these old blue jeans, no sirree. I bought a red chiffon dress with a skirt that swirls all over the place and looks absolutely gorgeous."

Lila saw her father watching the gray-haired woman and the little boy. For a brief, heart-stopping moment, she thought she actually detected the ghost of a smile on his face. But when she caught his eye, the expression vanished and he was instantly withdrawn again, staring down at his bowl of oatmeal.

Soon afterward Archie got up and wandered from the room, stopping in the hallway to gather up his block of wood and carving knife before he trudged silently onto the veranda.

Lila sighed and settled back with her coffee mug, thinking about all the unhappiness and buried secrets in this lovely, sun-washed place.

Kelly never talked to anybody or even smiled if she could help it, and neither did Archie. Marie was battling with painful feelings of loneliness and abandonment. Even Casey, who seemed so carefree at the moment, had some kind of deep emotional scarring that gave him night terrors and haunted his eyes at unguarded moments.

Lila's heart ached for the two children, but she didn't know how to help them if they wouldn't talk to her. And she was afraid to get too close, because she could already feel herself falling in love with them.

Not much point in that, when their father was planning to take them away as soon as he could travel.

She took a sip of coffee, absently patting the big black Lab who had roused himself to come and sit by her chair. Again Lila wondered exactly what it was that drove Tom to his life of aimless wandering.

She knew that as a boy he'd yearned to escape the bitter realities of life with his father, the grinding poverty and violence. And in those days he really believed that happiness lay over the next hill, just around the corner, somewhere beyond the sunset.

But Tom Bennet was getting close to forty now, and had two children to care for. He wasn't a boy anymore.

She shook her head, got up and took her car keys from the rack by the door. "I'll do my rounds," she told Marie, "and then check Tom out of the hospital. We should be back by lunchtime."

Marie paused in her dance, her cheek still pressed tightly against Casey's.

"Okay," she said. "Lila, are you sure you don't want me to make up a bed in the guest room for him? He may talk tough right now, but that man's going to feel pretty drained when he starts walking around here under his own steam. He's probably leaving the hospital at least four days too early."

"He insists he's going to sleep in his camper," Lila said grimly, "and I'm sure that's what he'll do. Tom's as stubborn as a mule once he makes his mind up about something."

"Daddy's coming home," Casey sang when Marie set him down on the floor. "Daddy's coming home, coming home, coming home…"

Lila bent to kiss him, and he clung to her for a moment. She buried her face in his curls, inhaling the pleasant scent of shampoo and warm small boy.

"Casey," she murmured in his ear, "try not to run and jump on Daddy when you see him, because his tummy is still sore. All right?"

Casey nodded, round-eyed and solemn.

Lila paused by the table to stroke Kelly's hair. "I'll see you soon, dear," she said.

But Kelly jerked away from her touch and went on reading.

Lila exchanged a rueful glance with Marie, shook her head and hurried into the glorious summer morning, heading for her car.

KELLY WAITED until Lila was gone, then closed the book and finished eating her cereal. She liked to have the book open in front of her whenever Lila was around. Otherwise she could feel those blue eyes resting on her, probing into her head and trying to make her talk about things, and she was terrified that one day she might give in and say a lot of stuff she shouldn't.

It was so nice here, Kelly thought wistfully. She gazed at the dogs sprawled comfortably in the warm square of sunlight on the hardwood floor, and the ruffled gingham curtains framing a view of the river as it sparkled in the morning sunlight.

She loved this place.

Everything about living here was wonderful, from waking every morning and hearing the birds singing in the cottonwoods to going upstairs in the evening and watching the moonlight as it glimmered on the water.

Kelly even enjoyed lying awake in her bed after dark and listening to the coyotes singing on the cliffs, though she knew they sometimes frightened Casey.

And she loved all the books and paintings on the walls, and especially the safe, solid feeling that everything had been here for years and years and would never change.

But these thoughts often made her feel disloyal to her father, who was doing the very best he could to look after Kelly and her brother.

Traveling around and going to rodeos was lots of fun, she told herself firmly. It was an exciting life. Thousands of kids would give anything to have the adventures that she and Casey enjoyed when they traveled all year with their father, seeing parts of the world that stay-at-home kids never got to visit.

Besides, the life they lived, the rodeos, the different places and the constant whirl of excitement, all helped to keep her from thinking about things that really hurt.

Awful things, stuff that Kelly never wanted to think about again....

Abruptly she got up, carried her dishes to the sink and rinsed them, putting the cereal bowl in the dishwasher. Casey and Marie had settled at the table, and Casey was practicing his slow, laborious printing with a crayon gripped tight in his fist.

"I can't believe how well he can do that," Marie said. "Only four years old, and the little tyke can already print his whole name. Kelly, you're a wonderful teacher."

Kelly warmed at the praise but kept her face stiff and impassive. "He can't make the *B* yet," she said coldly. "It still looks like a squashed bug."

"Does not!" Casey shouted, his cheeks turning pink with outrage.

Marie stroked his hair gently and murmured something, touching the paper. He subsided and began to print again, his face contorted with effort.

Kelly shrugged, gathered up her book and went outside onto the veranda.

The old man was there already in his accustomed place, whittling, with two dogs lying at his feet.

Kelly was getting more used to him by now, and had realized he wasn't angry, just sad. She could sense the depths of misery in him. In fact, it was a wrenching, bleak despair that she understood quite well, though his grim expression still frightened her sometimes.

She sat on the other end of the veranda and opened her book, pretending to read while she cast sidelong glances in his direction.

The old man was probably conscious of Kelly's presence but he ignored her, carving little curls of wood that fell away from his hands and piled up on the floor all around him.

At the end of the day when he was finished whittling, he always went into the kitchen, got a dustpan and broom and cleaned up his mess, depositing it neatly in the kindling box at the side of the house next to the stacks of firewood.

They hadn't used the big stone fireplace since Kelly's arrival because it was the middle of summer. But she sometimes lay in her bed at night and tried to imagine what it would be like here in the wintertime, when snow was drifted all around and the river froze into a sheet of ice so smooth that her father and Lila used to skate on it when they were kids.

On those chilly winter nights, Lila probably made a big fire in the hearth and sat on the couch watching the flames. She'd read a book and have a bowl of popcorn in her lap...

Kelly shook her head to get rid of the pleasant image, then cast the man a quick glance to see if he'd noticed. But he went on whittling as if she didn't even exist.

There was no point in thinking about how nice this place would be in the winter. By then, she and Daddy and Casey would be thousands of miles away, down in Texas or New Mexico, where the sun shone every day and they had rodeos all year round.

She got up restlessly and wandered back to the door, then paused by the old man's chair. The block of wood in his gnarled hands seemed to be gradually taking shape and form, and she was consumed with curiosity about what he was making.

Suppressing her fear, Kelly edged closer, then caught her breath, enchanted.

The object in his hands was a lifelike little prairie dog, and it was beautiful. The tiny animal stood comically erect on splayed hind paws, holding a flower stem to his mouth. His shiny wooden cheeks bulged as if he had been eating all day.

In spite of herself, Kelly laughed out loud. "Oh, he's so cute!" she said. "He looks like Casey with a bag of raisins to eat."

Clearly startled, the man glanced up at her from under his bushy eyebrows. She caught a quick flare of alarm in his eyes, and some other expression that she couldn't identify.

But immediately he masked the expression and went on whittling, turning his back on her deliberately. In fact, he actually moved his chair around on the wooden floorboards so he wouldn't have to look at her.

Kelly stared at his plaid shoulder and felt both fear and an outrage that were hard to control. To her horror, tears began to sting behind her eyelids and almost choked her. Of all things in the world, she couldn't bear being ignored as if she didn't exist. That was the worst thing a person could do to somebody else.

And we should know, she thought bitterly. *Casey and me, we know all about that...*

Without thinking, she reached out and punched the old man's shoulder as hard as she could.

"You're mean!" she shouted. "You're just as mean and nasty and horrible as you can be."

He turned his head to look up at her, his face registering such astonishment that it was almost funny. But Kelly was in no mood to be amused.

"You are!" she said passionately. "You just sit here all the time ignoring everybody, and act like they're not worth noticing. And what good are you to anybody? Lila works all day and then has to worry about you besides. Marie has to give up her holiday and come out here to look after Casey because you can't be bothered because you're too selfish."

Kelly was running out of breath and her courage was beginning to falter a bit, but she forced herself to continue.

"Selfish!" she shouted, bending close to him. "That's what you are. You're worse than Casey, and he's just a little kid. I don't even know how anybody as mean as you can make something that pretty."

She gestured at the whimsical prairie dog, now hanging limply in the man's gnarled hand.

"Because you know what?" She put her face closer to his, still fighting back tears. "I think you're just awful. You're a mean, awful, coldhearted old man, and I don't know why Lila even bothers with you.''

With that, Kelly swiped an arm across her face, marched into the house and slammed the screen door behind her. When she peeked over her shoulder, she could see the old man staring at the place where she'd vanished, his face a study in blank astonishment.

''Serves him right,'' Kelly muttered as she ran upstairs to the guest room she was sharing with Casey. ''Mean old thing.''

TOM HAD ALMOST NOTHING in the room with him in the way of personal belongings. The few things he'd used in the hospital were packed in a duffel bag, which they stopped to put away in the camper before they left.

''Have you seen my home on wheels?'' he asked Lila, pausing by the back door of the big vehicle.

She nodded awkwardly. ''That night when I found Kelly in the—''

''Look, don't talk about it,'' he said hastily, his face twisting with pain. ''That crazy kid. She knows I have almost two thousand dollars in cash hidden away in the saddle compartment, and yet she's eating garbage out of trash cans.''

''She didn't know where else to go,'' Lila said. ''She had no idea where to find a grocery store, and anyway, she didn't want to leave Casey alone in the camper. The whole thing was a huge responsibility for an eleven-year-old child.''

''I know, I know,'' he said wearily, tossing his duffel bag inside and closing the door. "But I still don't like thinking about it."

He stood erect and flexed his free arm, looking up at the bulk of the hospital.

"God, it's so good to be out of that place and have the sun shining on my face again."

"How do you feel?" Lila asked.

"I'll be better when I can get my jeans and boots on," he said wryly. "I'm getting pretty damn tired of wearing these sweatpants all the time, like an old man in a nursing home."

"Tom, a week ago you were in ICU, and your condition was listed as critical. Now you're released from the hospital and walking around, which puts you about two weeks ahead of your doctor's projected schedule. Quit pushing everything so hard."

"Pushing hard is the only way I know how to do it, sweetheart. Don't you remember?" He raised an eyebrow, watching her with such teasing intensity that she felt herself growing hot all over.

"I was going to bring Dad in to drive your truck back to our place," she said, keeping her voice deliberately casual. "But he seemed especially remote this morning and I didn't want to risk it. So the plan is that I'll come back in with Marie when she leaves this afternoon, and drive your truck home then. Okay?"

"You're going to so much trouble for me," he said, instantly contrite, "and I do nothing but tease and hassle you. I'm sorry, Lila."

Even when they were children, she'd never been able to resist him when he was being sincere and thoughtful, and a little abashed about whatever sin he'd committed.

She wondered if he was aware of that, and knew how devastating he could still be to her careful composure.

"Come on," she said curtly, heading across the parking lot. "My car's just around the corner."

As they walked, she adjusted her pace to his limping stride, wondering how he could even move with such painful injuries. But Tom Bennet had always been as strong as an ox, and twice as hardheaded.

He gave a low, admiring whistle when they stopped by her little silver Mercedes.

"It looks like doctoring pays well," he said with a grin.

"Especially when you have nothing else to spend your money on."

She held the door for him and gripped his uninjured arm as he lowered himself gingerly into the low-slung seat of the car. Sweat beaded on his forehead, and his face went white beneath the tan.

"Oh, Tom," she said anxiously, but he made an impatient gesture to cut her off.

"I'm fine," he said. "Don't keep fussing over me, Lila."

She walked around and got into the driver's side, tossing her handbag into the back seat. Then she started the car, backed expertly out of the lot and headed for home.

Tom watched her profile in silence. "You have nothing else to spend your money on?"

"Not much. My major luxury is helping a wasteful ex-husband," Lila said with a humorless smile.

"So you married a weak guy, Lilabel?"

"I guess you could say that. Poor Trevor, he's certainly no ball of fire, that's for sure."

"Then why did you marry him?"

"I was lonely," Lila said briefly. "And almost thirty, finally established in my practice. I wanted a home and children, and he looked like a reasonably presentable specimen."

"But the two of you didn't have any kids."

She shook her head. "It took me about three weeks of marriage to realize Trevor wasn't the man I wanted to father my children. Or to be any part of my life, for that matter," she added with another bleak smile. "But it took another two years to get rid of him, and the poor boy still needs my help from time to time."

"Poor Lila." He reached out to touch her hair, then stroked her cheek. As always, his touch made her quiver with fierce yearning. "A woman who was born to be a wife and mother," he said huskily, "and instead she's still living with her father."

"Don't touch me like that anymore, Tom." Lila summoned all her courage and turned to look at him directly. "Those days are over. We haven't been lovers for fifteen years. And I don't approve of your lifestyle any more than I ever did. In fact, now that you have two children, I think it's not only irresponsible, it's actually wrong to live the way you do."

He closed his eyes and leaned his blond head against the back of the seat. His face was still pale, and she wondered how much pain he was suffering.

"It can't be much fun to have a houseguest you disapprove of so strongly," he muttered.

"Well, I'm sure it won't be for long," she said

calmly. "Because I have no doubt you're planning to leave us long before it would be reasonable for anybody else in your condition to travel."

There was a brief, charged silence.

Finally Tom looked out the window at the road sweeping along the rugged cliffs, and the river sparkling far below in the midday light.

"God, I love this place," he muttered, almost as if talking to himself. "Sometimes when we're traveling, I get so homesick I can hardly stand it. Even though my boyhood wasn't much fun," he added, "except for you and the things we did together."

Lila gave him a quick glance. "Tom...you knew your father died a few years ago, didn't you?"

"Somebody sent me a notice." He gazed down at the massed cottonwoods along the shore, his face expressionless. "And you can bet I didn't shed any tears over him. That old bastard was always far too mean to live."

Lila looked ahead to the chimneys of their log house and took a deep breath. "About your wife..."

"Yes?"

He stretched uneasily and extended his long legs, wincing with pain. "What about her?"

"You told me she was dead, but I wondered if you could..." Lila hesitated, feeling awkward. "If you'd mind telling me something about how she died."

"Why?"

"Because it seems to me the children are quite traumatized by events in their past," Lila said. "There's something they can't bring themselves to talk about. Maybe it's just unexpressed grief, but I wondered if there's—"

"Lila," he said. His tone was gentle, but she heard the underlying firmness. "Don't get into any of this, all right? Just leave it alone."

She met his eyes, shaken by their blue-green depths. Years ago they had been a boy's eyes, sparkling with fun and melting with youthful passion.

Now they belonged to a hard-faced man with children and a murky past, and an aura of painful secrets that puzzled and distressed her.

"Okay," she said, keeping her voice light. "We'll do it your way, Tom. No questions, no probing. Just a few days for you to recuperate and then you and the kids can move on. If that's the way you want it to be, that's fine with me."

She parked in front of the house, got out and slammed the door a little more firmly than she'd intended, then strode around to help him out of the passenger side.

He unfolded his long body painfully, turned and limped up the walk toward the house, where Archie sat on the veranda with his carving in his hands, and the dogs stirred sleepily at their approach. In the distance, pelicans soared and dipped above the sunlit river, and cattle stood at the water's edge.

Lila cast a glance at Tom, and thought for a moment that she saw tears glistening in his eyes. But he turned away quickly and mounted the steps, just as his children came running out to greet him.

CHAPTER TWELVE

DINNER WAS AWKWARD and mostly silent. Lila had ridden to town with Marie earlier in the afternoon to bring Tom's truck back to the farmhouse. She and her father now shared their table with Tom and his children.

She'd prepared a simple meal of pasta and salad and was trying to ease the tension by showing Casey how to swirl spaghetti on his fork.

"Like this," Lila said, leaning toward the little boy. She speared a few strands of pasta and turned her wrist expertly so they wrapped around her fork. "Then you don't have to slurp those big long noodles and scatter tomato sauce all over."

Casey watched and struggled earnestly to imitate her. He had a bib tied around his neck, and his plump cheeks were smeared with red sauce.

Across the table Kelly watched Lila's technique, then twirled her fork deftly and captured a neat mouthful of spaghetti.

"That's very good," Lila said with a smile. "You learn everything so fast."

Kelly ignored her, eating stoically. From time to time the girl stole a glance at Archie, then glared down at her plate again. He ate in silence as always, so withdrawn that Lila wondered if he was even aware of Tom's presence.

But for her own part, Lila was aware of little else. The blond man seemed to fill the room.

He sat on Casey's other side, watching her with that disconcerting blue gaze that still made her feel warm and shaky. His shoulders seemed so broad in this confined, domestic setting, and his bigness was further exaggerated by the cast on his arm.

"I can write my name," Casey told his father proudly. "The whole thing."

Tom hugged the little boy with his good arm. "I sure missed you, son."

Casey looked curiously at his father's cast. "Daddy, how long do you have to wear that thing?"

"The doctor thinks it'll take about a month to heal," Tom said, taking a sip of water.

"So we get to stay here for a long, long time?" Casey's eyes brightened.

Tom shook his head and set the glass down. "I doubt that Lila and Archie want us around for that long," he told his son. "We'll be hitting the road again as soon as I can drive."

"Can you drive with one hand?" Casey asked.

"Sure can. In fact, I can do a whole lot of things with one hand." Tom caught Lila's glance, his eyes full of laughter.

She looked down quickly at her plate, toying with a crust of garlic bread.

When the meal was finished, Kelly got up silently and began to clear the table. She carried dishes to the sink for rinsing, then stacked them in the dishwasher while Lila took an apple pie from the oven and served hefty slices, topping each with a scoop of ice cream.

"Do you want some, Dad?" she asked.

Archie shook his head, got up and shambled from the room, heading for the veranda.

Lila watched him go, feeling miserable. Archie seemed even worse than usual today, and she wondered if something in particular had happened to upset him, or if he was just annoyed to have the house full of people and noise.

She was conscious of Tom's eyes resting on her in concern. He seemed about to say something but she gave him an imperceptible shake of the head, glancing toward the two children.

He nodded in understanding and accepted the piece of pie she handed him.

"Well, this looks great," he said heartily. "If I had to get hurt, we're sure lucky it happened in Lila's backyard, aren't we, kids?"

"Yummy," Casey said, attacking his pie. "I love ice cream."

Kelly finished stacking the dishes and sat down again with her dessert. The four of them ate in silence, listening to an owl hooting down in the cottonwoods as the evening shadows lengthened.

Anybody who peeked in the window would think they were a normal little family, Lila thought. And how wrong they'd be.

"I can skip stones on the river," Kelly told her father, breaking the long silence. "I practiced and practiced all day yesterday, and now I can do it as good as Marie."

"What's your best throw so far?" Tom asked.

"Nine skips with one stone."

"Hey, I can beat that," he said cheerfully. "Even with one arm."

"Bet you can't." Kelly's face brightened, and for a moment she looked like any ordinary, fun-loving child.

"Bet I can," Tom told her solemnly. "Tell you what, after we've finished eating and tidying the kitchen, we'll go out and have a stone-skipping contest, okay? Lila will come along and be the judge."

Both children began to bounce in excitement and argue about the rules of the contest. Lila caught Tom's eye over Casey's curly head. They exchanged a smile and she felt a treacherous flood of warmth.

If he doesn't leave soon, she thought in despair, *and take these kids with him, I'm really going to be in big trouble.*

But the thought of their departure left such a void that she could hardly bear to think about it.

"I LEARNED TO DO THIS when I was twelve years old," Tom said, bending at the shoreline to select a flat rock. "Archie taught me."

"That mean old man?" Casey asked in astonishment, running along at his father's side.

Tom glanced at Lila, his blunt cheekbones gilded by the dying rays of the sun. "That man is Lila's father," he told Casey sternly. "He also owns this house where you're staying, and you should show some respect. Don't call names, son."

"Okay," the boy said cheerfully. "Here's a good one, Dad." He selected a smooth flat rock and handed it to his father.

"If Casey's helping his dad, I'll be on Kelly's side," Lila said. "We'll find the best stones of all, won't we, Kelly?"

The girl gave her a startled glance, then returned to her study of the riverbank.

When they'd each selected half a dozen flat rocks and, after much amiable wrangling, established the rules of their contest, Tom and his daughter began to skip stones across the river.

Lila enjoyed the laughter and the pleasant warmth of the sunset and the feeling of being a child again. She and Tom had done this same thing twenty-five years ago, long before adult life intruded, with all its conflicts and responsibilities.

She could tell that Tom deliberately let Kelly win the contest. He was so skilled with his hands that he could easily have skipped a stone at least a dozen times, even throwing left-handed.

But all his efforts seemed to arch just a little too high, then plop into the water after a few ineffectual bounces.

Finally he acknowledged defeat, much to Casey's chagrin and Kelly's gloating triumph.

After the game, Tom and Lila walked together along the riverbank while the children shouted and played at the water's edge.

Tom glanced back at the house where Archie sat on the veranda. "It's sad to see him like this, Lila. I can hardly believe he's the same man."

"That's what everybody says."

"So, is he clinically depressed?"

"We assume he probably is." Lila squinted at the flare of gold etching the top of the cliffs. "I can't get him to see a professional, but I've talked his symptoms over with some of the doctors I know, and they all diagnose depression.''

"Isn't there anything you can do for him?''

"Not without his cooperation. If he were agreeable, there'd be all kinds of treatments we could try. Dietary changes, medication, activities, counseling.'' Lila shook her head in defeat. "But he just says no to everything and sits there with his whittling. And every day he seems to disappear a little more.''

Tom took her hand and held it. His touch was so comforting that she didn't pull away this time, just walked along beside him and listened to the gentle flow of the river.

"This feels good,'' she said, lifting her face to the warm twilight breeze. "It's like we're ten years old again.''

"That's not the way I remember it,'' he said with a grin. "If I'd tried to hold your hand when we were ten years old, you'd have socked me in the eye.''

She laughed. "I probably would have. You were still small enough in those days that I could give you a pretty good fight.''

He slanted a teasing glance down at her. "But then I grew and you didn't.''

"Hey,'' she protested. "I grew, too, you know. In fact, I'm a pretty big girl now. Taller than most of the men I date.''

"Do you date, Lilabel?''

"Not much.'' Unobtrusively she freed her hand and bent to rub some leaves of sage between her fingers, sniffing in pleasure at the oily fragrance.

He watched her, his thick hair lifting and stirring

in the breeze. "Tell me about this ex-husband of yours."

"There's nothing much to tell. Trevor's handsome and smart, but easily bored. Ever since I've known him, he's been drifting from one job to another. Any one of them would have a good future if he'd stick with it, but pretty soon he gets bored and moves on. Then eventually he comes and borrows money from me to tide him over."

"And you lend it?"

She smiled. "For a price, sometimes."

"What kind of price?" he asked with quick suspicion.

"Not what you're thinking."

Lila told him about Marie's broken marriage and the ballroom-dancing classes, and her requirement that Trevor escort her friend in order to be loaned the five hundred dollars.

Tom laughed so heartily that the children turned to look at them from the water's edge, then went back to their play.

"Same old Lila," he said at last. "Organizing people's lives, working busily behind the scenes to make everybody happy."

"Is that so bad?" Lila asked.

"No, sweetheart." He put his free arm around her and gave her a boyish hug. "It's not bad at all."

The feel of his muscular arm and his long hard body against hers was almost more than Lila could endure. She pulled away hastily and turned to face him.

"Tom, don't say a word to anybody about this, all right?"

"About what?"

"My deal with Trevor to take Marie out dancing. She would be so humiliated if she knew, and her confidence is shaky enough these days."

"I won't breathe a word," he said solemnly. "Hey, look, here's our rock."

They'd reached the natural stone bench where Lila often came to read by the water's edge when she had some free time. Tom lowered himself gingerly and patted the surface of the rock.

"Come and sit down, Lilabel. Remember how much fun we used to have down here? This big old rock was a stagecoach, a mountain, a fort...whatever we wanted it to be."

"Yes," she said briefly, sitting as far away from him as she could. "Of course I remember."

He extended his long legs carefully and grimaced with pain.

"Tom, we should go back," she said, frowning. "This has been too much activity for you on your first day out of bed."

"I feel great, and stronger by the minute. I hate those damn hospitals. They really sap a person's strength, you know."

"Well, that's good to hear," she said, "since I spend half my life in hospitals."

He touched her hair, then leaned close to lift a few strands and hold them to his face. "Your hair always smelled so good," he murmured.

"Tom," she began warningly. He straightened immediately and moved away.

"So what else have you been doing?" he asked. "You went to medical school, then nursed Bella while she was sick, and now you take care of Archie and your friends and your lazy ex-husband. Do you ever do anything just for Lila?''

For some reason the question was upsetting to her. She didn't want to answer him, or even think about what he'd said.

''Let's talk about you for a while,'' she said after a brief silence. ''What have you been doing all these years, besides going to rodeos?''

''My life hasn't been all that interesting,'' he said with sudden coldness, staring at the glittering water.

Lila could almost see the shutter falling over his eyes, and hear the curt, wary tone in his voice.

Even after all this time apart, she knew Tom Bennet well enough to understand that nothing was going to make him talk about his life or share details of his marriage and past experiences. And trying to probe would be as useful as flinging herself against a brick wall.

She sighed and got to her feet. ''I guess we'd better start heading back,'' she said. ''It's time for Casey to have his bath and go to bed.''

They walked side by side toward the house, while the children ran quarreling behind them. Lila cast a sidelong glance at his withdrawn profile.

''Tom...''

''Yes?''

''Are you really planning to move on and start going to rodeos again in only a few days?''

''As soon as I can drive, Lila. In the meantime, there are some chores I can do around the place to earn our keep.''

''What kind of chores?''

He waved a hand toward a nearby paddock. "That fence needs repairing. Otherwise you're going to have llamas wandering across the countryside. And the barn has to be painted, too."

"You're right, it does. I'm afraid things have been going downhill since Dad stopped tending to the place. I never have enough time."

"Well, the kids and I can do those chores. In fact, I'm getting them started on the barn tomorrow after you go to work."

"I'm sorry to upset your plans," she said lightly, "but you might have one more worker on the painting crew."

He raised an eyebrow and grinned in delight. "Really, Lilabel?"

She bent and plucked at a blade of grass, chewing on it with feigned casualness. "I'm thinking I'll take this week off to help with the kids until you're feeling better."

"Can doctors take time off just like that?"

"Tomorrow I'm off, anyway, and I have about a year of unused holiday time," Lila said. "It's only a matter of rescheduling some appointments, and they're usually lighter in the summertime when my patients are on holidays. I'll still do my hospital rounds and handle emergency calls, of course, but I should have most of the days off this week."

"Well, I'll clean an extra paintbrush, then. Remember our old painting contests, Lila?"

"I remember." She suppressed a smile and turned to look up at him. "So when are you planning to leave?"

He straightened as they walked and tried to lift his injured arm.

"I think by next weekend I should probably be strong enough to travel." He cast an inquiring glance at her. "Is that okay? Can you stand for us to hang around here that long?"

"Oh, Tom!" she said impatiently, her cheeks warming with annoyance.

Lila felt a sudden flood of anger, and another emotion that she was afraid to analyze. She broke away from him as they reached the house, ran lightly up the steps and paused in the doorway, looking back at the two children.

"Hurry up, Casey," she called. "I'm running your bath now, and I'm going to hide your rubber duck somewhere in the bathroom. You have to come and find him."

Casey squealed in delight and began galloping toward the veranda. Lila hurried upstairs, ignoring Tom, who stood in the shadowed doorway looking up at her.

A FEW MORNINGS LATER, when Kelly woke up, the sun was already reaching long golden fingers around the edges of the curtain. She lay against the pillows and smiled drowsily, loving the feeling of being in this cozy room where the same tree was right outside the window every morning.

When they were on the road traveling to rodeos, the scenery beyond their camper window changed every day, and sometimes it got really tiring and confusing.

But here in this place, the cliffs and the river had

been in the same place for thousands of years and nothing would ever make them move, except maybe a huge earthquake or a volcano exploding.

But Kelly wasn't afraid of things like that.

She rolled her head on the pillow and looked over at the cot where Casey slept. He was already gone, with only his rumpled nest of blankets remaining.

Casey was always an early riser, but here in this beautiful house, Kelly didn't have to worry about him at all. He wasn't her responsibility right now. When he got up and wandered downstairs, there were grown-ups to look after him, to make sure he washed his hands and put on his socks and had some breakfast.

She sighed blissfully and snuggled under the covers again, thinking about Lila and the old man in the house, and her father nearby, sleeping in the camper under the cottonwoods. That made her feel even better.

Dad had suggested that Casey sleep with him out in the camper so Kelly could have a whole room to herself for a change, but Lila had protested. She didn't think it was a good idea for Casey to sleep in the camper in case Dad had to lift him or something and hurt his insides again.

Kelly had been a little surprised at how meekly her father obeyed Lila. Normally, Tom Bennet never listened very much to anything people said. He just made up his mind about what he wanted to do, then went quietly his own way.

But Lila had some kind of influence over him that other people didn't. Maybe it was because they'd been friends for so long, ever since they were as young as Kelly.

She stared at the ceiling, thinking about the fairy tales her father used to tell her when she was a little girl.

Kelly's favorite story had been about a beautiful dark-haired, blue-eyed princess who lived in a castle by the river, in a kingdom full of animals. The princess had always been so wonderful, so sweet and good and gentle. Kelly loved those stories and used to beg to hear them again and again when she was Casey's age.

Now that she was older, she remembered the way her father's face would soften when he talked about the beautiful princess, and his voice sometimes got husky and sad.

Maybe the princess had actually been Lila, because it was easy to see how much he cared about her. Kelly could usually tell how he felt, even when he hid his emotions from others.

Briefly she entertained a fantasy where her father married Lila and moved into this big house with her, and Kelly and Casey had their own rooms and got to live here all the time, and make friends with all the dogs and llamas and go to school on a big yellow bus with other kids.

She sighed, then shook her head to dispel the wistful vision.

Nothing like that was ever going to happen, and there was no point in thinking about it.

Besides, Kelly thought grimly, those dreams weren't always so nice in real life. Sometimes they turned out to be horrible.

She felt tears prickling behind her eyes and wondered what was happening to her. Once she'd been so tough, able to stand anything. Now she seemed to be on the verge of tears half the time, as big a baby as Casey. It was very troubling.

Suddenly she had the feeling of being watched, and sat up in bed to look around. Then she stared, enchanted, hardly daring to breathe.

On the nightstand by her bed sat the little carved prairie dog.

CHAPTER THIRTEEN

THE PRAIRIE DOG was perched comically erect on her nightstand, holding his stem of flower, so lifelike that Kelly half expected him to jump down and snuggle into bed with her. His cheeks were as fat and glossy as Casey's, and his eyes were bright.

"Oh," Kelly whispered in wondering awe. "Oh, look at you...."

She reached out with a trembling finger to touch one of his dainty splayed paws, so finely carved you could see tiny claws at the tip.

Carefully she gathered the carving into her hand and held it, gazing into the prairie dog's eyes. He felt warm in her hands. She smiled and crooned in delight, stroking his smooth body.

After a moment she slipped out of bed, dressed rapidly and went to the window to look out, then picked up the carving, padded downstairs and slipped past the kitchen without making any noise.

Casey was in there, and so was Lila. Kelly could hear her brother's shrill chatter, punctuated by Lila's low, musical voice.

She flattened herself against the wall and strained to listen.

They were talking about painting. It had taken them most of the past two days to scrape off the old paint on the barn, and Casey hadn't been much help. But today they would actually start to apply the fresh red paint they'd bought. Casey was asking a thousand questions, as excited as if this were the first barn anybody had ever painted. Lila answered him with her usual calm patience, then started telling him a story about when she and his father had once painted a barn.

Tom had been thirteen and she was twelve, and they'd earned enough money from Lila's father to go into town for dinner and a movie all by themselves.

Kelly listened for a while, enjoying the story and the image of Dad and Lila as kids, having dinner in a big restaurant like grown-ups.

Finally she went down the hall and let herself out onto the veranda, where the old man sat in his accustomed place with the spaniel and the black Labrador lying at his feet.

He made no sign that he noticed her arrival, but then Kelly hadn't expected any. She passed by him and went to sit on the steps, holding the carving in her hands.

The prairie dog felt even warmer now since she'd been holding him so long, and his dear little face was bright with interest. Kelly cast a quick glance at the old man to make sure he wasn't watching, then kissed the prairie dog's wooden face and set him upright on the floorboards next to her so he could see out.

It was a beautiful morning, already warm and sunny. A few wispy clouds drifted overhead in a sky of pure blue, and the river danced and sparkled with light. Down by the cottonwoods, Kelly saw the camper begin to rock and shift. After a moment her father opened the door and climbed down stiffly.

He thought nobody was watching him, and Kelly noticed how slowly he moved, clutching at his stomach as he shifted his weight to the ground. But already he looked stronger and his walk showed more confidence, almost like the old hip-swinging stride that was so much a part of him.

Kelly watched while he buttoned his shirt and tucked it in his jeans, then went over to look at the fence next to the barn. A couple of llamas loped across the pasture and stood with their silly heads high in the air, baring their teeth at him. He smiled, and Kelly relaxed and leaned back.

Dad was feeling a lot better. He was happy here, just like she and Casey were.

Again she had a vision of what it would be like to settle down and never have to leave....

Abruptly she got up, lifted the little prairie dog and whispered to him so he wouldn't be scared, then went to stand by the old man's chair.

He'd begun a new carving, but it was too soon to tell what it was going to be. Right now it was just a block of wood with the corners hacked away.

"Thanks a lot for the prairie dog," Kelly said gruffly.

He went on whittling, and she was afraid he wouldn't answer at all. She could see how hard it was for him to be close to anybody. His jaw was clenched, and his hands tightened on the knife.

"You said you liked it," he muttered at last, not looking at her. "So I thought you might as well have it."

Kelly looked down at the carving in her hands, at its bright eyes and sweet fat cheeks and whimsical paws.

"I love him," she said. "He's the very best thing I ever owned."

The old man glanced up at her, and she realized his eyes were gentle under the beetling gray eyebrows that terrified Casey so much. They weren't really scary at all, just shadowed and sad.

"I'm sorry I yelled at you," she said. "It wasn't nice."

He shrugged. "Sometimes people have to yell," he said. "It makes them feel better."

His voice sounded rusty and unused. No wonder, when he hardly ever talked.

"Do you yell sometimes?" she asked.

The old man shook his head and went on carving. Kelly leaned against the wall, watching his hands.

"Well, it doesn't make me feel better," she said. "Yelling makes me feel sad and empty inside, and then I want to cry."

She was horrified to hear herself confessing such a thing.

Kelly never told anybody how much she yearned to cry sometimes. But there were days, lots of them, when she wanted more than anything to quit being strong and give in to the misery that pressed inside her head like a cold black cloud.

He carved a long peel of wood, which drifted to the floor as softly as a feather.

"So why don't you?" he asked.

"Why don't I what?"

"Just sit down and cry. Go out there on the prairie

somewhere, so far away that nobody can see you, and cry until you feel better. I doubt that anything bad will happen if you do that.''

Kelly gripped her prairie dog and stared at the man in astonishment. She had a sudden and wholly irrational desire to touch him, to crawl on his lap and burrow against him like Casey did with Lila, and start crying right here on his plaid shirtfront.

This grim old man, of all people!

Tentatively she reached out and touched his sleeve, but he ignored her, whittling in silence. She could sense the stillness coming over him again like a door closing, and knew that he felt as terrified as she did.

Kelly wanted to ask him what animal he was making now, and why he was so quiet all the time, and how he understood the way she wanted to cry until all the bad things left her mind.

But she was afraid to spoil anything, and besides, she knew he wouldn't answer.

''Well, thanks again,'' she said awkwardly.

Then she left and went inside the house, where a delicious aroma drifted down the hallway from the kitchen. Kelly could smell bacon frying, and the scent of pancakes. Lila was singing a nonsense song and Casey joined in, his voice loud and bubbling with laughter.

Behind her she could hear her father's boots on the veranda floor, and his cheerful greeting to the old man, which was met with a customary grunt.

Instinctively, Kelly knew that Archie wouldn't want anybody to see her prairie dog. She ran upstairs and put it away carefully in the drawer of the nightstand.

"It's just for now," she whispered to the dear little whiskered face. "Later on you can come downstairs again and see what everybody's doing."

She smiled and closed the drawer, watching regretfully as he disappeared from sight. Then she composed herself, made her face hard and cold again, and went downstairs to the kitchen, where her father, too, had now joined in Lila's song.

THEY WORKED all morning on the task of painting the barn, then stopped for a picnic lunch, which Lila served on the veranda because they were all too paint-smeared and dirty to go inside the kitchen.

Casey looked blissfully happy. He sprawled on an old saddle blanket on the veranda floor and leaned against the railing with the spaniel beside him.

"This is fun," he said, gnawing on a chicken wing. "I always wanted to have a picnic."

"Don't give chicken bones to the dog, sweetheart," Lila told the little boy. "They make him choke."

"Okay." Regretfully, Casey withdrew the bone he'd been offering the interested spaniel.

Lila spooned some potato salad onto his plate and rubbed his tousled curls. "I thought your life was just a picnic all the time," she said. "Traveling around and living in a camper…that's what people do when they're on holidays."

The little boy looked surprised. "But that's not a picnic," he said. "It's just hard most of the time and you get really tired."

Rendered temporarily speechless by a huge mouthful of potato salad, Casey waved his hand at the river, the murmuring cottonwoods, the animals in the pasture and the paint-smeared group eating on the veranda.

"This is more like a picnic," he said. "I wish we could stay here forever."

Lila exchanged a quick, involuntary glance with Tom, who sat impassively at the top of the steps, leaning against a pillar. He looked away and went on whistling between his teeth, watching the llamas in the pasture.

"You know, a person could make a pretty good business out of raising those fellows," he commented at last. "They do well in this climate and the wool's really in demand. Isn't it, Archie?"

The old man didn't answer, just grunted and went on whittling, his plate of food still untouched on a table nearby.

At Tom's words, Lila felt her heart beat a little faster but she tried not to show any emotion. "Tom, I didn't know you were ever interested in being a businessman."

"Really?" He turned that lazy blue gaze on her, and she felt her cheeks grow warm. "What did you think I was interested in, Lilabel?"

She concentrated on slicing a ham with neat strokes. "Wandering around," she said lightly. "Seeing the world and having adventures."

"Well, you're right." He extended his legs stiffly and flexed his hand within the paint-stained cast. "That's what I'm interested in, all right."

"Even if it kills you," she said, trying to keep the edge out of her voice.

"Well, honey," he drawled, watching her with the

slow, teasing grin that always infuriated her, ''at least I'll die happy.''

And what about your kids? she wanted to ask. *If you die happy while you're riding bulls at some godforsaken rodeo, Tom, what happens to these two kids?*

But she'd promised herself she wouldn't argue with him anymore, or allow him to push her buttons with his teasing. Tom Bennet's life, and even his children, were none of her business.

A car pulled up and parked near the front of the house. Marie got out, her gray curls sparkling in the midday sun.

''Well, look at this,'' she said happily, mounting the stairs. ''It's a picnic.''

''It sure is.'' Lila smiled when Casey set his plate aside and ran to hug the new arrival, then pulled her toward one of the chairs, chattering excitedly about the painting project.

Marie squinted in the direction of the barn, which was mostly weathered silver-gray but now sported a strip of bright red for about five feet up.

''Daddy's building a skeleton so we can do the high part tomorrow,'' Casey said.

''It's a scaffold, you dummy,'' Kelly muttered.

Marie smiled at the big man on the steps. ''Well, you're certainly an amazing specimen, Tom Bennet. Last week I didn't know if you'd ever be leaving that ICU room, let alone painting barns and building scaffolds.''

Tom grinned, his eyes crinkling. ''Thanks, Marie. Why don't you tell Lila how amazing I am? She just thinks I'm a pain in the neck.''

''He's both,'' Lila said lightly, busying herself with

the food. "An amazingly huge pain in the neck. Marie, have you eaten?"

"A leaf of lettuce and handful of dried apricots. I'm dieting so I can be sure to fit into my dance dress tomorrow night."

"Dance with me!" Casey shouted. "Do the tango again, Marie!"

She grinned and reached over to ruffle his hair. "Later, darling," she promised. "When we don't have quite such a big audience, maybe we'll strut our stuff for a while, okay?"

"Okay." He gave her a beaming smile, his face smeared with chicken and potato salad.

"Oh, for goodness' sake," Marie said, "just look at you." She picked up a napkin and drew the little boy closer to rub at his cheeks and mouth over his squirming protest.

Lila smiled, helping herself to a tiny sliver of apple pie. "This is the nicest holiday I could ever have," she said, gazing across the sunlit fields and placid river. "Much more enjoyable than last year when I went to Ireland and it rained every day."

"But I can't imagine how the medical community is surviving without us." Marie held Casey against her knee and kissed him noisily. "Have you been to the hospital today, Lila?"

"I went in early to do my rounds. Everything's fine. I've sent Tony home with a course of oral antibiotics, and Carrie's stabilized enough after her chemo that I released her, as well."

"Wonderful," Marie said. "Carrie loves it when she gets to go home. Any other problems?"

Lila thought of her sick little patients in the pediatric ward, then looked at the two children on the veranda, both tanned and radiant with health. But she was increasingly convinced they had unseen damages and scars....

"Not really," she said. "No problems."

"Good. So I can relax and enjoy the prospect of going dancing tomorrow night for the first time in years."

"Has Trevor called to confirm?" Lila asked, feeling a stab of worry when she looked at Marie's glowing face. "Sometimes he...forgets things."

"Oh, he'll remember," Marie said comfortably. "He was very specific about the date. You know, Trevor actually seemed excited at the prospect of doing some dancing, even with an old relic like me."

"The man's lucky to have such a beautiful partner," Tom said gallantly. "If I were in better shape, I'd escort you myself, Marie."

Lila glanced over at him, surprised. "Really, Tom? Are you a ballroom dancer as well as a bull rider? I never knew that."

"There are lots of things you don't know about me, Lila." He looked at her directly, his eyes darkening with emotion, then smiled to take the edge off his words.

But she shivered a little, caught in the intensity of his gaze.

He'd lost all his hospital pallor by now and looked like a man sculpted out of bronze. His exposed arm and face were tanned and his dark blond hair was ruffled by the cap he'd removed to eat his dinner. He wore an old paint-smeared T-shirt and a pair of faded jeans that clung to his lean, muscular hips.

Suddenly Lila was overwhelmed by a surge of physical yearning so intense it took her breath away. She wanted to hold him and lie with him, kiss the pulse in his throat, feel his naked skin against hers and his warm breath on her face and eyelids.

Her body moistened with sexual desire, and her cheeks burned.

She looked away to keep him from noticing and listened to Casey, who was chattering with Marie while Kelly watched in silence.

"Hello, Archie," Marie said, smiling at the older man when Casey paused to catch his breath. "I didn't mean to ignore you. What's that you're making?"

He didn't answer, just cast her a look of alarm and returned to his whittling.

"It's a llama," Kelly volunteered.

Lila looked up at the older child, startled, wondering when Kelly had gotten on good enough terms with her father to know what carving he was working on.

But then, Kelly didn't seem to be afraid of anybody. Not like Casey, whose sunny, outgoing nature concealed a great deal of timidity as well as that something dark and troubling that Lila still couldn't seem to analyze.

"What do you do with those carvings when you're done, Archie?" Marie asked in an easy conversational tone, as if the silent old man were a normal part of the group.

He said nothing, just went on carving, clearly uncomfortable at being the center of attention.

"I take them to a gallery downtown," Lila said,

"where they sell them to tourists for a whole lot of money. Dad's carvings are very much in demand."

Archie cleared his throat. "Sometimes I give them away," he muttered. "But only to people I like."

Lila gaped at him, astounded. These days it was almost unheard of for Archie to contribute to a conversation at all, let alone talk about liking people.

She held her breath, wondering if he would say more, afraid to follow up on his comment for fear of spooking him. But he lapsed into silence again, concentrating on his work.

Kelly got up and paused by his chair to look at the carving in his hands. "I bet that's going to be a beautiful llama," she said. "I bet it'll be the nicest llama anybody ever made."

Then she left, slipping inside the house and running upstairs on some errand of her own.

A drowsy and contented silence fell over the little group on the veranda. Lila gazed out at the river with a lump in her throat.

If only Tom and his kids could stay a little longer, who knew what miracles might happen?

She forgot how anxious she'd been the previous evening for him to leave, before she could be overtaken by feelings she had no way of controlling.

Now she found herself wondering if there was some way she could coax him to stay a little longer, so the children could benefit from a few weeks of stability and Archie might be drawn out further by their noisy, cheerful company.

Maybe tonight she and Tom would go for a walk, just the two of them, after the kids were asleep, and she'd ask him to stay until the end of summer. He could take time to heal properly while she paid him to tend to all the things that had fallen into disrepair around the farm in recent years.

It would be a business arrangement, nothing more, Lila told herself firmly. And even if they were alone in the moonlight walking along the river, surely she was mature enough not to give way to her feelings.

Because, of course, it was an impossible relationship, and it always had been. Two people could hardly be further apart in their goals and outlooks on life than she and Tom Bennet. The attraction between them was partly physical and partly a remnant of her childhood, and Lila was strong enough to resist it.

She had to be…

Marie was dancing with Casey on the lawn, holding him in her arms while he squealed with laughter. Tom sat and leaned against the pillar, watching them with an absent smile.

Lila finished gathering up the food and putting lids on containers, then went and sat on the step next to him.

"The kids are really having a good time," she ventured at last. "Aren't they?"

"They seem to be." Tom laughed aloud when Marie dipped and twirled around the lilac hedge with Casey in her arms.

"Tom…" Lila looked down, aimlessly fingering the hem of her shirt.

He reached out with his good hand and touched her shoulder, stroking it gently, kneading her collarbone with his thumb. His touch was both soothing and arousing. Lila was torn between the urge to pull away and the equally strong desire to nestle close to him and feel the hard warmth of his body.

Kelly came out of the house again, and Lila glanced over her shoulder to see the girl pause by Archie's chair. She leaned over to whisper something to the old man. He listened, then nodded.

While Lila watched in openmouthed astonishment, Kelly reached into her pocket and took something out, setting it carefully on the floor next to his chair.

"Only till we're finished painting," she said to him as she moved toward the veranda steps, edging past Lila and her father. "Okay?"

"Okay," Archie said as casually as if this were an everyday occurrence.

When Kelly started down the steps, Lila caught the tail of the girl's shirt. "Hey, what's going on here?" she asked, smiling. "What secret do you have with my father?"

"No big deal. He's looking after something for me," Kelly said evasively.

"I see." Lila released the shirt and Kelly ran off toward the barn, calling something to Casey and Marie as she went.

Tom and Lila exchanged a glance.

"What are you looking after, Dad?" Lila asked her father.

Archie didn't answer, but she thought she detected a glimmer of amusement cross his brooding features.

"Tom," she said with sudden decision, "can we have a talk later? This evening, maybe?"

He grinned, his eyes crinkling. "Just you and me, Lilabel?"

"If you don't mind," she said, avoiding his teasing glance. "I wanted to...ask you something."

"Sure." He leaned back, still holding her shoulder. "We'll go for a walk by the river in the moonlight. It'll be like old times."

CHAPTER FOURTEEN

THE SUMMER DAY seemed to go on forever, fading gradually from afternoon heat to mellow twilight to the fragrant coolness of dusk.

They finished their painting for the day and ate the remnants of their picnic meal on the veranda, talking and laughing as the sky turned from blue to mauve and the first star twinkled in the southwest.

Marie got in her car and left, heading to her home in the city, while Lila and Tom bathed Casey and got him ready for bed.

Both children were tired enough to be fretful, and Casey had managed to get paint all over his plump little body, even in his hair. Finally he and Kelly were settled in their beds in the spare room.

Lila tidied the bathroom and tossed a load of wet towels into the washer, then came back to listen while Tom sang to Casey.

"'Oh, Casey boy, the pipes, the pipes are calling, from glen to glen and down the mountainside...'"

She sat in the rocking chair, smiling, resting her head against the cushioned back.

Casey's eyes fluttered shut, then opened again. "Kelly's got something," he complained sleepily to his father. "It's under her blankets, Daddy. She's hiding it."

"Shut up," Kelly said.

But her voice wasn't nearly as fierce, and when Lila glanced at her she seemed placid, almost gentle.

A far cry, Lila thought, from the prickly, belligerent child she'd first discovered in that garbage bin.

And now the little girl and Archie actually seemed to be building some kind of relationship.

With fresh resolve, she got to her feet and moved toward the door, pausing to kiss both children before she left.

"You promised me a walk by the river, remember?" she said to Tom.

"Lilabel, how could I ever forget something like that?"

She was almost frightened by the look of warm intensity on his face.

This was for the kids, she told herself firmly. And for her father. Besides, nothing was going to happen.

Nothing at all.

"I'll just get myself cleaned up a little," she told him, "and meet you by your camper in half an hour or so. All right?"

"I'll be there. Kids, say good-night to Lila."

They joined in a sleepy chorus and she paused in the doorway to look back at their shining faces against the pillows.

Lila smiled, her heart aching with tenderness. Then she became conscious of Tom watching her and turned quickly to leave, heading down the hallway toward her own room.

HALF AN HOUR LATER, she met him in the cotton-woods near the river. The night was dark by now, the

sky splashed richly with stars. A soft breeze murmured and rustled in the leaves overhead, and an owl
hooted near the water.

Tom was wearing a plaid shirt and clean faded
jeans, and smelled pleasantly of soap and shaving
cream. Lila's heart beat faster when she drew near to
him, but she forced herself to smile casually.

"How do you get clean in there?" she asked, waving at the camper. "Wouldn't you rather use one of
the bathrooms in the house?"

"It's small but very self-contained," he said.
"There's even a little shower next to the bed. Why
don't you come in and see?"

She pictured herself alone with him in the tiny enclosed space that was mostly bed.

"I don't think so," she said. "Maybe later, all
right? It's such a nice evening, I'd rather go for a
walk. But it's getting a little windy. Do you think
we'll need our jackets?"

She realized that she was chattering in nervousness,
and that he knew it and was amused.

"No, honey," he said. "You won't be needing that
coat."

Lila left her jacket on the hood of the truck and
turned away, heading along the path through the trees
to the water's edge. She was conscious of him following, moving along behind her with the prowling,
catlike grace that she remembered so well, though
occasionally she saw him wince with pain when he
thought he was unobserved.

"Remember when we were kids," she said over
her shoulder, "and we spent all those months one

summer mastering the art of slipping through the trees without making any noise?''

''We were terrific woodsmen,'' he recalled. ''But we never did manage to build a fire with kindling and a forked stick, did we?''

She laughed, feeling more comfortable now that the conversation had moved away from campers and beds. ''No,'' she said. ''We always had to give up and use matches to make a fire for our tea.''

''God, those days were fun, weren't they?'' He caught up with her as she emerged into the clearing by the shore, and fell in step next to her.

''Yes,'' she said. ''We had a lot of fun.''

They walked along in silence, the prairie breeze warm against their faces.

With spectacular, breathtaking suddenness, the moon rose above the river cliffs to the southeast. It was almost full, and painted so brightly orange from the summertime dust hanging along the horizon that it resembled a new sun in the black, star-dazzled sky.

''Oh, Tom. Look at that.'' Lila stopped and gazed upward, enchanted.

''That's another thing I've dreamed about,'' he said, standing next to her. ''So many years I've stretched out in hundreds of different beds in places all over the country, and thought about the moon rising on those cliffs.''

She looked at his finely etched profile and his hair lifting in the wind. ''Did you ever—'' She stopped abruptly.

''What?'' he asked, turning to fall into step beside her as she moved off along the riverbank, hands deep in her pockets.

"Nothing. Listen to the owls. That's one of my favorite sounds. The owls and nighthawks, the crickets and coyotes…all together they make a whole symphony orchestra."

Tom smiled, his teeth flashing white in the darkness. "I know. While we were painting the barn, Casey told me how the crickets all wear little black suits and sit in chairs playing tiny musical instruments."

Lila sighed with pleasure. "What a lovely image. You know," she added dreamily, "I've always thought I'd like to write children's books and get Dad to illustrate them. Some of the artwork he could do in paintings, and for others we could use his carved animals in different poses and have them photographed."

"That would be a great idea. Why don't you do it?"

"My job doesn't leave me enough time. And Dad is hardly what you'd call a dynamic creative partner these days, you know."

"Poor Archie."

There was a brief silence while the water lapped against rocks along the shoreline and the muted animal chorus sang all around them.

"A minute ago you were going to ask me something." Tom touched her arm. "What was it?"

Her heart began to beat faster. "I don't remember."

"It was about the moon. I told you how homesick it made me whenever I thought about a full moon over these cliffs, and then you started to ask me if I ever did something, but you didn't say what."

"I forget." She quickened her steps a little and

plunged her hands deeper into her pockets, though her cheeks were warm.

He kept pace with her, his face tense with effort, and she slowed her steps again. "Should I tell you what you were going to ask, Lila?"

"You still think you can read my mind?" she asked with a touch of annoyance.

"I know I can," he said calmly. "So stop and look at me."

Reluctantly she glanced over at his face, so close to hers in the moonlit darkness. The wash of light on his cheekbones, the outline of his sculpted mouth, the weathered lines around his eyes and the breadth of his shoulders all made her feel weak and light-headed with urgent longing.

He stopped in front of her and looked down steadily. "You were going to ask me," he said, "if there was ever a time during these past fifteen years when I looked at the moon and wondered if somewhere you were doing the same thing, watching the moon and thinking about me."

She forced herself to turn away and started off down the shoreline again, plunging blindly toward the distant curve of water.

"So I was right," he said, catching up with her. "Wasn't I, Lila?"

She shook her head and looked across the water, biting her lip to keep from responding.

He put a hand on her arm, holding her so she couldn't walk away. "Hey, don't you want to know my answer?" he asked.

"No!" she said with rising tension. "Tom, I don't want to have this conversation at all. I really don't."

"My answer," he said as if she hadn't spoken, "is yes. Every time I looked at a full moon for fifteen years, Lila, I thought of you. I wondered where you were, and if you were happy, and if I'd ever see you again. I ached to hold you and touch your face and hear you laugh. Every time I saw the moon," he repeated softly, looking up at the sky.

"Well, that wasn't right," she muttered, shuffling her feet uneasily in the damp, shimmering gravel. "If it's true, you shouldn't have been thinking things like that, Tom."

"Why not?"

"Oh, come on. It's obvious why not. Because you were a married man. You had a wife and children and other responsibilities. It's not right to spend your time brooding about…something that's past and gone."

"Married!" he echoed with so much bitterness that she looked at him in alarm. "My God, what a farce."

"Can you tell me about it, Tom?" she pleaded, falling into step beside him. "Can't we just talk for a little while about what your wife was like and what happened to her, and why the children seem so—"

"No," he said harshly. "We can't. It's all over, Lila. Those days are finally behind us. Maybe someday I'll tell you more, but for now the best thing is to bury it, forget the past and keep moving on. Those poor kids have suffered so much. I don't want them to start dealing with it all over again."

She glanced at his hard profile with its familiar look of stubbornness. When Tom Bennet retreated into himself, he could become more remote and inaccessible than anybody she'd ever known.

"You brought me out here to talk about something," he said. "Not just to enjoy the moonlight. I can always tell when you get that purposeful look, Lilabel."

She smiled wryly. "I guess you really do know me pretty well, Tom."

He glanced down at her, his face softening. But his eyes remained hard and intent. "I know you all the way to the center of your soul, Lilabel. You've been the woman in my heart for as far back as I can remember."

"Tom," she pleaded, "we were just kids."

"Maybe so. But we aren't kids anymore."

"I know we aren't. Look, I don't want to..." She floundered a moment, then took a deep breath. "I really came out here tonight to offer you a sort of business proposition."

With one of his unsettling shifts in mood, he gave her a sexy, irrepressible grin. "Well, that's great. I'd love to be propositioned by you, Lila. Especially if you've got the same kind of business in mind as I do."

Lila swatted him impatiently, but this was unwise, because touching his hard-muscled arm made her knees go weak with sudden fiery longing.

"I think it would be best for everybody if you stayed here a while," she said. "The kids are enjoying the place, my dad seems to be getting a little better, you're looking stronger every day and we're actually getting all kinds of work done around the farm. So," she concluded lamely, "it would be a good idea if..."

Her voice trailed off when she saw how intently he was watching her.

"If what, Lila?"

"You know what I mean," she said. "If you just…let me hire you as a farm supervisor for the rest of the summer. You could spruce up all the things that need doing, and the kids would…"

He waved a hand to stop her halting voice.

"What you really want," he said, "is for me to join the ranks of 'men Lila used to sleep with,' like poor old Trev? The loser-type guys that Lila looks after by paying them money to do little chores for her. Is that what you're planning for me?"

He looked unbearably sad. Lila moved closer and put a hand on his forearm, stroking it with an automatic, caressing gesture.

"Come on, Tom," she pleaded. "It's not like that and you know it. I'm just trying to hold on to you and the kids for a while, until it's safe for you to travel. Why are you so upset?"

"I'm not upset." He stared down at her, his eyes unfathomable. "I'm just hurt."

"Why?"

"Because you seem to think…"

He turned and strode away. This time it was her turn to quicken her steps, and she almost had to run to keep up. "What do you mean?" she asked. "Why are you reacting this way?"

He picked up a fallen branch and began absently to strip the loose bark. "I don't like being treated the same as that boy-toy you married, as if you need to come up with a nice little plan to manage my future so I won't go astray."

"Tom, I never…"

"I'm not that kind of man, Lila. I thought you knew me better."

She faced him, though it took a considerable amount of courage to meet that intent gaze. "Maybe I don't know you after all. So why don't you help me out? Tell me what kind of man you are."

He moved closer, still watching her with the same unfathomable expression. Finally he put his hands on her shoulders, gripping so tightly she almost cried out with pain.

"I'm a man who adores you, Lila Marsden. I've never forgotten a single thing about you in almost thirty years of loving you. Wherever I travel I take you with me. You're almost always the first thing I think of when I wake up in the morning, and the last thing in my mind when I drop off to sleep. You always have been, and you always will."

"Tom," she whispered, staring at him in amazement. "I didn't mean to…"

He dropped his hands abruptly and moved away from her.

"So don't go putting me in some kind of box," he said over his shoulder. "Don't make plans for my next few weeks and tell me how it's going to be best for me and everyone else if I fall in line. I'm not Trevor."

"I never said you—"

"I thought you learned a long time ago that I can't be managed and organized."

She waited miserably, hugging her arms in the thin cotton shirt. By now the moon had faded to a disk of cold silver, as high and pale as a coin tossed into the sky, and the wind was freshening.

Tom hesitated, and she could sense that he was struggling with himself. At last he crossed the gravel between them and took her into his arms, rubbing her back against the evening chill.

"Sorry," he murmured against her hair. "I shouldn't yell at you, because none of this is your fault. I know you're just trying to help me and my kids. But being alone with you like this, especially back here where it all started…this is more than I can stand, Lila. It makes me crazy."

His voice was husky, almost on the edge of breaking. She reached up to touch his face, laying her palm tenderly on his hard cheek.

"Tom," she whispered, "let's stop fighting. I'm so tired of fighting with you."

He kissed her then, his mouth gentle and tentative at first, but growing more purposeful.

Shameless with need, Lila clung to him, drowning in the sensations that flooded her body. Her passion rose to meet his until, almost frantic, she rubbed her body against his, ran her fingers through his hair, stroked his face and throat and shoulders.

This was how it was supposed to feel. No wonder she'd never been able to fall in love with anybody else. All others were pale imitations of this powerful, complex, infuriating and utterly desirable man she now held in her arms.

He whispered broken endearments, his hands roaming over her waist and hips, pulling her shirt from her belt and touching her naked skin, reaching up to cup her breasts.

"You still don't wear a bra," he murmured. "And

your breasts are even more beautiful than they were twenty years ago.''

Slowly his thumb caressed her nipple, making her shiver and press against him. ''Tom...''

''Come on,'' he said, putting an arm around her shoulders and striding off downriver again. ''Come with me.''

She stumbled along at his side, dazed and disoriented by the sudden urgency of her sexual arousal. ''Tom, where are we going?''

''It's a surprise.''

In a few minutes she realized what he was doing. They reached the secluded bend in the river where their old childhood fort had once been, and he drew her into the dark shelter of the willows. A cozy, inviting nest of blankets was arrayed on the sand.

Lila stared at the blankets, then at him.

''Well, look at this. You were pretty damn confident, weren't you?'' She tried to sound accusing, but her mouth twitched with laughter and betrayed her.

''Let's just say I was hopeful.'' He grinned in reply, then moved closer to grasp her shoulders. His smile faded as he gazed down at her. ''I love you, Lila.''

''Tom...''

''Tell me you love me. Say it out loud.''

''Tom, I can't...''

''Say it!'' His mouth closed hungrily over hers. ''Say it,'' he said again, his lips moving against her face. ''I want to hear you tell me.''

He kept kissing her, his lips roaming over her throat and eyelids until she was weak with longing.

''Say it, Lila.''

She gave in at last, abandoning herself to the flood
of need that had been pent up for fifteen years. "I
love you, Tom."

"That's my girl." Smiling, he sank onto the blankets and drew her down next to him. In the shelter of
the willows, out of the breeze, the night was warm
and sweet. When he unbuttoned her shirt and pulled
it off, she felt no chill at all, just a rich, tingling excitement as his eyes devoured her.

"So beautiful." He reached out to stroke the line
of her throat, the curve of her breast, while she
watched him in grave silence. "You were the first
woman I ever saw like this, and nobody else has ever
come close. You're a goddess."

She wanted to parry the compliment with some
kind of self-deprecating joke, but no words would
come. In the star-dazzled summer night with this
man's eyes worshiping her, she truly did feel like a
goddess.

"I've missed you so much," she whispered, tears
stinging behind her eyelids. "After you went away, I
thought I'd die."

"You sent me away, Lilabel. It was all your idea.
Wild horses couldn't have torn me from you, but you
said I had to go."

"I know."

She watched while he stood to strip off his shirt,
then bent, a little gingerly, to remove the rest of his
clothes. Working with only one arm, everything took
a little longer. Finally the white bandage around his
ribs gleamed like dull silver in the pale light as he
settled next to her again.

"Do you still have a lot of pain?" she asked, running her fingers through the mat of golden hair on his chest above the bandage.

"It's getting better every day."

"You're such a strong man, Tom." She looked down in admiration at his lean, powerful shoulders, his hard-muscled legs. There had been a time when she knew every slope and plane of that naked male body. Now it seemed both familiar and infinitely exciting.

"I'm strong, all right, but I don't know how good I'll be at loving just now," he said with a wry grin. "I might need a little help from the doctor."

Overtaken by recklessness and a sudden heady joy, she took off the rest of her clothes and lay close beside him, wrapping a bare leg around him, kissing his face and chest.

"Where does it hurt?" She raised her head to look at him, smiling. "I'll kiss it better."

"It hurts right there. Oh, yeah…" He sighed blissfully as her lips trailed kisses down to the edge of the white bandage. "That feels so good, Doctor."

"And here? Does this need some attention?"

"Yeah, that hurts too. It hurts a lot."

"Poor baby," She knelt beside him, her mouth moving lower down his abdomen, seeking and caressing. "Look, this must really hurt. It's all swollen."

His body shook with suppressed laughter, which turned to shivers of lust as she continued her gentle ministrations. She couldn't believe how good it felt to caress him, how sweet and familiar. After so many years, they slipped back into their old ways of playfulness and passion as if they'd never been separated.

"You were born to love me, Lila," he whispered, echoing her thoughts, his voice rough with emotion. "You don't know how I've missed you all these years."

She lay down again and arched against him, ravenous for him, aching with a pain and hunger that she could barely contain.

"I'm just beginning to realize," she said, bringing her face close to his again, "how much I've wanted you."

He ran his hand the length of her body, stroking her with worshipful tenderness. His palm was as callused and firm as she remembered, and he knew exactly how to touch her.

"You've always liked this, haven't you?" he whispered, reaching lower. "I still remember the funny little noise you used to make when I—"

"Oh, Tom." She melted against him.

"And this," he said dreamily. "This was one of your favorites."

"Tom," she gasped, "I'm dying for you. I can't bear any more of this."

"Sure you can. You can stand hours and hours of lovemaking, and that's what you're going to get. My little Lila." He smiled at her, his face just a few inches away. "Out on her fishing rock with a can of worms and a book. You had no idea how much I loved you."

He freed her hair and let the silken strands fall loose. Grasping her head in both his hands, he kissed her with unrestrained passion, and she felt her body opening to receive him.

"Please," she whispered. "Please, darling..."

He maneuvered her on top of him and held her, guiding her carefully downward.

"Are you sure?" she whispered. "It's not going to be painful?"

"It'll be too damn painful," he muttered, "if you wait another minute."

Then he was inside her, and she thrilled at the rich fulfillment. Slowly and gently, mindful of his injured body, she began to move astride him, rotating her hips, pleasuring herself with his thrusting hardness while he reached up to grasp and caress her breasts.

Nothing had ever felt so right, so sweet and true, so like a homecoming. She realized, here in the moonlight, their bodies united, that Tom was the man for her and always would be. They had been created to fit together.

The simple, wondrous truth of it brought tears to her eyes, and then a swelling climax that left her throbbing and gasping for breath.

She kept moving until he, too, was spent, his face rigid with pleasure, the moonlight glistening on his closed eyelids. At last she pulled a blanket over their linked bodies and nestled beside him, kissing his shoulder.

"Not such a bad thing," he whispered, his eyes still closed, "to happen to a poor old wounded cowboy."

"We were always good at this, Tom."

His good arm tightened around her. "I can't believe we've wasted fifteen years. We shouldn't be apart for a single night, Lila. Bodies that are matched like ours should be sleeping together in the same bed.''

''So you'll stay?'' She ran her fingers idly over the firm line of his mouth.

He opened his eyes and looked at her so long that she began to feel uncomfortable. Finally he sat up and reached for her shirt, still hanging from a nearby willow branch.

''Here,'' he said. ''You'd better put your clothes on. It's going to be getting chilly.''

Puzzled by his sudden change in manner, she dressed rapidly and helped him to retrieve his clothes and pull on his jeans.

Finally, fully dressed, they settled back together in their nest of blankets, basking in the warm, sated aftermath of lovemaking. He caressed her hair with long gentle strokes, gazing up at the stars flung across the black arch of sky.

''Remember when we got that book and tried to memorize all the constellations?'' he said.

''We couldn't make much headway, as I recall.'' She burrowed against him, kissing the warm curve of his throat.

''That was because your mother wouldn't let you outside at night anymore. She put you on a curfew.''

Lila rose on one elbow and looked down at him, her hair falling onto his cheek. ''Really? I don't remember that.''

''Well, it's true. I was fifteen, and she suspected I had other heavenly bodies on my mind.''

Lila chuckled, then sobered and kissed him again. ''You probably did.''

''Damn right. I was your mother's worst nightmare.

And this...'' He gestured at their bodies nestled close together. "This was what scared her most of all."

"Do you think so?"

"Of course. She knew who I was and where I came from. Bella loved you, and she was afraid I'd screw up your life. And I guess," he added, his voice suddenly bleak, "she was right, wasn't she."

Lila glanced at him, taken aback. "What do you mean, Tom?"

"I can't stay here with you," he said quietly. "I can't, and I won't."

"But..." She gaped at him, too surprised to answer. "You're leaving again?"

"Yes." He touched her hair with a tender, sorrowful look that she didn't understand. "I'm leaving again. And I want you to come with me."

CHAPTER FIFTEEN

LILA SAT ERECT and drew away to stare at him. "You want me to do what?"

He lay with his hands behind his head, watching her. His pose seemed relaxed, even casual, but she could see the tension around his eyes. "You heard me, Lila. I want you to come with me."

"But..." She laughed nervously. "It's a joke, right? You're kidding me."

"No, I'm not kidding. We'll be leaving soon, and I want you to come along. Share my life, Lila. Help me raise my kids. Be my partner."

"But that's..." Despair rose in her throat, almost choking her. "Tom, it's just ridiculous. You can't be serious."

He continued to fix her with the same grave, thoughtful expression. "So let me get this straight, okay? When you ask me to stay here and share your life, it's a reasonable, serious kind of proposition. But if I suggest instead that you become a part of my life, that's just ridiculous?"

Her cheeks flushed with annoyance. "Oh, come on. I have a career. I have responsibilities, patients who need my care, a home to look after, a father who's not well. I have a whole life! You want me to throw it all away so I can..."

Just in time, she caught herself and fell silent, staring at him.

"So you can what?"

"Nothing," she muttered, toying with the fringe on the blanket.

"So you can what, Lila?"

She remained silent, shaking her head.

"Again," he said quietly, "let me finish your statement for you. You don't see why you should throw away a rich, valuable, productive life so you can follow me around like a vagrant while I play at being a child for the rest of my life. Right?"

Lila looked up. "You're the one who said it. Not me."

"God," he muttered wearily, rubbing a hand over his forehead. "Fifteen years later and we're having the same damn conversation. You haven't learned anything, Lila. Not a goddamn thing."

"Me!" she said, stung. "*I'm* the one who hasn't learned anything? Really, you've got to be joking."

"I'm not joking, Lilabel."

He continued to watch her with that strange puzzling look she couldn't understand. His expression seemed almost pitying.

Lila's growing confusion made her angry. She got up and began to stride around the little clearing, searching for words.

"You, of all people," she said, "to accuse me of being immature! For God's sake, Tom, you're living the same life as when you were a teenager! You still wander around the country like a circus performer, only now you're dragging a couple of little kids with you, probably doing them all kinds of harm in the process. And you dare to act sanctimonious, as if I'm the one who's making some big mistake in my life! Tom, you've always been so—''

''Be careful, Lila.''

But she was beyond caution. ''You could have done so much with your life! You could have been anything you wanted. Instead, you squandered your youth and now you want me to join in while you waste the rest of your life. Well, you can forget it!''

She stopped at last, feeling spent and miserable, and leaned against a cottonwood to stare out at the shimmer of light on the water.

''Are you finished?'' he asked quietly.

''Yes,'' she muttered without turning around. ''I guess I'm finished.''

''Good. Then I get to talk for a while. Come back and sit down, Lila. I like to see your face while I'm talking to you.''

Reluctantly she came back and settled on the blanket where he was still lying. He pulled himself upright and sat leaning against the trunk of a tree, watching her in a silence that contained so much sadness it made her heart lurch briefly, then begin to pound in alarm.

But when he spoke, his words surprised her. ''Why did you marry Trevor Applegarth?''

''What kind of question is that?''

''A serious question, Lila. Tell me, why did you marry him?''

''Because…I don't know,'' she said in despair. ''Because he was handsome and dressed well. Because he was fun at parties and made me laugh. Who knows why anybody marries someone else?''

"Not because they're fun at parties," Tom said quietly. "Not if they want a long and contented marriage, anyhow."

"And what would you know about long, contented marriages? You won't even talk about your own."

"You're right," he said. "I've had no firsthand experience with happy marriages. Everything I know, I've learned from living the way it's not supposed to be."

"So why are you preaching to me?"

"And why are you so angry? This isn't like you, Lila. You're always so gentle."

She avoided his eyes, folding the edge of the blanket into little ridges, distressed to see how badly her fingers trembled.

"When you married Trevor," he went on gently, "was there any suggestion that you might move into his house or apartment?"

"Trevor's apartment wasn't even big enough for him, let alone two of us," she said.

"So he moved into your place?"

"Yes, he did."

"And was there any question of moving away, maybe relocating your practice to be closer to his place of business?"

She laughed without humor. "Trev didn't have a place of business. He didn't even—" Lila stopped abruptly. "Look, I see where you're going with this."

"Where am I going, Lila?" His blue eyes met hers steadily.

"You're saying I only look for men I can manage. You think I want to be in control and run things, so

I collect people who can be fitted into my life and then I'll never have to compromise.''

"That's not what I'm saying." He shook his head. "I could never be so harsh with you, Lila. I love you too much. Besides, I don't think it's true."

"Then what are you saying, for God's sake!" Frustrated, she got up and flung herself away from him again, picking nervously at the bark of the cotton-wood tree.

But his voice continued behind her, quiet and inexorable. "I'm saying you're afraid. You can't bear to put your life in any man's hands. The idea terrifies you."

"Is that so?" she muttered.

"Yeah, it is. I knew it fifteen years ago when you sent me away. You had no choice back then, because if you went with me, I was going to turn your world upside down and that was too frightening for you to contemplate. So you made me leave and robbed us both of all those happy years. And now you're doing it again."

"I can't believe this." She turned to face him, so angry that she could barely speak.

Tears burned in her eyes but she fought to hold them back. If she started crying she'd never be able to talk, and there were things she needed to say.

"Of all the arrogant, small-minded, self-absorbed things I've ever heard, Tom Bennet, this takes the cake! We have two choices here. We could live on this farm in peace and comfort, take good care of your kids, my patients and my father and have a nice life. Right?''

"That's right," he said. "We could have a real nice life."

"Or, on the other hand, we could wander around like vagrants, living and eating and sleeping God knows where, disrupting everybody's lives for no reason I can see. Yet when I make the obvious choice, you dare to tell me it's because I'm afraid?"

She leaned closer, glaring at him while he watched her in silence.

"I think," she said, "that it's easy enough to see who's afraid, Tom."

He met her eyes with that same disconcerting steadiness, making her feel uneasy and confused.

"Oh, you're right, Lila," he said. "I'm scared, all right. I'm scared as hell that I'll have to live without you again, because after holding you tonight, I don't think I can stand it. It took me years to learn how before, and this time will be so much harder because now I love you even more."

"Then tell me why, Tom," she pleaded, kneeling beside him on the blanket. "Why won't you just give up this wandering life of yours?"

"And what if I do, Lila? What if I choose to stay here like a pet dog because that's what you want from me? Will you have any more respect for me than you do for Trevor? Or will you wind up someday giving me pocket money to take your friends to dancing class?"

"Of course I won't! The two situations are completely different."

"How are they different?"

The question took her by surprise, and she had to search for an answer.

"Because I...I love you," she said at last. "And I never loved Trevor."

"But how long will you keep loving me when you realize I've been bought and paid for, and placed neatly under your control like everything else in your world?"

"Then don't stay here at the farm!" she said. "I could pose the same choice to you, Tom. If you love me and you're not afraid of commitment, prove it to me. Get a job somewhere here in the city, looking after livestock or something, and find a way to build a life for us and your kids. But don't go wandering off into the sunset and expect me to trot along at your side."

He stared at her intently, as if searching for something deep in her eyes.

"You just don't understand," he said at last. "Do you, sweetheart? You don't understand at all."

"Why you have to live like a vagrant, and if I want to love you, my only choice is to share that life?" She shook her head. "No, Tom, I don't understand."

His face twisted with pain. He looked away toward the shimmering river. "God," he muttered. "It's happening all over again. The worst nightmare of my life, and now it's back."

Lila wanted to shake him. "But it doesn't have to be this way!" she said in baffled frustration. "If you could only see reason..."

"See reason, Lila?" He smiled bitterly. "That's all you want from me?"

She stared at him, mesmerized by his intensity. For a moment as she gazed into the shadowed depths of his eyes, a glimmer of understanding stirred in her, a sense of the important truth he was trying so desperately to impart. But as soon as it came, the illumination was gone, swallowed up in her anger at his unyielding stubbornness, and by something else....

Reluctantly she understood this other emotion was fear, the very thing he'd accused her of. But that was too painful to think about.

Instead, she got up and started off down the riverbank, heading for the lighted house.

"Better get to bed in your little camper," she said over her shoulder, trying to keep her voice light and casual. "If you're planning to leave on the weekend, we'll all have to be up early tomorrow and work hard to finish painting the barn before you go, won't we?"

He said nothing, and long after she'd plunged off down the graveled bank and past the overhanging branches of cottonwoods, Lila still imagined she could see him sitting quietly among the remnants of their makeshift bed, watching her with that same bewildering look of sadness.

SHE TOSSED AND TURNED all night long, torn by conflicting emotions. His lovemaking had set her body on fire, arousing all those wild, sweet emotions she'd worked so hard to suppress for the past fifteen years. With almost unbearable intensity, she wanted to slip out of the house, go down to his camper and climb into bed with him.

He was right, their bodies were created to fit together. Nothing had ever felt so right, or ever would again.

The blankets were hot and stifling in the warm summer night. She kicked them off and lay staring

blankly at the darkened ceiling, listening to the murmur of wind in the trees beyond the window.

How could anybody endure this kind of pain a second time?

What a cruel trick of fate, when your body was
drawn so intensely to a man whose mind and outlook
could never, ever mesh with your own.

But he had no right to ask for the kind of sacrifice
that he was demanding of her.

To throw everything away and follow him.... It
might be a romantic notion for a couple of teenagers,
but so impractical at this stage of her life that Lila
couldn't even bring herself to think about it.

If Tom really loved her, how could he ask such a
thing? He was just being selfish, and any man so completely self-absorbed wasn't worthy of a woman's
love.

But the maddening thing was, Tom hadn't seemed
self-absorbed when he'd been talking to her on the
riverbank. Instead, his manner had been wise and sad
and insightful, as if he were looking into a part of her
soul that she herself couldn't begin to understand.

Lila rolled onto her stomach and grasped the pillow, which also seemed hot and prickly. She turned
it over, welcoming the brief coolness against her face.
But sleep refused to come, and she was still warring
with her troubled thoughts when the eastern sky began to lighten above the cliffs.

At last she got up and had a long hot shower, then
put on her painting clothes and went downstairs to sit
on the veranda with a cup of coffee, looking out at
the glorious freshness of the summer morning.

Tom's camper stood silent in the pearly glow of

dawn under its bower of cottonwoods. She wondered if he, too, was lying awake in there.

Probably not, she brooded, sipping from her steaming mug. After all, he seemed to believe he had right on his side in this ridiculous ultimatum, as if he knew something she didn't.

She studied the outline of the camper, wondering what it would be like to live in such a confined space with a man and two children.

To drive off into the sunset with no kind of order or routine to life, waking up in a different place every morning, seeing the horizon change from day to day...

Of course she couldn't do it. The very concept was ridiculous. Lila got up abruptly and went back into the house to mix a batch of pancakes.

Her father was the first to come downstairs. He went directly out onto the veranda and began whittling, as usual.

Casey arrived soon afterward. He appeared in the kitchen doorway with tousled hair, wearing his Star Trek pajamas.

"What smells so good?" he asked.

"Bacon." Lila crossed the room and knelt to hug him, holding his warm body until he squirmed in her arms. "You like bacon, don't you?"

"I love it." He kissed her cheek. "Are we painting the barn again today?"

"Yes, darling." Lila released him and went back to turn the slices of bacon. "You'll have to put your old clothes on."

"I like painting." Casey dragged a chair over by

the counter and climbed on it to watch her at the stove. "I love everything here. It's so nice."

She glanced at the little boy. "Do you like it better than traveling to rodeos all the time?"

He nodded so emphatically that his curls bounced. "Much better. I don't like being in different places all the time."

Lila looked at him thoughtfully, then went back to turning the sizzling strips of bacon. "Casey," she said, trying to sound casual, "do you remember very much about your mother?"

"My mother?" She could see the sudden tension in his body, the whiteness of his knuckles as he gripped the edge of the counter.

"Did she ever travel to rodeos with you?"

"No," he whispered. "She didn't like being in the camper. We just…" He gulped and swallowed hard. "We stayed at home all the time when she…when Mommy…"

Tears gathered in his eyes and rolled down his plump cheeks. His face contorted with pain. Lila looked at him in alarm, then reached to hold him. But he was gone, scrambling down from the chair and running out of the room.

Kelly came in, looking worried. "Casey's crying," she reported. "What happened to him?"

Lila felt close to tears herself. "It was my fault. I asked about his mother, and it upset him."

"I told you not to do that," Kelly said, but she didn't sound as fierce as usual. "He always cries."

"Why?" Lila asked, looking directly at the girl.

Kelly went to the fridge and poured herself a glass

of orange juice. "Because he can't forget what happened. He still has nightmares sometimes."

"About what?" Lila asked. "Please tell me, Kelly. I can't help him if I don't know what's wrong."

Kelly's face went carefully blank. "It's best if we don't talk about that."

"I should go and see if he's all right." Lila wiped her hands on a dish towel and turned the heat off under the bacon. "Kelly, could you keep an eye on—"

"It's okay," Kelly interrupted. "Dad's coming in. He'll look after Casey."

As the child spoke, Lila heard Tom's footsteps coming up the veranda stairs two at a time, and then the low murmur of his voice as he talked to Casey. She returned to the stove, feeling increasingly troubled.

Archie came in and seated himself at the table. "Something smells good," he commented.

Lila gaped at her father. His manner seemed casual and offhand, as if there were nothing momentous about this event. But she couldn't remember the last time Archie Marsden had walked into the kitchen for breakfast and volunteered any sort of cheerful comment.

Kelly sat next to him and glanced at him shyly, then reached in her pocket, removing a small wooden object, which she placed by her plate. Lila realized that it was one of her father's carvings, the little prairie dog he'd been working on recently.

"His name is Flower," Kelly said.

Lila looked from the child to the old man, completely at a loss for words. She set a plate of bacon on the table, then began to fill a serving platter with hot pancakes.

"Does Flower like pancakes?" Archie asked.

Kelly considered the question gravely. "I think mostly he likes nuts and seeds." She touched one of her prairie dog's fat cheeks. "But he might eat a pancake if he was real hungry."

"I'll bet he would," Archie agreed. "You know, I love pancakes."

"Me too." Kelly slathered butter on her pancakes and poured warm maple syrup over them from a ceramic jug, which she handed to Archie. He accepted the jug with a smile.

Lila went back to the stove to pour more batter onto the griddle, feeling as dazed and astonished as if she'd just overheard a conversation between the sun and the moon.

She was still trying to think of something to say when Casey and Tom came into the kitchen. Casey looked red-faced but calm. He trotted over and hugged Lila's legs, burying his face against her while she stroked his freshly brushed curls.

"Are you all right, sweetheart?" she whispered.

He nodded, keeping his face hidden. Lila knelt to hug him while he burrowed against her. At last she moved him away gently and lifted him into a chair, then bent to kiss him.

"I'll get you some bacon," she murmured. "I saved you a few of the crispy pieces."

Involuntarily she met Tom's eyes across the table. He watched gravely, his handsome face calm and unrevealing. Her heart pounded and she felt unsteady again, almost ready to burst into tears and run from the room as Casey had done a few minutes earlier.

His presence was so overpowering here in the cozy, domestic confines of the kitchen, so utterly desirable and so far beyond her reach that she couldn't bear to look at him.

Kelly glanced at her sad-eyed little brother, then leaned over to cut up his bacon. "Hey, Casey," she said. "Look at Flower."

"Who's that?" he asked, his voice still hoarse from crying.

Kelly moved the prairie dog closer to the boy's plate. "See, he's going to watch you eat your bacon. Isn't he beautiful?"

Casey's brown eyes widened as he looked at the prairie dog. He gulped and swallowed, then gazed up at Archie with mute, passionate appeal.

"You can have the next one, son," Archie said. "It's going to be a nice little llama. We can even make a saddle and bridle for it."

"But you won't have time to finish the llama," Kelly said. "We'll be leaving in just a couple of days. Won't we, Dad?"

"Yes," Tom said, watching Lila over the children's heads. "We're leaving on the weekend."

"I want the llama!" Casey looked stricken again. "I don't want to go away until I have my llama!"

Archie watched the boy in concern, then glanced from Tom to Lila. She turned away hastily to flip pancakes.

"I'll try to get it finished," he said to Casey at last. "And if I can't, I'll send it to you. Your daddy can let me know where you're going to be, and as soon as the llama is finished, we'll put it in the mail for you. Then you'll get a nice big package with your own name on it.''

Casey nodded, looking only slightly mollified, and began to eat his bacon.

The meal dragged on, with Kelly doing most of the talking. She chattered determinedly about prairie dogs and barn painting while her little brother and the three adults ate in silence.

CHAPTER SIXTEEN

THEY WORKED on the barn all morning, while Archie sat on the veranda whittling and watching them across the farmyard.

Lila concentrated her efforts on the lower portion of the weathered clapboards. The two children were farther along the wall, slapping white paint on the big door and the trim that surrounded it. Tom moved carefully back and forth on the scaffold above them as he painted the upper walls and eaves.

She worried for a moment over the prospect of his partially healed arm being exposed to possible trauma, then forced the thought from her mind.

Not much point in worrying, she thought grimly. After all, in a few days he was going to be driving hundreds of miles, looking after two kids on his own, riding bucking horses and bulls again. An injured arm was probably the least of his concerns.

He climbed down from the scaffold and stood next to her, looking up critically at the expanse of eaves that remained unpainted.

"Today's Thursday," he said. "I doubt if we're going to be able to get the whole building painted before the weekend."

His face looked tanned and boyish again. Only when she looked at him closely did she see the bleakness in his eyes, and the depths of misery that he was hiding from the children.

"I won't be able to help tomorrow," Lila said with forced casualness, turning away from him. "I think I'll go back to work for the day, just to get caught up and make sure things aren't getting backlogged at the clinic."

"What about the barn?"

"Dad and I can hire somebody to finish painting the barn."

"I see." He glanced at the two children, who were brushing the door with great energy down at the other end of the building, then moved closer to her and lowered his voice. "Our last day together and you won't even stay here with me?"

"What's the point, Tom?" She bent to dip her brush in a bucket of red paint, then pressed it against the rim to squeeze off the excess.

Tears burned in her eyes.

"I thought you were enjoying this," he said, taking a long drink from the cooler of lemonade that stood in the shade of the barn. "I thought you liked being out in the sunshine, doing something wholesome and physical for a change."

He was so close that she was conscious of his warm maleness, coupled with the oily tang of paint. A memory flashed into her mind from the night before, so vivid she could actually feel their naked bodies wrapped together in the moonlight, and the powerful thrusting strength of him as he held her with his injured arm and caressed her body.

"You're thinking about it, too," he said, watching

her closely. "Aren't you, Lila? You're remembering what it was like to be with me last night."

She glanced quickly at the two children, then pulled her cap lower over her eyes and brushed with nervous determination at the old wooden shingles.

"I'm not denying," she said evenly, "that we're a good match physically. We always have been. If a relationship was nothing but sex, we'd probably have a great future together."

"Why are you afraid to admit what's right in front of your eyes?" he asked.

Lila took a deep breath, then stood up and faced him. "Why does Casey cry whenever anybody says something about his mother?"

His face hardened, and his blue eyes were suddenly wary and full of pain.

"Come on, Tom," Lila said in a low voice. "Tell me about your marriage. Tell me what happened to these kids that upset them so much."

He bent to tip some paint into an empty pail while she watched the muscles knotting in his back and shoulders under the shirt.

When he stood erect, his expression was guarded and noncommittal again. "If you'll agree to come with me," he said at last, "I'll tell you about it. Otherwise, I don't see why I should share all the details of my past with you."

"You don't see why," she began in fury, then stopped herself when she saw Kelly watching from the corner of the barn. "Why not tell me because I'm your friend, Tom," she whispered. "Tell me because we've loved each other for most of our lives, and I'm concerned about you."

"Are you?"

"Of course I am. Just because I can't throw my life away to follow you into the sunset doesn't mean I don't care."

He leaned against the unpainted portion of the barn, watching her with disconcerting steadiness. "I don't believe you really love me, Lila. I don't think you could ever allow yourself to love anybody. It's too scary for you."

"Oh, come on," she said wearily. "Don't start that again, all right? I hate it. Do you think you can just drop back into my life after fifteen years and tell me what's going on in my psyche?"

"I know you hate it," he said with maddening calm. "Nobody else has ever done this to you, have they? You've never allowed anybody close enough to know what you're thinking."

"Nobody's ever been arrogant enough to pretend to know." She began to paint again with short, furious strokes. "In fact, there's probably nobody in the world as arrogant as you are."

"Then why do you love me?"

"I don't know," she said in despair. "I guess it's a bad habit I picked up when I was a kid, and I've never quite been able to shake it."

He hefted his bucket of paint and moved toward the scaffold, then paused, watching her intently. "You still have two days to sort out your priorities," he said. "I'll wait until Saturday afternoon. By Sunday I plan to be in Montana."

"I'm not going with you, Tom."

He hooked the handle of the paint bucket to a dangling rope and hoisted it over a projecting arm of the scaffold, hauling it up close to the eaves and fixing the rope with a slipknot.

When he had built it, Lila had admired this simple invention, which allowed him to climb the scaffold with his undamaged arm, and he'd told her with a jaunty smile that a man could do anything he set his mind to.

Not everything, she thought now, her heart aching as she watched him.

"You'll be dying of loneliness on Saturday when you sit on that veranda and watch us drive away," he said quietly.

She bit her lip to stop its trembling and went on painting. "I know I will."

"You'll spend the rest of your life being sorry you missed this chance at happiness."

"No I won't," she said, avoiding his eyes.

He reached out and grasped her arm. "Tell me you haven't spent these past fifteen years regretting the first time you sent me away."

"Tom, I've had a really good life." She looked down at his hand on her arm. The paintbrush dangled, and slow drops of red fell onto the ground like blood.

"Tell me you haven't regretted anything."

"I've built a world for myself," she said. "A lot of children have benefited because I went to medical school and set up my practice here. I don't regret a minute of the work I've done."

"That's not what I'm asking, Lila."

She looked up at last and met his eyes. "I'm not going with you, Tom. Please stop asking me, because I'm not going."

He held her gaze for a long time, and again she

saw in his face that puzzling look of sadness and concern that had troubled her the night before. At last he turned away and began to climb the scaffold.

Lila watched him for a moment, battling tears, then forced herself to go on with her work.

AT THE OTHER CORNER of the barn, Casey dipped his brush and slapped paint on the barn door under Kelly's watchful eye.

They thought he was just a little kid and didn't know how to help, but he was going to show them. Today Casey intended to work all day just like Kelly and the grown-ups, and not get tired and wander off to play under the trees with his toy soldiers.

But he knew Lila and his father were arguing about something, and it frightened him. Even when he didn't look, he could feel their anger and sadness drifting toward him on the summer wind.

He glanced up at Kelly, who worked silently next to him, her face cold and withdrawn. She had a long smear of white paint on her cheek.

Casey liked the way the paint looked. Experimentally, he lifted his brush and dabbed some paint on his own face, then a little more, until Kelly saw what he was doing and came over.

"Stop that, you dummy," she said in a fierce whisper. "You're making a big mess."

Obediently he dipped his brush into the paint and slapped more white on the door. While he worked, he thought about the people around him…his father up on the scaffold, and the old man on the veranda with his scary eyebrows and gentle hands, and the way Lila looked at night in her bathrobe, all white like an angel.

Casey sighed blissfully, remembering the night when she held him in her arms and talked about the baby coyotes, and then put him to bed and sang to him.

He loved Lila with all his heart. Being close to her satisfied a deep, aching hunger and filled the place inside him that always felt raw and empty. She was like ice cream, or a warm bubble bath, or playing on the swings in the bright sunshine.

When Lila hugged him, Casey felt safe and happy, like nothing terrifying could ever happen.

The Bad Thing popped into his mind suddenly, so violently that he almost dropped the brush. He whimpered aloud and Kelly glanced at him sharply.

Casey lowered his head and scuttled away from her to dip more paint onto his brush.

He wouldn't think about it. He wouldn't let it get close again.

But the memory had been trying to get back into his head ever since breakfast, and he didn't know how to make it go away.

Frantically, he tried to think about all the good things at this place. He remembered the dogs, especially the black one that he was slowly making friends with. And the way the river looked all golden at night when the sun was setting, and how soft and comfy the big couches were, like leather arms wrapped around him. And the birds outside his window that sang so loud in the morning, and the llama the old man was making for him....

Lila's father wasn't scary at all anymore in spite of

his eyebrows. He was nice, just like Lila and Marie. They were all nice.

Casey saw his father saying something to Lila, and the way she looked so sad when Daddy climbed back up the scaffold. He swallowed hard and blinked to hold back the tears so Kelly wouldn't get mad at him again.

He knew they would be leaving soon, and he didn't know how he was going to be able to bear it.

Never to see any of the dogs anymore, or have Lila hug him, not to get the llama the old man was making and play with its little saddle and bridle.

Despite his best efforts, tears began to roll silently down Casey's cheeks. He brushed at them with his arm and got paint on his shirt, but it didn't matter because he was all covered with white smears anyhow.

He felt hot and prickly and miserable, but suddenly a cool hand touched his forehead and gentle arms enfolded him. Lila was there, kneeling to hold him as she wiped his face with a tissue.

"What's the matter, darling?" she whispered. "Why are you crying?"

Casey leaned against her and buried his face in her shoulder, loving the safe feeling of being in her arms. Kelly stood nearby and watched them silently.

"I don't want to go away," he whispered. "I want to stay here."

"Oh, sweetheart."

Lila said something to Kelly, then took Casey's hand and led him off toward the house.

He trudged along at her side, feeling nervous, wondering if Lila was mad at him for crying all the time and not wanting to go away when he was supposed to. Kelly said only babies cried and wanted everything their own way, and grown-ups didn't like it when kids acted that way.

But when he cast a surreptitious glance up at Lila, she didn't look angry. Her lovely face seemed as gentle and sweet as ever, and from time to time she gave his hand a comforting squeeze.

Casey started to feel a little better.

When they climbed the veranda step, the old man looked up, raising his eyebrows.

"Looks like somebody's been crying," he said in a gruff voice that still sounded rusty, like he was just learning how to talk again after being quiet so long. "Did you fall and hurt yourself again, son?"

Casey felt a deep relief that nobody was asking about the Bad Thing. They thought he was just hurt.

He did a brief search of his body, where there was usually some kind of fresh scrape or bruise to be found.

Wordlessly, he held up his left knee, which he had grated harshly on the rocks when he'd fallen while running along the riverbank yesterday. Lila had covered the wound with a bandage, but he'd pulled it away in the night. Now the sore had a dark red scab with some discoloration around it. It looked wonderfully satisfying to Casey's eyes.

Archie leaned forward to examine the wound. "Well, now," he said, whistling aloud. "That looks pretty mean, son. I'd say that's enough hurt to make a grown man cry. Here, look what I've got."

Before Casey's dazzled eyes, he held up a wooden

carving that was the image of Pablo, the big white llama out in the pasture.

Casey laughed, studying the haughty head, the lips rolled back over long front teeth, the fat little tail and shaggy legs, the long graceful neck.

"It's finished," he breathed, touching the carving with a grubby, paint-smeared forefinger.

"Not quite," Archie said. "We need a few more touches to bring out that shaggy hide, and then I'll have to figure how to make a little saddle and bridle and some saddlebags for you to carry things around."

"And it'll all be ready before we go?" Casey asked, jumping from one foot to the other.

"If I have to sit here and work all night," Archie promised solemnly.

Casey flung himself on the old man and held him tight, and the dreadful images in his mind began to fade. The old man patted him awkwardly, as if he didn't really know how to hug somebody.

But he was Lila's father, and Lila said he used to hug her all the time when she was little, so probably he'd just forgotten.

After a while Casey disengaged himself from Archie's clumsy embrace, kissed his cheek and followed Lila into the house, leaving the old man watching the door with a bemused expression.

"It won't be so lonely to go away if I can take my llama with me," Casey said, trotting behind Lila into the kitchen.

Her face looked so sad that he was briefly frightened again, but then she smiled and lifted him onto the counter by the sink, moistened some paper towels and wiped his face.

"You don't need to be lonely, sweetheart," she said. "You'll have Daddy and Kelly with you, and they always take good care of you."

He squirmed under the face-washing, which he hated. But it felt better when Lila did it. Her touch was so gentle and quick, it was over almost before he knew what was happening.

"There." She stood back to look at him, then smiled and hugged him. "Now you're the best-looking little boy in the whole world."

He nestled contentedly in her arms. "I love you, Lila," he whispered.

"And I love you, darling." She moved away to get the cookie tin while he watched in surprise.

"Are you crying?" he asked.

"Maybe a little." She came back with a plateful of oatmeal cookies and sat opposite him. Each of them munched a cookie.

"Why?" he asked.

"Because I don't want you to leave, either. I'm really going to miss you."

"I wish we could just stay here forever," he said passionately, "and not have to leave."

"But you have to go to the rodeos, Casey. It's what your father does to earn a living. He's always done that."

"No he didn't," Casey said, shaking his head violently. "We never used to go to rodeos and live in the camper. We lived in a big house and Daddy was home all the time. We had a dog and a cat and three turtles, and a swimming pool outside, and Kelly had a tree house but she wouldn't hardly ever let me inside it."

"Really?" Lila watched him, her face all puckered with surprise. "But that sounds so beautiful. Why didn't you just stay there?"

"Because…"

The Bad Thing filled his mind again, bloodred and screaming. He dropped the cookie and put his hands over his eyes, shaking with dread.

Lila took him onto her lap and rocked him slowly, stroking his body, singing to him. Her gentle softness and fragrance were so soothing that Casey found himself lulled, comforted, wrapped in safety.

His mind emptied slowly of terror, like water dripping from a bucket.

Lila kept whispering in his ear, talking about the dogs and the river, the birds and the baby coyotes and the beautiful little llama with his new saddlebags, until gradually there was no room at all for the bad thoughts and they had to disappear.

Sometime later Casey realized his father had arrived in the kitchen and was watching in concern. Lila murmured something and Daddy came near and lifted him. Casey was transferred from Lila's scented softness to his father's hard strength, and that felt wonderful, too.

Daddy carried him outside onto the veranda and settled on the porch swing with Casey, while Lila followed them. They all sat watching the old man whittle, and Daddy sang to Casey until he felt warm and safe and his eyelids started to droop.

The last things he heard before he fell asleep were the gentle flick of the carving knife and the birds calling from the cottonwood trees.

And over it all was his father's voice, telling Casey how much he would always be loved.

CHAPTER SEVENTEEN

THE NEXT DAY, Lila went to work and left all of them behind having breakfast and discussing the upcoming day of work on the barn. She was filled with mixed emotions as she drove up the valley road and watched in the rearview mirror while the river and the big log house vanished behind the cliffs.

Partly it was a relief to escape the swirling emotions at the farmhouse for a few hours and get back to a world where she was in charge and able to make all the decisions that affected her own life.

In the presence of Tom Bennet and his children, and even her own father, Lila had the miserable sense that things were slipping beyond her control, spiraling into a tornado of raw emotion that would someday grow powerful enough to pick her up and carry her off at will.

These feelings, especially the lack of control and nervousness about what might be coming next, were emotions that she hated above all others.

But another part of her ached to turn around and head back home, so she wouldn't miss a second of the precious remaining time.

This was Friday morning. By tomorrow night, Tom and the children would be packed and gone.

As she drove east into the pale green light of sunrise, the meadowlark song rising joyously from the prairie all around her, Lila finally acknowledged to herself just how deeply she loved Tom Bennet and his son and daughter.

All children were dear to her, but these two were something different altogether.

Brave little Kelly, with her stubborn independence and prickly reserve, and her face so much like Tom's as a boy...

Lila's heart lurched briefly.

And Casey. Dear Casey...

She smiled at the grass-lined stretch of country road, her eyes misty with tears.

He was such a darling. Even now her arms ached to hold the little boy, to seek out and soothe the terrors that seemed to haunt him. If Tom would only talk to her, tell her more about their past!

Casey's story about a big house and pets and a swimming pool, and their father being home every day didn't correlate with the image she'd always had of Tom Bennet's vagrant life-style. But then, she had so little idea of what he'd actually been doing these past fifteen years.

And if he refused to tell her...

Lila gripped the wheel, frowning, and pulled onto the highway.

In fairness, she had to admit it wasn't all that surprising Tom didn't want to confide in her. He clearly interpreted her refusal to give up her life and follow him as a lack of trust, so he felt he couldn't trust her in return.

And he was right, of course. She realized it now,

when she was forced to examine herself with uncompromising honesty.

Lila didn't trust any man enough to give up everything she'd struggled fifteen years to build and run off with him on some kind of adolescent whim.

It wasn't fair of him to ask, she told herself for the thousandth time.

But then, with maddening vividness, she recalled the sad wisdom of his eyes and his voice telling her that she hadn't changed at all, hadn't learned anything in all these years.

Lila pulled into the doctors' parking lot and got out of her car, gathering up her shoulder bag and briefcase, still thinking about Tom.

There was something so different about him now. In reality, very little actually remained of the carefree boy she'd known, except for the familiar physical beauty of his body and the sweet lovemaking that still thrilled her whenever she thought of it.

But in his heart and mind, Tom had changed a lot, become stronger and more distant, much harder to understand. The knowledge troubled her, made her feel even more uncertain.

At last she put him firmly out of her mind and went inside the hospital, heading for the children's ward to do her rounds.

By now Carrie was back home and in remission, happily buying a whole collection of hats and preparing to return to kindergarten. Tony was out of danger, as well, responding to the antibiotics, and would soon be living a normal boy's life again. Even baby Jamie had recovered fully from his dangerous croup and was back tormenting his day-care providers.

But, of course, the ward was now filled with new little patients, each with a heartbreaking story that absorbed Lila's full attention.

At nine o'clock she checked her watch and realized she had only half an hour to grab a snack before heading to the downtown clinic. She went into the cafeteria and found Marie Korman sitting alone at a side table, staring out the window at the green expanse of lawn.

"Hi, Marie. I thought I'd grab something to eat on my way to the clinic." Lila set her tray next to her friend's, then slapped her own forehead in dismay. "Hey, I just remembered. Yesterday was Thursday! So how was your ballroom-dancing class?"

Marie shrugged and looked up. Lila was appalled by the sadness in her eyes.

"I didn't go," she said.

Lila sank into the opposite chair, her heart pounding. "You didn't? Why not? I thought you had a dress picked out and everything."

"Trevor just never showed. I was all dressed up," Marie said tonelessly. "And as excited as a teenager, Lila. I waited and waited but he never came. So finally I got undressed and went to bed."

"Oh, Marie…"

"What a pitiful sight I must have been," Marie said bitterly. "Pacing back and forth between the window and the phone in my cute little red chiffon dress."

Lila put her hand over her friend's. "I'm so sorry. He's always been an unreliable man. But I was sure," she added grimly, thinking about the check she'd written, "that he wouldn't break this date with you."

"Well, he did." Marie looked up with a brave attempt at a smile that almost broke Lila's heart. "Anyhow, who can blame him? Something must have come up. It wouldn't take much to be more appealing than going dancing in the basement of the library with a dried-up old grandmother, now, would it?"

Lila felt a rising anger at her feckless ex-husband. "Please don't keep talking about yourself that way, Marie. I can't stand it. You're a beautiful woman, and still so trim and fit…"

For the first time she noticed her friend's jeans and plaid shirt.

"Why are you here, anyhow?" she asked. "Aren't you still on holidays?"

Marie shrugged. "I couldn't stand sitting around the house twiddling my thumbs. I thought I might as well come down and see how things are going, maybe grab a cup of coffee and a muffin."

Lila picked anxiously at a plate of fruit salad, trying to think of something that might ease the hurt of Trevor's betrayal.

"I should ask you the same question," Marie said. "How come you're going to the clinic? Didn't take the rest of the week off to paint the barn?"

"I'm like you, Marie. I can't stand being at home anymore."

Marie's eyes widened. "Really? When I was out there, it looked like you were all having so much fun."

Lila's cheeks warmed and she looked down hastily at the salad again. "It was fun at first. But the situation's been getting…complicated."

"I see." Marie watched her shrewdly. "So he's gotten to you, has he?"

Lila gave her friend a bleak smile. "Well, I was hardly an unwilling participant."

"You never really got over that man, did you?"

"Apparently not." Lila pursued a bit of melon around the plate with her fork. "But it's just impossible, Marie. It really is."

"Why?"

"Tom gave me an ultimatum the other night. They're leaving tomorrow and he wants me to go with them. Otherwise the relationship is over."

"Go with them?" Marie said, staring. "In that little camper? You've got to be kidding."

"I'm not kidding."

"Leave behind your father and your home and job and everything?"

"That's what he wants," Lila said bitterly. "Not much to ask, right? Why, any woman would do it in a minute if she really loved a man."

"So put him right out of your mind," Marie advised. "Anybody who'd ask such a thing is too selfish to worry about. Hell, this guy even makes Trevor Applegarth look like a prince."

"That's what I keep telling myself," Lila said. "But it's so confusing."

"Why?"

Lila searched for an answer. "It's like Tom… knows something."

"He knows something?" Marie echoed. "What do you mean?"

"I'm not sure," Lila said in despair. "Almost as

if he has some deep insight into my character, and he feels sorry for me.''

''Because you won't give up your own medical practice to travel around the country with him in a truck and camper?''

Lila gave her friend another wry smile. ''Crazy, isn't it?''

''Pretty crazy.'' Marie shook her head. ''How are the kids taking all this?''

''Well, Kelly's just quiet and self-contained, like always. Maybe even more than usual, except for one thing.'' Lila's spirits lifted for a moment as she told Marie about Archie and his astonishing interaction with the little girl.

Marie's face softened. ''Yes, I noticed a bit of that when I was at the farm. It must make you happy to see him beginning to respond.''

''Yes, as long as it doesn't all stop when they leave,'' Lila said. ''Somehow Kelly has managed to get through his wall of silence, but I'm still not sure if anybody else can.''

Marie drained the last of the coffee and set her mug down. ''And how's my darling little Casey?''

''Not so good.'' Lila told her friend about Casey's sorrow over leaving the farm, his upset whenever his mother was mentioned and his puzzling tales of living in a big house with a swimming pool and having his father at home all the time.

''Do you think he's making it up?'' Marie asked. ''Maybe he wanted so much for their life to be that way, he imagined it was really true.''

''I wondered about that, too,'' Lila said. ''But he

seemed so matter-of-fact about it. And he certainly falls apart at any mention of his mother.''

"It could be he just hasn't been able to work through the grief and loss."

"But it doesn't seem like grief," Lila said slowly. "It's more like terror."

"I'd say there's definitely something traumatic in their background," Marie said. "They show all the classic signs, poor kids. Can't you get Tom to tell you what happened?"

"He says he has no reason to trust me with his life story unless I can show some trust in him."

"And how would you go about showing this trust?"

"By giving up my whole existence and going away with him," Lila said in despair. "This is all just a great big depressing circle, Marie. There's no end to it."

She gazed out the window at a pair of black-capped chickadees in the juniper that bordered the lawn. They pecked at the masses of silvery berries, hopping daintily from branch to branch, their feathers glistening in the morning sunlight.

But while she watched the birds, she was seeing Casey's tear-filled eyes, and Tom's powerful bare shoulders in the moonlight, and Kelly's stubborn little freckled face....

Sadness washed over her, and she had to choke back a cry of pain.

"I think I'll drive out there tonight for a visit, if that's okay," Marie was saying. "If they're really leaving tomorrow, it'll probably be my last chance to say goodbye to the kids."

"That'll be nice," Lila murmured. "They'll be happy to see you."

Marie got up, patted Lila's shoulder and left the cafeteria. Lila sat by the window and watched her friend's slim erect back, wondering how happy anybody would be at the farmhouse that night.

Finally she left her tray at the counter and went out into the hallway, stopping briefly at the doctors' lounge to call Trevor at work.

"Hi, sweetheart." He sounded startled but jaunty. "To what do I owe the pleasure?"

Lila pictured him sitting at his desk in Friday casual wear. Probably pressed khakis and loafers and a polo shirt with a designer logo.

"Trev," she said wearily, "it's hardly worth the effort to be mad at you. You're hopeless."

"Mad at me?" he said. "What for?"

"Did you forget something last night?" Lila asked. "A little something that slipped your mind, maybe?"

"Last night I was…" He sounded genuinely puzzled. "Oh, no!" he exclaimed suddenly. "The goddamn dancing lesson!"

"Yes, the dancing lesson," she said coldly. "You had a date, Trevor. You promised me."

"Lila, I'm so sorry. We had a client meeting that ran late. I'm trying so hard to line up this account so I can pay off a bunch of debts, including yours. But I swear to God, if I'd been able to—"

"Don't bother swearing, Trev. I assume you were tied up in the desert somewhere, a hundred miles from a telephone? You couldn't possibly have called the poor woman and at least let her know you weren't going to be able to make it?''

''I completely forgot about it.''

''She waited all evening, Trevor. She bought a new dress and had her hair done and sat by the window watching for your car.''

''Dammit, I told you I'm sorry. If there's anything I can do to—''

''Goodbye, Trev.''

Suddenly Lila was too angry to trust her voice any longer. She hung up the phone and left the hospital, heading outside to the parking lot, where she took deep, ragged breaths of the fresh summer air in an attempt to settle her emotions.

But while she drove downtown to the clinic, Lila kept remembering Marie's unhappy face, her listless air of misery.

Maybe Tom had been right when he accused Lila of enjoying power. He said she wanted to be in charge, to organize people's lives and manage everything.

But when she tried to help, her efforts led to this sort of ruin.

Poor Marie, Lila thought, gripping the wheel and looking at the crowded downtown streets.

Her friend would have been so much better off without somebody meddling in her life. After being callously rejected by her husband and then making this shy, tentative venture back into the social world, how was she ever going to recover from the embarrassment and humiliation of such a terrible evening?

"I'm sorry," Lila whispered aloud, close to tears. "Oh, Marie, I'm so sorry."

THE DAY PASSED in a merciful blur of work. Lila had no appointments scheduled so she was able to spend her time updating charts, checking out the new drug monographs and research literature that had been piling up in her office, and talking with her colleagues and their nurses about the fall schedule at the clinic.

Their patient load was increasing, government funding was down and the coming year promised to be busier and more stress-filled than ever.

But when she left in the late afternoon, walking out through the waiting room where a few children still played in one corner while their mothers leafed anxiously through magazines, Lila knew she could never leave this job. She loved it too much.

Unwilling to go home and face the tumult of emotions in the big log house, she had dinner downtown and spent some time shopping aimlessly for clothes. All the while she remained haunted by Tom's accusations about her need to manage her own life and everybody else's.

Twilight was gathering and a couple of stars sparkled in the southwest by the time she pulled into the yard and parked next to a low-slung silver convertible that she recognized as Trevor's new BMW.

Her heart beat faster as she climbed the steps to the deserted veranda and went inside the house. Everybody was gathered in the living room, where a rodeo played on the corner television set.

Casey had his toy soldiers spread out on the Navajo

rug and was playing some complicated game, while Kelly curled up in an armchair, reading a book, her wooden prairie dog standing next to her on the chair arm. Neither appeared at all interested in the televised rodeo.

Archie, Tom and Trevor sat around the room, their eyes fixed on the television screen.

Lila was sharply conscious of the differences between her former lover and her ex-husband.

As she stood in the doorway for a moment before anybody noticed her arrival, she could see how Trevor lounged in the chair, his trousers carefully arranged so the creases remained sharp. From time to time he glanced up at his own image in the wood-framed mirror above the sideboard.

Tom had changed after the day of painting and wore clean faded blue jeans, moccasins and a T-shirt. His injured arm rested on the arm of the chair.

He watched as Casey played, bending to murmur something to the little boy, who listened gravely, then smiled.

Anybody looking at these two men, Lila thought, would automatically select Trevor as her life partner, the man who could best share the life-style and aspirations of a successful young doctor.

But the fact was, Trevor had never really had the slightest idea what she thought or what went on in her heart. And Tom Bennet, the rough-and-tumble rodeo cowboy, had always been able to look all the way into the depths of her soul.

She shifted nervously on her feet and Casey glanced up, his face breaking into a happy smile.

"Lila's here!" The little boy scrambled to his feet and ran across the room.

Lila lifted him and gave him a fierce hug, kissing his plump cheek. "Did you have a good day, sweetheart?" she asked.

Casey nodded vigorously. "We finished painting the whole side and all the doors. Dad says we might even get the other side done tomorrow before we leave."

"My goodness," Lila said, putting him down after another hug. "You must have worked very hard."

She smiled at her father, then at Kelly, who glanced up from her book with a noncommittal expression and went on reading.

But Lila avoided Tom's eyes. He was watching her from the chair with a grave, thoughtful expression that made her feel nervous and even more miserable.

"Trev," she said quietly, "could I see you out here for a moment, please?"

Looking awkward for once, Trevor got up and left the living room, joining her in the hardwood foyer.

Lila glanced toward the living room, where the noise from the distant television was loud enough to drown out their conversation.

"You rotten bastard," she said in a low, furious voice. "If you could have seen how hurt Marie was..."

He spread his hands wide in a gesture of mute appeal. "Lila, I said I was sorry. What else can I do? Go to her house in sackcloth and ashes?"

"If I thought it would make Marie feel any better,

I'd make you do just that, you sorry excuse for a man!''

His face reddened suddenly, and Lila looked at him in astonishment. Apparently, even a man with as little conscience or sensibility as Trevor Applegarth had a point where he could be hurt.

''Look,'' he said coldly, ''none of this was my idea in the first place.''

''What do you mean?''

''You can't always go around fixing everybody's lives the way you want them to be, Lila. It doesn't work out. People aren't that easily managed, but you just never give up trying, do you?''

This observation, so similar to what Tom had said but coming from such an unlikely source, was surprisingly upsetting.

''Trev,'' she said, ''don't start lecturing me, okay? After all, you're a thirty-five-year-old man who has to be paid money to take a nice lady out dancing.''

''Hey, it was just a loan,'' he muttered sullenly. ''Don't make me sound like a gigolo on top of everything else, okay?''

''Loan or gift, the fact remains that we had a deal. I gave you the five hundred dollars you needed, and you agreed to take Marie for some ballroom dancing. I don't see why—''

She saw Trevor's eyes widen in alarm and turned to see what he was looking at, then felt almost sick with shock.

Marie stood in the open doorway, staring from one of them to the other, her face white and twisted with pain.

"Paid him?" she asked slowly. "Lila, you paid him to... Oh my God!"

Marie uttered a strangled cry and covered her face with her hands, then turned and stumbled off across the farmyard toward her car.

Lila tried to run after her but Tom was there, holding her arm.

"Not now," he said quietly. "There's nothing you can do for her right now, Lilabel."

CHAPTER EIGHTEEN

LILA STOOD next to Tom and watched Marie's car drive out of the yard and up along the river road, winking in the moonlight with false brightness. Trevor got into his car and left, as well, after muttering an embarrassed farewell that got little response from anybody.

At last Lila turned away, aching with misery, and found Tom watching her. His face was gentle and sympathetic.

"I'm such a fool," she muttered, hugging her arms. "I'm bossy and selfish, and I do nothing but harm."

"That's not true," he said. "You're a good woman, Lila. You've always been the most generous person I know. You spend your life giving to others without thinking about yourself."

Lila shook her head, bewildered. "Then why are you so angry with me? Why do you keep acting like I'm a disappointment to you because I can't just dump all my responsibilities and follow you?"

He met her gaze so long that she began to feel uncomfortable.

"I'm waiting," he said at last.

"What for, Tom?"

"I'm waiting for you to understand."

"How can I understand," she said in despair, "if

you won't explain anything to me? You refuse to tell me what's happened to you and these children, or where you've come from, or why you want me to pull up stakes and travel with you. I feel so helpless, Tom.''

He put his arms around her and drew her close. She nestled gratefully, loving the muscular warmth of him, the familiar sense of strength and shelter.

In Tom's arms she was at home again, after years of loneliness. She was safe from all the world....

But soon reality intruded in her thoughts and she pulled away, rubbing her forearms nervously.

Most of her problems were of her own making, and this man couldn't solve them. Besides, Tom Bennet would be gone tomorrow. He would vanish from her life as completely as he had once before.

''Maybe it'll be another fifteen years before I see you again,'' she said. ''Kelly will be in her mid-twenties and Casey will be finishing college. And I'll be...'' Her voice choked. ''I'll be fifty-one, Tom.''

''Lila...''

''I love you,'' she whispered, turning to stare at the river, ''and I love those kids. I don't know how I can bear this.''

''Then come with us. Just make the choice and then act on it.''

''I can't!'' she said desperately. ''Tom, you're a smart man and you understand me, you always have. You must be able to see how impossible it is for me to do what you want.''

''Yes,'' he said quietly. ''I can see that, all right. But it doesn't stop me from hoping you might change your mind before tomorrow.''

She made a weary gesture of defeat, then turned and started walking toward the river.

"Where are you going?" he asked.

"Just for a walk."

"May I come?"

"No," she said. "You have to go and put the kids to bed. Besides, I want to think. And when enough time has passed, I'll try to call Marie at home and see if there's anything I can say to make her feel better."

"All right." He stood quietly and watched her go. She moved down along the bank and around the projecting branches of the cottonwood grove. When she looked back through the screen of greenery, he was still there, a tall, lean figure with moonlight washing over his shoulders and his blunt cheekbones, staring at the place where she'd disappeared.

Lila walked for almost an hour, wrestling with her chaotic thoughts.

When she came back she was relieved to find the house plunged into silence. The upstairs lights were off, and the camper down in the trees glowed faintly behind its flowered curtains.

That meant the kids were asleep and Tom was getting ready for bed. She didn't have to talk to anybody.

Now there was only one more day to get through. By tomorrow night they'd be gone, hopefully before she even came home from work.

And then one kind of hurt would be over and a new pain would start...the long, slow agony of learning once again to live without the man she loved.

Lila took a phone upstairs and got ready for bed, then dialed Marie's number.

"Hello," Marie said, her voice quiet and expressionless.

"Hi, it's me. God, I'm so sorry."

"That's okay," Marie said. "You meant well, Lila."

"But it wasn't the way it sounded. Trevor really was happy at the prospect of going with you, Marie. He knows you're a good dancer, and he didn't..." She paused, searching for words.

"Didn't have to be bribed to dance with me?"

"I'd already agreed to loan him the money. Trevor just asked you as...a favor to me," Lila said, stumbling awkwardly.

"Honey, you're not making this any better," Marie said with a touch of her old dry humor.

But Lila could still hear the pain in her friend's voice.

"I'm so sorry," she said again. "Look, Marie, can we get together tomorrow? Do you want to have lunch or something?"

"No, I'm working all day in my garden. It'll be good therapy," Marie said. "What about you? Tom and the kids are leaving tomorrow. Don't you want to be there to say goodbye?"

"No!" Lila said. "I can't bear to watch them leave. I think I'll get up early before anybody's awake, drive into town and spend the day working at the clinic. And when I come home they'll be gone."

"You poor dear," Marie said, moving Lila almost unbearably.

In the midst of her own pain and humiliation, the woman was still generous enough to sympathize with a friend's pain.

"Marie," she said, "you're such a sweetheart."

"Sure I am," Marie said with a gallant attempt at lightness. "Who cares if we have to pay the boys to dance with me?"

"Oh, please don't say that."

"Lila, it's okay. It truly is. I know you meant well. I'm not saying I didn't get a bit of a shock when I overheard your conversation with Trevor, but I'll get over this. I promise I will. Now go to sleep."

"Sleep," Lila said bitterly. "What's that?"

"Just go to sleep," Marie repeated firmly, "and I'll see you soon, and our lives will get back to normal. You hear me?"

"I hear you," Lila said. "Thanks so much, Marie. You're a good friend."

But for a long time after she hung up, sleep was slow in coming. Lila watched the cold play of moonlight and shadow on the wall, trying not to cry.

At last the effort was too much and she dissolved in lonely tears, muffling her sobs in the pillow for fear of waking the children.

KELLY WOKE just after sunrise and lay very still in her bed, listening while Lila got up and went quietly downstairs. Soon afterward she heard the sound of a car starting and driving out along the river road.

She glanced at the cot where Casey slept deeply, his bright curls outspread, his face pink with creases from the pillow. He held his teddy bear in his arms but wasn't sucking his thumb. In fact, he'd practically stopped that habit since they'd come to the farm.

Rolling over in bed, Kelly lay with her hands behind her head and stared at the ceiling.

Lila was already gone, which meant that she didn't plan to be around when they left.

Kelly understood the feeling because she, too, hated saying goodbye to anybody. But this time was going to be the worst of all, since it wasn't just people they were leaving, but also a place she'd come to love.

She reached over to the nightstand and grasped her prairie dog, laying him next to her on the pillow. He stared at the ceiling along with her.

"At least I don't have to leave you behind, Flower," she whispered. "You're coming with me no matter where I go. You'll always be with me."

The prairie dog lay and watched her while she got up and pulled on her paint-stained jeans and shirt, then tied the laces of her running shoes and fitted the baseball cap on her head. For once Casey didn't stir, though he was usually awake before she was.

He must be really tired from all that painting.

Not that he worked very hard, Kelly thought scornfully. The little boy mostly just fooled around and wasted time, and got more paint on himself than on the barn.

But he was still only a baby, he didn't know any better....

At last she picked up the prairie dog and carried it downstairs to the kitchen, where Archie and her father already sat at the table, eating breakfast in silence.

"Hi, sweetie," her father said, pulling her close and planting a lusty kiss on her cheek. "How's my best girl this morning?"

His words were cheerful but his eyes looked sad, and she could hear the strain in his voice.

"I'm fine," Kelly said.

She put Flower near her plate, setting him up carefully so he had a good view of the kitchen and the dogs lying by the back door. Then she slipped into her chair and watched while Archie padded around putting more toast and cereal on the table.

Casey appeared in the doorway when Kelly was partly through her bowl of cereal. He stood blinking like a little owl in his pajamas, and her father got up and took him away to get washed and dressed.

"You know, I do believe that prairie dog has been growing," Archie said when they were alone. "He looks bigger to me."

Kelly looked on while the old man buttered a slice of toast. She liked watching him do things, because his hands were so gentle and strong.

"When I was a little kid," she said, "I used to pretend my toys came to life at night and ran around playing with each other."

"So did I."

They smiled at each other for a moment, then looked away hastily and went on eating.

Kelly's father came back into the room with Casey, who wore clean jeans and a T-shirt instead of his painting clothes.

"I don't think we'll work on the barn this morning," Tom said in response to Kelly's startled glance. "I have to pack the camper and get everything ready to travel. Casey's going to help me, aren't you, son?"

Casey's face crumpled. "Daddy, I don't want to go away."

"Sure you do," Tom said. "It'll be fun to drive

down to Montana. Remember how much you liked the little animals in the petting zoo at Great Falls?''

''I like the llamas better,'' Casey said stubbornly. ''And they're right here.'' His chin began to jerk and tremble ominously.

''Speaking of llamas,'' Archie said to the small boy, ''I just might be able to get that little critter finished today if I work real hard. But you're going to have to help me, son.''

Casey swallowed a sob and looked up. ''Me? How can I help?''

''Well,'' Archie said thoughtfully, buttering another slice of toast, ''if you get busy and help your daddy, and pack your things without any fuss, I might just find the time to get that llama finished before you leave.''

Casey knelt on the chair, his tears forgotten for the moment. ''And the saddle and bridle?'' he asked. ''And the little saddlebags?''

''The whole shooting match,'' Archie said solemnly. ''But you'll have to be good.''

Kelly watched as her brother subsided and began to eat his cereal.

Casey was small enough to be bribed with a promise like that, but it never lasted very long. He might get his new llama and be happy with it for a while. Still, a few hours down the road when he understood that they were really going away and he wasn't going to see Lila or the farm anymore, he'd start bawling and he probably wouldn't quit for hours.

She sighed and felt her father's eyes resting on her with thoughtful concern. Expressionless, Kelly got up and took her prairie dog in hand, left the kitchen and wandered out onto the veranda. She sat on the top step and set Flower down beside her so he could see the river, then hugged her knees, brooding over the view that had become so familiar.

She could feel the beginning of tears burning in her eyes, and it terrified her. All this time, she'd never once cried. If she started now, how would she ever be able to stop?

She kept her face cold and withdrawn as her father and brother came out onto the veranda and paused beside her.

"Casey and I are going to take the truck into town and get the tires and oil checked," Tom said. "And maybe have a lighter bandage put on this arm of mine if we have time. Do you want to come along?"

Kelly shook her head, not trusting her voice.

"Kelly?" her father said above her head. "Do you want to come? We're going to have lunch at the Dairy Queen. You always like that."

She knew he wouldn't be satisfied unless she said something, but she had to keep her voice gruff so it wouldn't break.

"That's okay," she said, staring down at her hands. "I'll just stay here and clean up our room and pack all Casey's stuff so I can put it in the camper when you get back."

Tom sat on the step and put his arm around her. "Are you all right, sweetheart?" he asked.

Go away, Kelly thought fiercely. *Just go away, before I start bawling like Casey.*

"Sure," she muttered, watching her prairie dog's face. "I'm fine. I can't wait to leave, that's all."

She felt her father's eyes resting on her for a long

thoughtful moment, and was terrified he might be going to ask something else. But at last he got to his feet, took Casey's hand and walked down to the truck.

Kelly rested her chin on her knees and watched them drive away, out of the yard and up the river road. The big Labrador padded over and sprawled next to her in the sunlight. Absently she patted his head.

But within her, a void of despair grew and darkened like a huge black hole.

Gradually she became aware that Archie was sitting behind her, whittling. In the stillness of the morning she could hear the comforting little flick of his knife, the swish of metal on wood, even the feathery softness of shavings drifting onto the floorboards.

They sat for a long time, she and the dog and the old man, while beside her the wooden prairie dog perched on his haunches and surveyed the world with bright carved eyes.

"Looks like bad weather coming," Archie commented behind her. "See that line of cloud along the horizon? Whenever clouds mount up in the west like that, it means a storm's on the way."

Kelly looked across the trees bordering the river and watched the clouds that massed and mounted, white and fluffy as popcorn in the pale blue arch of sky.

"They're thunderheads," she said, clearing her throat. "Like in that book I read."

"I reckon they are," Archie said, and she could hear the smile in his voice. "Too bad we don't have a colt being born today. We could name him Thunderhead."

"Maybe if…" To her horror, her voice faltered and broke. Kelly took a deep breath and forced herself to continue. "Maybe Casey will call his llama Thunderhead," she said at last. "If you get it finished today."

"Maybe he will," Archie agreed placidly.

Again she heard the comforting snick of the knife. Kelly wanted to ask if he thought he'd get the toy done, and how he planned to make the saddle and bags. But she didn't speak.

I should go away, she thought desperately. *I should get right up and walk away from here before something awful happens.*

But for some reason, she couldn't bring herself to leave the veranda. She just sat there, patting the dog and staring at the masses of white puffy clouds.

Gradually the sky darkened and her mind filled with bleakness and horror. It was unbearable to know they were leaving. In a few hours they'd be gone, traveling down the road again, just the three of them. It was a misery too awful to endure.

A tear trickled down her cheek and fell on her jeans, making a little dark spot. Then another one followed. Furtively she dabbed at her face, trying to look as if she were brushing at a mosquito or something.

"You know," Archie said behind her, his voice casual and conversational, "I always heard it helps to cry. Folks tend to feel a whole lot better if they let themselves cry."

She wanted to argue, to tell him that it was impossible to start crying because the prospect of losing control was too horrible to contemplate. But she couldn't speak. Her throat felt choked and tears blurred her eyes now, making her shoulders tremble.

At last Kelly got up and stumbled blindly toward him, gulping and sobbing. She wasn't even sure how it happened, but she was in his lap, nestled against his clean plaid shirtfront.

And, wrapped close and safe in those sinewy arms, she was crying her heart out.

He held her awkwardly, patted her back, murmured soothing words of comfort. She couldn't make out what he said because she was crying so hard, as if she might be going to turn inside out with the force of her grief.

"It's all right," he whispered, taking off her cap and patting her hair. "It's all right."

She kept on crying for a long time, while the clouds rolled over to block out the sun, and shadows fell long and cold across the farmyard. She cried until she felt drained and empty, as light as air, hardly even tethered to the earth anymore. If a strong wind came up, it would pluck her right out of his arms and carry her away across the treetops.

When the storm of weeping finally began to subside, he took a clean white handkerchief from somewhere and wiped her face, then held it for her to blow her nose as if she were no bigger than Casey.

"Now then," he said in a casual, gentle voice, as if they were still talking about the weather. "Now then, maybe you should tell me what this is all about."

Kelly took a deep ragged breath and sobbed a few more times. Finally, halting and trembling, shuddering with emotion, she began to talk.

CHAPTER NINETEEN

ARCHIE LISTENED to the little girl tell her story, rigid with shock and horror at the things these children had endured. He had no words to comfort her and was distressed by his clumsiness until he realized that she really didn't need him to say anything. She only wanted to talk, and the way the words spilled out, she must have been needing this release for a long, long time.

Still silent, he held her close, rocking her gently in his arms.

Finally she stopped talking and nestled against him, clearly exhausted. He looked down and saw the pale line of her forehead, the eyelashes fluttering against her cheek. She relaxed in his embrace and gradually became solid and heavy, until he knew that she was asleep.

Gently, moving with great care so as not to disturb her, he got up and carried the little girl into the house, placed her on one of the big leather couches and covered her with a Navajo blanket. Her face in repose had lost all its customary cold, guarded expression and looked open and vulnerable.

Archie gazed down at her, his heart wrenched with love and sympathy.

She was so much like young Tom at the same age.

Archie remembered the manly, forthright little fellow who'd first made his way across the river to play with Lila, and how much he'd always liked the boy.

He settled in a nearby chair and spent a long time watching the child sleep. Her thin chest rose and fell steadily under the blanket, and after the storm of grief, her face was so drained of color that the freckles stood out sharply.

Archie leaned back in his chair, still watching Kelly's face as he mused over the past.

Right from the beginning, Bella had been unnerved by young Tom and what he represented. She'd been afraid of what he might mean in Lila's life. Archie wondered if that concern had been pure snobbishness on his wife's part, or just the natural protectiveness of a mother trying to keep her only child from harm.

Instead of blaming Bella, perhaps he should look deeper.

Maybe he'd been the one who gave Lila her cautious instincts, her fear of opening herself up to love and pain. Could it be that he was responsible, after all, for her loneliness and isolation now?

Because, Archie thought grimly, he was certainly responsible for his own.

Thoughts and impressions crowded his mind, memories of the miserable years he'd just passed, almost overshadowed by the pain and terror of being dragged from his self-imposed isolation. But he saw as well the images of people who'd shaken him so badly with the knowledge that their pain was equal to his own and required action from him.

At last he got up and went into the kitchen. He found Lila's list of numbers on the bulletin board next to the phone and hesitated for a long time in an agony of indecision. When he finally forced himself to dial the phone, his hands were shaking.

At the other end the phone rang and rang, so long that he was about to hang up in relief, when a woman's voice answered.

Archie cleared his throat nervously and tried to speak.

"Hello?" she said again, more sharply. "Hello, who is this?"

"Marie?" he managed to say at last. "This is…it's Archie Marsden."

"Archie!" she said. "I was out in the garden, and I didn't hear the phone ringing at first. Is something wrong?"

"No." He glanced through the archway at the couch, where Kelly's bright hair shone above the blanket. "No, everything's fine. I just…wanted to ask you about something."

"All right. How can I help you, Archie?"

"Well…" He shifted from one foot to the other, overwhelmed by shyness, and cleared his throat again. "Well, you see, I was thinking I'd like to…to go out dancing tonight. And I wondered if you might be able to go with me."

"You're asking me to…"

He could hear the break in her voice, the quick catch of pain, and it emboldened him a little. Archie could never bear to see another person hurting.

"Listen," she said, "this is really very sweet of you, but it's not necessary, Archie. I told Lila last night, I'm fine. That business with Trevor was all just…it was a misunderstanding."

"I'm not asking because of any misunderstanding, Marie," he said with more courage. "I'm asking because I'd truly like to go dancing tonight instead of sitting on my front porch. And I'd rather go with you than anybody I can think of."

"Archie, I don't...I really don't know what to say."

"Well," he said, "then maybe you could just say yes. Because, you know, it's not all that easy for an old curmudgeon like me to ask a pretty lady out for the evening."

"Old curmudgeon," she scoffed.

He could hear laughter in her voice, and a rough touch of emotion.

"Nobody was ever less of a curmudgeon than the Archie Marsden I remember," Marie said. "And I think you're probably the best dancer within a hundred miles."

Her warmth made him feel better. In fact, he was beginning to feel wonderful, better than he had for years. "I'm pretty rusty, Marie. In most every way," he added ruefully. "I might just disgrace you out there on the dance floor."

"You know, I think that's a risk I'd be happy to take."

"Then you'll go?" he said.

"I'd be delighted."

"We might as well do it up right, Marie. How about dinner first? Would that be pushing my luck?"

She laughed, with her old bubbling amusement that he'd always found so attractive. "I think your luck is running pretty good today, Archie."

"Well, in that case," he said, "maybe I could just ask for one more thing."

"What's that?" she asked with a sudden note of suspicion.

"I wonder if you could wear that pretty red dress of yours," Archie said shyly. "Because that's something I'd really love to see."

"Oh, Archie…"

For a moment he wondered if he was going to have another crying female on his hands.

"Seven o'clock?" he said in a brisk, businesslike manner. "Would that be all right with you?"

"That would be fine." To his relief, she laughed again. "Seven o'clock would be just fine."

Archie hung up, smiling, and went back to check on Kelly, who still slept soundly.

He decided it would be best for her to sleep off the draining emotional outburst, and that she'd probably be more comfortable if she didn't wake and find him staring at her.

So he went back onto the veranda and picked up the little wooden llama to put the finishing touches on its shaggy hide.

While he worked, he thought about how miraculously his existence had changed since Lila brought these children home, and the intricate ways that people's lives were intertwined.

In a way, his new course of action still frightened him terribly, because it seemed so fraught with danger after the protective cocoon he'd wrapped himself in for so long. But there was no turning back at this point, and he knew it.

The clouds filled the sky now, rolling and massing

overhead. Thunder rumbled ominously in the west, and a jagged bolt of lightning cut the sky. Rain began to patter down, onto soil so parched and dry that the first few raindrops bounced straight upward from the ground in big dusty bubbles.

But the squall had settled into a steady downpour by early afternoon when Tom's truck rolled back into the farmyard, and the tall man and his little boy came running up onto the veranda.

Casey paused to lean against Archie's chair, gazing at the llama.

"It's almost done," Archie told the little boy. "I just have to make the saddle."

With spontaneous gratitude, Casey stood on tiptoe to hug Archie and kiss his cheek, then went into the house. Soon afterward, Archie heard voices and a clatter of dishes from the kitchen. He realized that Kelly was awake, preparing lunch for herself and talking with her little brother.

Steeling himself, he glanced up at Tom, who stood by the railing, staring off across the pasture with raindrops sparkling on his broad shoulders and a sad, faraway look in his eyes.

"Sit down, son," Archie said gently, waving his hand at one of the empty chairs. "I think it's time for us to have a little talk."

LILA LEFT the clinic before six o'clock and drove home through pounding rain. The darkness and gloom matched her mood. She couldn't bear to contemplate the emptiness of the house she was going to, to the life that now stretched ahead of her.

She could hear Tom's voice in the drumming of

raindrops on the windshield and in the sigh of the
wind as she drove. Through the dark chill of the summer storm, she could feel his arms enfolding her, and
the warmth of his big body.

"Oh, God," she whispered aloud, staring straight
ahead at the highway awash with puddles. "How am
I ever going to endure this?"

But when she pulled into the farmyard, she saw
Tom's camper still parked under the dripping cottonwoods, its windows glowing with light.

Her sudden stab of fear and alarm was almost as
intense as the burden of sorrow. It was impossible to
say goodbye to them. Some things were simply too
painful to bear.

For a moment she considered turning around and
heading back to town, driving around aimlessly until
the truck was gone. But the storm had begun to in-
tensify, and the road down to the river was becoming
so soggy with rain that she feared she might not be
able to make it home later in the evening.

I can just go straight up to my room, she thought,
getting out of the car and running across the muddy
yard to the veranda. *If I slip upstairs and lock myself
in, they'll be gone before they even know I'm here.
They must be almost ready to leave....*

Her father sat on the veranda, whittling as usual,
his form half-obscured by gathering shadows and the
darkness of the storm.

"Hi, Dad," she said, trying to keep her voice casual. "Where is everybody?"

He jerked a thumb over his shoulder. "The kids
are inside watching television, and Tom's finishing
up his packing in the camper. He figures if he waits

to leave until it's almost bedtime, the kids will fall asleep right away when he starts driving and the trip won't be so hard for them.''

"I see."

"There's still some pasta in the fridge, and a bit of leftover pudding.''

"Okay." She hesitated by the door. "I'm not really hungry, so I think I'll just run upstairs and have a bath. You can…" Her voice broke. "You can say goodbye for me, all right?''

"Sit down, Lila."

"But I don't…"

"Sit down," he repeated.

She sank into the chair and gazed at him in surprise. This purposeful man was so unlike the father she'd been living with for the past few years, she hardly even recognized him.

When Lila examined him more slowly, her bewilderment increased.

"Dad, what are you wearing?"

He looked down at his gleaming white shirt and leather jacket, his finely polished boots. "I'm dressed in my best," he said placidly.

"You certainly are, and you look wonderful. But why?"

"I'm going dancing," he said with a ghost of a smile.

"Dancing?" she asked blankly.

"With Marie." He glanced at his watch. "In fact, I'll have to leave in half an hour, but that should give us enough time."

She was too bewildered to ask what he needed time

for. Her mind still struggled to absorb what he was saying. "You're going dancing with Marie?"

"Yes indeed." He looked down at the llama in his hand, for which he'd now fashioned a tiny leather saddle. "Dinner first, and then dancing."

"Dad, I just...I don't know what to say. How did this happen?"

"I called and asked her, and she said yes." Archie looked at his daughter with mock sternness. "Is it so amazing, my girl, that a pretty lady would want to go dancing with me?"

"No, of course not. You look really handsome, Dad. But I can't..." She shook her head in disbelief.

"So I have to leave soon," he repeated. "But first I want to tell you a story. Just sit back and listen, all right?"

Still dazed, Lila huddled in the chair and wrapped her arms tightly around herself as she stared through the sheets of silvery rain at the lighted windows of Tom's camper.

"I'm going to tell the story of Tom Bennet's life after he left here fifteen years ago," Archie said.

Lila turned to him in renewed astonishment. "Where did you hear this story?"

"Kelly told me this morning."

"Kelly?"

"Tom and Casey were in town. She got real upset at the prospect of leaving and cried for quite a while, then told me a lot about their family history. After Tom got home, I asked him to fill in some of the blank spaces, and he did. So now I have a pretty clear picture."

Lila's heart began to beat faster with excitement

and dread. She had a feeling that what her father was about to say would change her life forever in ways she couldn't begin to imagine. Part of her wanted urgently to cover her ears and run upstairs without listening, but she couldn't seem to move from her chair.

"Tom set out on the rodeo circuit when you sent him away," Archie said, his voice barely audible over the steady drumming of rain on the veranda roof. "He was wild and careless, and he felt that after he'd lost you, there was nothing to hold him. So he traveled all over the place, hundreds of thousands of miles back and forth across America. He went with other cowboys by plane, by truck, however he could get from one rodeo to another."

"I'm not surprised," Lila said. "I knew he was a rolling stone."

"But in Texas a few years later, he met a girl who fell hard for him and wouldn't let him go. She was barely out of her teens and obsessed with him. Tom had no strong feelings for her, but she ran away from home and followed him from rodeo to rodeo. He felt responsible for her because she was so young."

"And I'll bet I know what happened next," Lila said. "This girl got pregnant, right?"

"Yes, that's what happened. Tom's whole outlook changed when he had a child on the way. He married the girl and swore he was going to give his baby everything he'd never had as a kid."

"Poor Tom." Lila stared at the windows of the camper, still gleaming through the rain like a beacon. "He never had much, did he?"

"He sure didn't." Archie was silent for a moment, then resumed his story. "A friend of his on the rodeo circuit was down on his luck and sold Tom an old ranch in British Columbia. Tom scraped together a bank loan and put all his rodeo winnings toward the ranch, and they moved there to settle down. Kelly was born soon afterward, and he started working like a madman to make the place into a paying proposition.''

Lila stared at her father. "You mean he quit traveling?"

"Quit cold," Archie said calmly. "Never went to another rodeo for years. Tom just worked all the time and did a lot of baby-sitting because his wife wasn't all that interested in being a mother."

"What was she interested in?"

"Just Tom, apparently. She was still obsessed with him, and she started having jealous delusions. He'd go out to work for the day and she'd accuse him of slipping off to visit the neighbor's wife or going to town to see a girlfriend. He could never convince her he was being faithful."

"But...that must have been awful for him."

"Yes," Archie said. "And it got worse and worse. He built a rodeo arena at his ranch and started making a lot of money by renting the place out for cowboys to practice and train their horses. But it brought people to the ranch, pretty cowgirls and rodeo riders' wives, and his own wife went almost out of her mind with jealousy. She was one of those women who wanted her man all to herself, never seeing another living person."

"Even then she wouldn't have been secure," Lila said. "That kind of jealousy is a symptom of mental

illness, Dad. It goes way beyond ordinary possessive-
ness.''

"Tom was beginning to realize that. He felt so
sorry for her, kept trying to get her some counseling,
but she refused to go. And he worried a lot about
Kelly, because he had to work so much of the time
and he didn't know how his wife was treating the
little girl.''

"But he still let her have a second child?''

"It wasn't Tom's idea. She deceived him and quit
taking birth control pills without telling him because
she thought she'd get more of his attention if she was
pregnant again.''

"And I'll bet she did," Lila said.

"She sure did. By then he was terrified most of the
time because she was getting more and more unstable.
She accused him of doing all kinds of things behind
her back and caused horrible scenes, threatening to
harm herself or Kelly if he didn't stop.''

"But he couldn't stop what he wasn't doing in the
first place," Lila said, her heart aching. "Poor Tom.''

"When Casey was born, things got better for a little while. Tom was thrilled to have a son, and she
was satisfied that she was getting his full, undivided
attention. But as soon as he had to go back to work
and concentrate on running the ranch, she began to
fall apart again. Nothing he could do was enough to
make her feel secure. He started being even more
afraid about how she was treating the kids, and he
took them with him around the ranch as much as he
could. That meant leaving her alone in the house to
brood and get bitter, but she'd still never agree to see
a doctor.''

"What a mess," Lila whispered. "And how terrible for the kids."

"Tom tried to hire a nanny or housekeeper, but the ranch was pretty remote and nobody wanted to live out there. Especially when any woman who came to work at the place was a threat to his wife, no matter how old or plain. The slightest things would set her off into wild rages. Tom suspected she was hurting the kids, but he never caught her at it and Kelly wouldn't tell him anything. She was always protective of her mother, but at the same time she was also doing her best to keep Casey from being abused."

"What a burden for a little girl," Lila said. "Taking care of everybody when she was just a child herself, and getting no emotional support except from her father."

"It was hard, all right. The poor little mite's been tired and stressed for years, I reckon. You should have heard her cry this morning, Lila."

Archie looked down at the toy in his hands as if reluctant to continue.

"So what finally happened, Dad?"

"Tom's wife was having one of her peaceful spells. Tom let her keep the kids for the day because she said she was going to take them up to the pasture to have a cookout and go sledding, and they were both excited."

"How old were they? When was this?"

"In the winter, over a year ago. Kelly was ten and Casey was three."

Lila felt a growing dread and a sick feeling in her stomach. "What happened?"

"The woman got upset about something and

started to rant, so they never went on their outing. She put Casey down for his afternoon nap. Kelly was upstairs in the playroom with her toys, watching television and building a model farm, keeping out of her mother's way. That afternoon the woman killed herself.''

"She…when she was alone in the house with the kids?'' Lila looked at her father in horror.

"She put on her wedding gown and veil and slashed her wrists,'' Archie said. "But she didn't do a good job of it, just bled a lot all over the dress. By that time she was totally unhinged. She took one of Tom's ropes and hung herself from a beam in the downstairs foyer of the house. When Casey woke up from his nap and cried because he was hungry, Kelly brought him downstairs and they found her hanging there in her bloodstained wedding gown.''

Lila covered her face and began to cry, her shoulders shaking.

"They were both completely traumatized,'' Archie said. "Tom took them to a psychologist, who told him they needed a change of scene. They'd suffered too much in that house, and the memory of her hanging from the beam would never leave their minds. So Tom sold his ranch and put the money in the bank.''

"And he took his kids on the rodeo circuit,'' Lila whispered through her tears.

"He and the doctor both thought it would be good for them, having a constant change of scenery and a lot of different people in their lives.''

"Did it work?''

"Tom thinks it was helping. After a while both of them started getting better. They still don't really like traveling very much, but he's been afraid if they settled down anywhere, they'd start to be haunted all over again.''

''Why wouldn't he tell me all this himself, Dad?''

''Well, Tom's always been a proud, independent kind of person.'' Archie watched her gently. ''I guess he wouldn't want you to make any decision out of pity for him, would he?''

''I said such awful things to him. I should have known...'' She stared at the camper, stricken with remorse. ''I'm trained to deal with kids. Marie and I knew those two had been through some kind of awful trauma, but I didn't probe enough to find out what it was. I think I was afraid of what might come out because there was a danger of getting involved. I'm such an emotional coward, Dad.''

''Don't be so hard on yourself, sweetheart. You've done a whole lot to help these kids. Tom's very grateful to you.''

But Lila couldn't hear her father's voice anymore. She was unaware of anything but the pounding of her heart and the wild pull of emotion within her. A wave of feeling crashed through all the careful barricades she'd erected over the years, and suddenly they were gone like mist on a summer day.

Like a woman in a dream, she got up and walked down the steps toward the distant glow of windows, oblivious to the cold rain on her face or the wind tearing at her hair.

CHAPTER TWENTY

SHE PULLED OPEN the door of the camper and climbed inside. Tom turned to look at her, clearly startled. His big body seemed to fill the warm, lighted space as he took groceries and tinned goods from a cardboard box and stored them away inside the little refrigerator and the tiny cupboard.

"Lila," he said, glancing away so he wouldn't have to meet her eyes. "I didn't think you'd make it home before we left."

"I'll need about a month." She brushed raindrops from the shoulders and sleeves of her jacket, then took it off. "Is that all right?"

"A month? What for?"

"To wind up my practice and get my patients settled with other doctors. I think a month should probably do it, Tom."

"You're quitting your practice?"

"Yes, I am."

"And then what?"

"I'm going with you," she said.

They were so close together that it was almost impossible not to touch him. With a huge effort she kept herself from reaching toward him, wrapping her arms around him and pressing her body against his.

"Why?" he asked.

"Because I love you and your kids. Because I can't bear the thought of living without you again, and it's time I started having enough courage to manage my inner life as carefully as the one I live on the surface."

"Archie told you the whole story, didn't he?"

"Yes," she said quietly. "He did. Why couldn't you tell me?"

He looked at her then, and she was torn by the bleak pain on his face. "You know why," he said.

"Oh, Tom…"

He lifted handfuls of soup tins and stacked them automatically inside the cupboard. "I always felt guilty," he muttered. "I felt like the whole mess was my fault, and my punishment. But it seemed so wrong that my kids should have to suffer."

"Your punishment?" she asked. "For what?"

"For loving you." He turned to her again. "I could never stop loving you. All those years when she accused me of being unfaithful, I kept trying to tell her there was no other woman in my life. But it wasn't true. You were always there, Lila."

She put her arms around him and nestled against his chest. "We can't control our thoughts and memories. You were always in my heart, too."

His arms tightened around her. "You'll really come with me? You're prepared to throw away everything you've built here and travel off into the sunset without even knowing where you're going?"

"Not only prepared, I'm excited about it," she said. "And I'm not afraid of anything except losing you again." To her astonishment, she realized that what she said was true. "All that counts is being with you, Tom, and not losing this one last chance for love and happiness. Whatever happens afterward, wherever life decides to take us, this time we're going to deal with it together.''

He sank onto the bed, looking dazed with happiness, then pulled her down beside him, stretching out and cradling her in his arms.

"Think how different our lives would have been if you'd made this decision fifteen years ago."

"I wasn't ready then." She looked gravely into his eyes, so close to her own. "I needed to grow up a whole lot and learn all kinds of things about myself and life before I could decide I was ready to follow you."

He gathered her closer with a warm, teasing laugh. "Oh, Lilabel! And you always said I was immature."

She burrowed against him, kissing his throat. "But if I'd gone with you back then," she murmured, "Kelly and Casey wouldn't exist, and they're both such wonderful people. So maybe it's just as well that things worked out the way they did."

"I love you, Lila," he whispered, his voice husky with emotion. "We'll have such a wonderful life together, darling."

"Tell me what we'll do. What will our lives be like, Tom?"

"Well, let me think…" He stretched out on the bed, still holding her, and ran a finger over the line of her forehead, nose and chin, then caressed her lips with a slow, delicate touch.

She caught his finger gently between her teeth, took his hands and began to kiss the rest of his fingers one by one.

"Tell me," she said.

"Okay. First I think we'll finish painting the barn and get the pasture fence repaired. And then I'm going to rent some land from Archie and go to a few llama auctions. Maybe we'll even travel to South America to find some top-grade breeding stock and start building a herd. I've been reading about llamas. They're a great moneymaking prospect, Lila."

"You're..." She leaned up on one elbow, staring at him in confusion. "But, Tom, I don't understand. You're talking about staying here? Now that I've agreed to leave my job and travel with you, you're saying you want to settle down instead?"

He pulled her back into his arms and kissed her, then held her tenderly.

"I'm tired of traveling, Lilabel, and after this past year I don't enjoy it much anymore. Neither do the kids. I didn't really want you to come with me, I just needed you to be willing to come. I knew when that happened, it would mean you were finally ready to commit everything you had to this relationship. And I couldn't be with you on any other terms."

"But..." She shook her head against his tanned throat, still dazed. "But if all you wanted was to settle down here and go into business with my father, why didn't you agree to it when I first made that offer?"

"Lila," he whispered, "you still don't understand how much I love you, do you?"

"Maybe you should tell me." She smiled and began to caress his long body.

"I love you so much that living here and seeing you every day would have been hell unless I could be certain you felt the same way about me. After a while the frustration would have driven me away again. And the last thing those poor kids need,'' he said, his eyes darkening suddenly with pain, ''is to be uprooted from a place they're happy in.''

A light was slowly beginning to dawn inside her mind, glowing from a joy so bright and intense that she was dazzled by its splendor.

''But this is…Tom, it's wonderful!''

''What's wonderful, sweetheart?''

''This means you'll stay here with the kids, and I can keep my practice, and we'll all live together and love each other, and Kelly and Casey will go to school…''

''And we'll sleep together every night,'' he murmured against her hair. ''And we'll raise kids and llamas and make love every time it rains.''

''Every time it rains?'' she asked.

He grinned down at her, his eyes sparkling. ''That's going to be a family rule, Lilabel. And guess what?''

''What?'' she asked, smiling.

''It's raining now,'' he whispered.

She stretched luxuriously in his arms, listening to the rain drumming on the aluminum roof of the camper. They felt so warm and enclosed within the roar of the storm, as if they were the only people in all the world.

''But the kids are going to be alone in the house soon,'' she told him, suddenly remembering Archie's leather jacket and polished boots. ''Dad's going to town. As if enough miracles haven't already happened today,'' she added, shaking her head, ''it seems my father has a date with Marie.''

"Damn, you're right." Tom kissed her and sat up reluctantly. "We'd better go up to the house and look after them. They're both going to be so happy to hear we're not leaving after all."

Lila sat up, too, hating to leave his arms. "Tom," she said.

"Yes, sweetheart?"

"I think it's going to be raining all night," she told him. "And you should hear how nice the rain sounds rustling through the trees outside my bedroom window."

He grinned, his eyes kindling with emotion. "I think I'd like to hear that, Lilabel."

They kissed one more time and strained together in a wild, sweet embrace that thrilled her all the way to the core of her body, rich with promises of the night to come.

Finally, still clinging together and laughing, they climbed down from the camper and splashed through the puddles toward the big lighted house where the children waited.

EPILOGUE

Three years later

ON A BEAUTIFUL SPRING morning, Kelly came through the front door and walked across the veranda to sit on the steps next to Casey, who was holding his old carved llama. By now, the llama, called Thunderhead, was worn and discolored from years of constant play. The little leather saddle and woven bridle had each been replaced twice.

But Thunderhead was a star, because he had appeared on the cover of Lila and Archie's first book for children. Nowadays, children from all over the world wrote letters to ask more about the llama and to tell how much they'd loved the book.

Their baby sister, Bella, sat next to Casey in her padded lounge chair. He showed her the llama and she reached for it, puffing in excitement, but Kelly frowned at her brother and shook her head.

Bella was sure to chew on the llama. She was only five months old and put everything in her mouth.

When Casey withdrew the toy, Bella screwed her eyes up and waved her feet in their little white socks, which meant she was about to yell. Hastily Kelly gave her the set of colored plastic keys tied to the handle of the lounge chair. Bella settled back, pulling at the keys and murmuring contentedly to herself in her own strange language.

Casey was seven years old now, halfway between his two sisters. Kelly was fourteen and Bella had been born just before Christmas. When Lila went to work three afternoons a week at the clinic, she always packed Bella up and took her along. Everybody at the clinic loved the baby.

Kelly loved her, too, just as much as she'd always loved Casey.

Now that Kelly was older, she didn't fight as much with her brother. And Bella wasn't her sole responsibility the way Casey used to be, so she was able to relax and enjoy being a big sister.

Their parents were both nearby, rocking in the porch swing and reading the newspaper as they liked to do on Sunday mornings.

But at the moment there wasn't a lot of reading going on, Kelly realized when she stole a glance at them. They were nestled close together and kissing, apparently thinking themselves unseen behind the fringed canopy of the swing.

"They're doing it again," she murmured, bending close to Casey.

Bella cooed and tried to grasp her hair.

Kelly patted the baby's fat cheek, smiling.

Though she and Casey pretended to object, even called it "gross," they loved to see Tom and Lila kissing and cuddling, or looking all warm and misty as if they wanted to gobble each other up. Their parents' warm, constant love for each other, and for their children, was like a thick stone wall that enveloped the family in safety and kept all the dangerous things out.

Kelly had never felt so safe, so utterly, completely happy. And today was a special day....

"When are they coming, Mom?" Casey called in the general direction of the porch swing.

"Anytime now, dear," Lila's voice said.

Casey called her "Mom" all the time now, and so did Kelly. When they first started, Lila had been so happy that she cried, but she was used to it by now.

The little boy nodded and squinted at the road again, galloping his llama up and down the veranda post to amuse Bella, who laughed with deep throaty chuckles.

Archie and Marie were coming home today in the big motor home they lived in while they wandered all the way down to Arizona during the winter, and then back up the coast to Canada again in the spring.

"Whoever would have thought," Marie often teased, "that Tom would be the one sitting on the veranda, and Archie would be off drifting around the country like a tumbleweed!"

But Kelly's father didn't seem to mind staying at the farm. In fact, he was so happy that he sang and laughed all the time, and hugged any of the kids that happened to be nearby.

While Casey was watching the road, Kelly spotted somebody walking in the distance. Her throat went dry and her heart pounded with excitement as she watched a boy strolling along the graveled trail by the river.

The new arrival was Lanny McGregor, who lived on the next farm. He was a big, sturdy, quiet boy, an honor student and a football player, and lately his voice had begun to get deep and manly.

Lanny and Kelly had been playing together for years, ever since she came to live at the farm. Today, Lanny was obviously coming down to do some fishing. He had a pole over his shoulder, and he carried a metal stringer and a bucket.

"Looks like Lanny's heading off to go fishing. And he's all by himself," Kelly's father said.

"Poor boy. He does look lonely, doesn't he?" Lila said, with the solemn, teasing note in her voice that Kelly secretly loved.

"You know, I remember being that age," Tom said, "and having a pretty girl to go fishing with. What a great time that was."

Kelly heard him chuckle, and glanced over in time to catch the meaningful look that passed between her parents. Lila was smiling up at him, her face gentle with emotion.

"I guess maybe I'll go down later and see what he's doing," Kelly said casually, peering at Lanny's tall form between the cottonwoods.

He had settled on the big flat rock with his fishing equipment, and she was anxious to join him. But first she wanted to see Archie and Marie.

"Well, ask him to come in for lunch," Lila said. "I like that boy."

Tom bent to kiss his wife tenderly and pushed the floor with his toe to set the porch swing moving again, just as the morning light flashed on the big flat windshield of Archie's motor home when it rounded a bend in the river road.

Casey bounced up and down in excitement. "Here they are! They're coming!"

Kelly lifted her face blissfully to the warmth of the sun while they waited for the motor home to get closer.

All around she could hear the gentle, familiar cadences of her life…the creaking of the swing and her parents' murmured conversation, the baby's contented chatter, the birds singing in the cottonwood trees and the quiet flow of the river where Lanny was waiting for her.

"Bella," she whispered to the baby. "You know what? You should look around and try to remember this, because it's probably the nicest place there's ever been in the world."

Bella gazed up at her and Casey with a serious, quizzical expression, then began to laugh and kick her legs. Kelly laughed with her.

She got up and took Casey's hand, and they ran down to greet Archie and Marie as the motor home drove into the yard.

HARLEQUIN SUPERROMANCE®

**From April to June 1999,
read about three women whose
New Millennium resolution is**

By the Year 2000: *Satisfaction!*

April—*The Wrong Bride* by Judith Arnold.
Cassie Webster loves Phillip Keene and expected to marry
him—but it turns out he's marrying someone else. So
Cassie shows up at his wedding…to prove he's got
The Wrong Bride.

May—*Don't Mess with Texans* by Peggy Nicholson.
Susannah Mack Colton is out to get revenge on her
wealthy—and nasty—ex-husband. But in the process
she gets entangled with a handsome veterinarian,
complicating *his* life, too. Because that's what happens
when you ***"Mess with Texans"!***

June—*If He Could See Me Now* by Rebecca Winters.
The Rachel Maynard of today isn't the Rachel of ten
years ago. Now a lovely and accomplished woman,
she's looking for sweet revenge—and a chance to win
the love of the man who'd once rejected her.
If He Could See Me Now…

Available at your favorite retail outlet.

HARLEQUIN®
Makes any time special ™

IN UNIFORM

There's something special about a man in uniform. Maybe because he's a man who takes charge, a man you can count on, and yes, maybe even love....

Superromance presents *In Uniform*, an occasional series that features men who live up to your every fantasy—and then some!

Look for:

Mad About the Major
by Roz Denny Fox
Superromance #821
Coming in January 1999

An Officer and a Gentleman
by Elizabeth Ashtree
Superromance #828
Coming in March 1999

SEAL It with a Kiss
by Rogenna Brewer
Superromance #833
Coming in April 1999

Available wherever Harlequin books are sold.

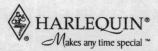

COMING NEXT MONTH

#834 DON'T MESS WITH TEXANS • Peggy Nicholson
By the Year 2000: Satisfaction!
Veterinarian R. D. Taggart is the innocent bystander caught in the cross fire between a blue-eyed Texas hellcat and her vindictive ex-husband. Susannah Mack Colton inadvertently destroys Tag's reputation in what *appears* to be nothing but a vendetta against her ex—and Tag intends to collect on his damages!

#835 THE DOCTOR'S DAUGHTER • Judith Bowen
Men of Glory
Lucas Yellowfly was always in love with Virginia Lake. More than a decade ago, the half-Indian boy from the wrong side of town spent a memorable night with the doctor's daughter. Now they're both back in Glory, Lucas as a successful lawyer and Virginia as a single mother with a five-year-old son. Virginia's looking for a job—and Lucas finds he needs someone with *exactly* her qualifications!

#836 HER SECRET, HIS CHILD • Tara Taylor Quinn
A Little Secret
Jamie Archer has a past she wants to keep hidden. She's created an entirely new life for herself and four-year-old Ashley—a life that's threatened when Kyle Radcliff reappears. Kyle doesn't immediately realize who she is, but Jamie recognizes *him* right away. Her child's father.

#837 THE GUARDIAN • Bethany Campbell
Guaranteed Page-Turner
Kate Kanaday is a widow with a young son. Life is hard, but she manages—right up until the day a stalker leaves his first message on her doorstep. Before long she's forced to quit her job and run. And there's only one place to go—to the home of a stranger who has promised to keep them safe whether he wants them there or not. From the bestselling author of *See How They Run* and *Don't Talk to Strangers*.

#838 THE PULL OF THE MOON • Darlene Graham
9 Months Later
Danielle Goodlove has every reason to believe that marriage and family are not for her. As a dedicated obstetrician, she's content to share her patients' happiness. Until one moonlit night, when firefighter Matthew Creed is brought into the emergency room. Now she wishes things could be different....

#839 HER BROTHER'S KEEPER • K.N. Casper
Family Man
Krisanne Blessing receives a call from her ex-lover, Drew Hadley, asking her to come back to Coyote Springs, Texas. Drew is now a widower with a young son—and he's also a close friend of her brother, Patrick. Krisanne is shocked to discover that Patrick wants her and Drew to give romance another try. She's even more shocked when she discovers *why* he's encouraging their relationship.